Shelter for Adeline

D1563915

SHELTER FOR ADELINE

BADGE OF HONOR
TEXAS HEROES
BOOK 7

By Susan Stoker

Table of Contents

Chapter One   1

Chapter Two   15

Chapter Three   40

Chapter Four   51

Chapter Five   72

Chapter Six   87

Chapter Seven   117

Chapter Eight   131

Chapter Nine   150

Chapter Ten   163

Chapter Eleven   195

Chapter Twelve   207

Chapter Thirteen   220

Chapter Fourteen   236

Chapter Fifteen   253

Chapter Sixteen   284

Chapter Seventeen   297

Chapter Eighteen   323

Chapter Nineteen   347

Chapter Twenty   356

Discover other titles   384

Connect with Susan Online   386

About the Author   387

Chapter One

ADELINE REYNOLDS TOOK a deep breath and crossed her fingers before walking through the door of the small diner. She didn't mind online dating, but the last few men she'd met had been so far from what she was looking for it wasn't funny. Dirk was twenty-two, way too young; John was forty-eight, too old; Roman was about a hundred and fifty pounds heavier than depicted in the picture he'd posted in his profile; and Mark was just plain weird.

She had high hopes for Bud, despite his name.

Her younger sister, Alicia, thought she was insane for looking online for someone to spend the rest of her life with, but then again, Alicia had met the love of her life in high school and hadn't had to worry about finding good men to date as an adult.

Adeline was careful. She never gave out her address or phone number to any of the men she met online. She chatted with them on the Internet for at least three weeks before agreeing to meet them in person. When she did meet with someone, she made sure it was for a quick lunch date in a public place first. And she stalked the man online, trying to find out everything she could about him before deciding to take the next step and meet in person.

Bud was around her age, thirty-four, had a full-time job, he'd never been married and had no children, and looked normal. Looking normal was important, because she herself was nothing special. She had about twenty...or thirty...extra pounds on her shorter frame, her black hair was medium length, and she had a perfectly boring job, which she hated.

She also had a dog. And that's where being normal ended for her.

Adeline had epilepsy and would most likely always have it. And really, epilepsy wasn't actually that rare, three million people, or one out of every twenty-six, had some form of the disorder. As best the doctors could tell, it was caused by her very long delivery at birth. Her mom had a hard time and Adeline's brain was starved of oxygen. Other than the seizures, Adeline was as healthy as a horse.

"Seriously? You want to leave now? We just ordered," her date exclaimed in disbelief.

"I don't *want* to, but Coco is alerting. I'm going to have a seizure, and I don't know if it's going to be a big one or not. I need to get somewhere safe before it happens."

Bud looked at her in horror. "You're gonna start spazzing now? Here? In front of everyone?"

"Not if you help me find somewhere private I can go to," Adeline said dryly, ignoring the offensive "spaz" remark.

"I can take you home."

Adeline shook her head. "I won't make it. I only have about ten minutes. It would take me around twenty-five to get home." Not to mention she didn't want him knowing where she lived. It was a rule she had with the men she met online. No allowing them to know where she lived until after at least the third date.

She preferred not to beg, but didn't have a choice at the moment. She gave him one more chance to be a good guy. "Please, Bud. I know you weren't expecting this, and honestly, neither was I, but I can't control when they happen. Will you please help me?"

Bud shook his head and threw his napkin on the table and stood up. "This is way over my head. I can't handle this. I only wanted to have lunch and see if we had any chemistry. You're nice and all that, and having a dog around all the time is one thing, but this is something else altogether. I wish I could help you, but I can't. Sorry."

Adeline didn't bother watching as Bud stalked away. It was disappointing, but not the end of the world. It had happened before, a guy walking away from her after finding out the realities of being with someone suffering from a disease like hers. If she could turn her seizures off, she would. But since it wasn't possible, she'd come to terms with them.

She tried to reassure Coco that she understood his alert, and get her purse and jacket together at the same time. It wasn't the first time she'd had to deal with an imminent seizure in a public place, and it most certainly wouldn't be the last.

"Are you all right?"

Adeline whipped her head up in surprise and stared at the man standing next to the booth. She hadn't noticed him walking up to her, more concerned about getting her stuff together and trying to reassure Coco.

He was tall; she had to crane her head up pretty far to look into his eyes. He was looking down at her in concern, his brows drawn together. Even though she was nervous about her pending seizure, she couldn't help but notice how good looking the man was. He was tan and had a five o'clock shadow, as if it'd been more than a day since he'd last shaved.

But the thing that really struck her was what he was wearing. The navy-blue cargo pants, along with the T-shirt that had "Station 7" emblazoned on the front with a large Maltese cross under it, made her entire body sag in relief.

"You're a firefighter?"

"Yes, ma'am."

"An EMT or paramedic?" she clarified, knowing that just because someone was a firefighter didn't necessarily mean they'd gone through medical training.

"Yes…?" The word was stretched out into a question.

"I'm Adeline. I have about ten minutes or so before I'm going to have an epileptic seizure, as Coco,"—she gestured toward the dog currently panting in her face and pawing at her leg—"has warned me. I need to get to a safe place, I can't drive, and the person who could've taken me somewhere,"—she paused for a precious moment to glare at the door Bud had disappeared through—"seems to have ditched me. I'm incredibly embarrassed, but I'd appreciate the help."

The firefighter held out his hand and said in a calm and controlled tone, which went a long way toward making her feel better about the entire situation she'd found herself in, "My name is Dean. It's good to meet you. Trust me; I'll take care of you."

Crash closed his hand around Adeline's, threw a twenty-dollar bill on the table, then helped her to her feet. He had no idea if the money would cover whatever she and her date had ordered, but he had other things to worry about at the moment. He kept hold of her hand and led her to the front of the restaurant and out the door. Luckily they were across the street from Station 7.

He'd gone to the diner to eat lunch with Hayden, a sheriff's deputy, who was one of his good friends. They'd been talking about everything that had happened to her boyfriend when he'd been abused and stalked by an ex-girlfriend. Crash would never understand how people could be so crazy when they were in a relationship—or when that relationship ended.

"Where are we going?"

Crash glanced over at the woman walking next to him and was impressed at her composure. "Sorry, I should've reassured you already. The station I work out of is right across the street. We have a room where you can relax and be safe."

"Thank you," she breathed, obviously pleased with his answer. "I was going to ask the manager if there was an office or someplace I could lay down in, but I wasn't sure about how clean it might be."

Crash chuckled. "I can't guarantee how clean the fire station is, but I can guess that it'll be better than lying on the floor over there." He gestured back to the diner. They served amazing food, but he knew the owner was a pack-rat, and any office in the place was probably stuffed to the gills with paper, boxes, and who knew what else.

He held open the door to the station then followed Adeline and Coco inside.

"Yo! Crash, that you? That was a fast lunch," a deep voice called out from down the hall.

"Crash? I thought you said your name was Dean?" Adeline asked.

"It is. But I don't usually go by it. Crash is my nickname. Come on, let me introduce you real quick to the guys before we get you settled."

She glanced at her watch, then nodded reluctantly.

"It'll be fast, promise," he reassured her, putting his hand on the small of her back and encouraging her to walk ahead of him down the hall.

They walked into a large open room, which had a couple of couches and a huge television. A professional-looking kitchen was to the right of the room, complete with stainless steel appliances.

"Hey. Guys, this is Adeline and her dog Coco—"

Driftwood interrupted him before he could explain what they were doing there. "Wow, you work even quicker than me, Crash. Maybe you should be the official playboy of the station instead of me."

"Fuck off," Crash told him. "Adeline, this is Drift-wood, Chief, Taco, and Sledge. Tiger, Squirrel, and Moose are around here somewhere I'm sure." He looked her in the eyes as he said, "They're jerks most of the time, but I trust them with my life, and they're the kind of men I'd want around me in a medical emergency. Okay?"

She nodded.

Crash turned back to the room. His friends might be jokesters, but they obviously understood that something more was up than one of their buddies bringing a chick to the station. "We'll be in the back office."

"What's up?" Chief asked, standing.

Adeline answered before Crash could open his mouth. "I'm epileptic and my dog alerted that I'm going to have a seizure."

"Go," the tall Native American demanded, waving Crash toward another hallway in the back of the room. "Let us know if you need anything."

Crash nodded in thanks and moved his hand so it rested between Adeline's shoulder blades. "Come on, let's get you settled."

They headed across the room and into the hallway Chief had indicated. Crash opened the first door to the right and ushered Adeline and her four-legged friend inside. He kept his hand on her until she was sitting on the leather couch.

"Is this okay? Do I need to clear a spot on the floor?" Crash knew if Adeline had a grand mal seizure, it would be better for her to be on the floor, so she couldn't fall off the couch and possibly get hurt, but he wasn't sure what to expect just yet. There were so many different kinds of seizures someone with epilepsy could have, he didn't want to assume. "Do you need to go to the hospital afterwards? Should I get an ambulance en route?"

Adeline didn't answer him. She was staring off into space and didn't seem to be aware of where she was. Coco whined at her feet and nudged her with his nose.

"Easy, boy. I've got her," Crash soothed, putting one arm around Adeline's waist and shifting her body until she was lying supine on the leather cushions. He sat at her hip so he could keep her from tumbling off the edge if it came to that, and to keep a close eye on her. Her dog jumped up onto the couch at her feet and laid his head on her shins.

Her hands began to jerk at her sides as the seizure progressed.

Crash had seen people in the midst of seizures before, so he wasn't surprised or bothered by what was happening. From his observation, she was having a complex partial seizure. He'd seen them plenty of times over his career. Patients seemed to be out of it or staring into space as their brain sent electric impulses through their body, and many times it was paired with the jerky motions of their hands, as was Adeline's.

He kept his eyes on her the entire time, monitoring her breathing and watching the pulse beat in her neck. Eventually her jerky arm and hand movements slowed, but she continued to stare off into space.

Crash ran his eyes over her flushed cheeks, using his

medical training to continue monitoring her condition. After several minutes, a small sigh slipped from between her lips. Crash moved the hand he'd been using to take her pulse and brushed it against her cheek. She quieted immediately, and he would've sworn she'd turned into his touch.

He'd seen Adeline enter the restaurant the moment she stepped through the door. The smile on her face as she'd walked toward the table was beautiful. When he'd realized she was meeting a man, he'd felt a pang of remorse so strong it had almost taken his breath away. He'd only partly been listening to Hayden while covertly watching Adeline interact with the man sitting across from her.

It was obvious after only a few short minutes that the two didn't really know each other. Crash figured it was probably a first date, or second at most. But it wasn't until the man threw down his napkin and got up, leaving the woman looking nervous and unsure, that he'd moved.

Crash couldn't remember if he'd even said goodbye to Hayden or not; he'd seen the woman in distress and wanted to do something about it. Immediately. Thank God he had. The thought of her lying on the dirty floor of the diner, with people staring at her as she seized, was repugnant to him. No one should ever have that indignity foisted upon them.

Crash continued to monitor Adeline's breathing long after she'd stopped twitching. The skin of her cheek felt warm, but not overly so. After a while, her dog whined at the same time she gave a slow blink, licked her lips and took a deep breath. She turned her head slightly and looked up at him with a dazed expression, as if she wasn't quite sure where she was or what was going on.

"Hey, you with me?" Crash asked in a low, steady voice.

She looked confused, as if she'd just woken up after a twelve-hour nap. She swallowed and one of her hands moved down toward her dog. Coco whined and shifted at her feet enough so he could reach her fingers and lick them enthusiastically. Adeline smiled and took another long, slow breath.

Crash was impressed by how quickly she came back to herself, and realized where she was and what had happened. "Yeah, Dean, I'm good. How long was I out of it?"

"Only ten minutes or so. Want a glass of water?"

"Yes, please."

Crash put his hand on her forearm, which now lying across her stomach, and gave it a little squeeze before standing up and striding out of the room. He'd offered to get her something to drink because he was worried about her and also to give her a little time to get her equilibrium back.

If he was being honest, he needed a moment to get himself under control as well.

He was a professional. Had assisted many people with the aftereffects of a seizure, but none of them had ever affected *him* as Adeline did. He felt protective of her, as any good medic would, but it was more than that.

It was also ridiculous. She could be a raving bitch or in a relationship. He had no idea what she was really doing in the restaurant, only his suspicions. Feeling protective was a normal reaction for him; it was nothing more than that. At least that was what he told himself.

When Crash came back into the small room with a bottle of water, Adeline looked more like she had when he'd first met her thirty or so minutes ago. She'd sat up on the couch and was petting her dog absently with one hand. She smiled up at him when he neared and reached out for the water.

She took a deep swallow and sat back with a sigh. As quickly as she relaxed, her body tensed and she sat forward as if she was about to stand up. "Well, thank you for helping me out, I appreciate it. I should get going."

"Stay," Crash immediately protested. "At least for a while."

"I'm really all right," Adeline said softly. "Unfortunately, I'm used to the seizures and they don't wreck me like they used to."

Crash sat on the couch next to her. He felt exactly like he did the first time he'd asked a girl out in the seventh grade. Nervous and hopeful at the same time. "It's not that, I…damn. Okay, if you're sure."

"What is it?" Adeline asked, looking concerned now. "Did something happen while I was out of it?"

"No," Crash protested immediately. "Nothing like that… Are you seeing anyone?"

She looked taken aback at his question, but Crash was relieved when she answered immediately without looking away from him. "No. Why?"

"The guy at the diner wasn't your boyfriend?"

Adeline wrinkled her nose adorably. "No. First— and last—date."

"You never got to eat. Want to go back across the street and grab something…with me?"

"Are you asking me out?"

"Yes. Obviously very badly, since you have to clari-fy," he said sheepishly.

"Oh…well…you don't have to babysit me. I'm okay. Honest."

"I don't want to babysit you," he said immediately.

The fact of the matter was he *did* want to keep his eye on her for a while to make sure she was okay after the seizure. But it wasn't just that. He was nervous…which was out of character for him. Asking women out usually didn't faze him. But for some reason, Adeline had gotten to him.

"I'd like to get to know you," he told her honestly. "And you have to be hungry." He added the last bit to try to cajole her.

"You don't care that I have epilepsy?"

"No."

"Or that I have a dog?"

"No. I love dogs."

She considered him for a long moment, then finally nodded. "Okay. Then yes, I'd like to have lunch with you."

"Thank God," Crash breathed out and pantomimed wiping sweat from his brow.

Adeline chuckled.

Crash stood and held his hand out to her. "Lunch awaits."

Taking his hand, she stood as well. He kept hold of hers as he led the way to the door. Feeling her small, smooth fingers around his as they walked made Crash smile. There was just something about her that made him feel as though he could do anything.

Maybe he was an idiot. Maybe Adeline was a horrible person. But as stupid as it seemed, for some reason, Crash felt as if he was taking the first steps toward his future.

Chapter Two

—————◆—————

"EVERYTHING ALL RIGHT?" Chief called out as Crash and Adeline made their way back across the main room to the front of the fire station.

"Yup." Crash didn't even slow down, but continued on as if his friend hadn't spoken. The sooner he could get Adeline to the restaurant, the sooner he could start to learn more about her.

They headed out the front door and across the street toward the diner. "Are you on shift right now?" Adeline asked.

"Yeah, but I can take the time to buy you lunch. No worries," Crash told her. "There's a chance I might have to bail on you though, and I apologize in advance for that. If I get toned, I'll have'ta run."

"It's fine," Adeline told him. "I understand."

"You'll be okay to drive home?"

She nodded. "After I get something to eat, I'll be fine. Promise."

Crash stopped outside the doors to the restaurant.

"I've learned never to let the possibility of a call stop me from getting out and about," he said seriously. "I spent the first years of my career as a firefighter sitting inside the station, afraid to go anywhere because I was scared we'd get a call. But the fire chief sat me down and had a talk with me. He told me that as long as I wasn't off doing anything irresponsible, I wasn't tied to the station. I don't go more than a couple miles away, but I've learned, for my own health, that sometimes it's good for me to get some space from the other guys."

"I totally get that," Adeline said. "Well, not getting space from guys, but not being afraid and sitting around waiting for something to happen. I was that way with my epilepsy too. I was so afraid I'd have a seizure that I barely went anywhere. I hid inside my house and I think that actually made it worse. Since I've had Coco, I've been able to feel more confident about going about my daily business."

They smiled at each other.

"See? Something we have in common already then," Crash said warmly.

Adeline smiled shyly and examined the man standing in front of her. She hadn't really had much chance to check him out with everything that had happened. But now she looked her fill. Dean was good looking. *Really* good looking. He had dark brown hair in a short cut. It kinda stuck up on the top of his head, but in a natural way, not one that took a ton of hair goop to achieve.

He was muscular, but not overly so. He had a strong jawline, deep brown eyes, almost the exact color of the dark brown coffee table she had at home. All in all, he kinda reminded her of Chris Hemsworth. An even more gorgeous version, if that was possible.

He grinned at her, and for a second Adeline was afraid he could read her thoughts, but he merely said, "After you." Dean held the door open and gestured toward the entrance, inviting her to walk through.

"Thanks." Adeline had only partly been cognizant of Dean as they'd left the small restaurant not half an hour ago. She'd been more concerned with her imminent seizure and getting to a safe space. But now, she was definitely aware of the man behind her. His fingertips rested lightly on the small of her back as he guided her into the waiting area. He didn't pull away as they stood side by side waiting for the hostess to find them a table.

Adeline probably should've felt crowded or pressured by his touch, but instead felt protected. Her hand tightened on Coco's leash. She hadn't ever felt that way before. Her parents had always been worried about her, to the point they hovered and really weren't comfortable going anywhere in public with her because of her frequent seizures. She'd always felt nervous when they were out together, hypersensitive about not wanting to embarrass them. But, for just a moment, standing there with Dean, she almost felt like any other woman would on a first date.

"Right this way," the hostess told them, walking in the opposite direction from where they'd both been sitting earlier.

Still feeling the light pressure on her back, Adeline followed the woman to a large booth along the back wall.

"Will this work?" the hostess asked.

"Perfect," Dean told her.

Adeline scooted in on one side of the booth and Co-co settled in without a fuss at her feet. Dean waited until Adeline was seated before moving to the other side. Without asking, he looked up at the hostess and said, "A large water for the lady and an ice tea for me, please."

The woman nodded. "I'll tell your waitress. Ruth should be right with you."

Adeline bit her lip in nervousness after the woman had left. She hadn't been anxious before, but now she was. She wasn't sure what to say to the man sitting across from her. Before, he was there to help her and she wasn't worrying about making small talk. But now, it felt like they were on a date, which was ridiculous. It was only lunch.

"Relax, Adeline," Dean told her, putting his fore-arms on the table and leaning forward. "I won't bite."

She laughed nervously. "I don't know why I'm nervous. You'd think I'd be used to this by now."

"What do you mean?"

"Blind dates. I've had quite a few in the last couple of weeks."

"Really?"

"Yup. I've been trying the online dating thing."

"And I take it that hasn't been going well?" Dean asked.

Adeline shook her head. "No. You saw Bud today." She took a breath to continue, but Dean interrupted her.

"Bud? His name really was *Bud*?"

Adeline giggled. "Yup. I should've known, huh?"

"Yeah, definitely. Who else?"

"Well, there was Dirk, who was twelve years younger than me. Not my kinda thing. Then John was fourteen years older than me, and that didn't work for me either. Roman looked nothing like his picture on the site and Mark was simply odd." She shrugged. "I know people find their true loves online all the time, but I'm beginning to think it's not for me. It's just too easy for people to misrepresent themselves online and it's frustrating to think that I'm really trying to find someone I'm compatible with, and they just...I don't know what they're doing."

"Full disclosure here and all that," Dean said. "One

day we were bored on shift and a bunch of us went online and made profiles on one of those sites. It was kind of a joke and I was shocked a week later when I checked it out and I had a ton of messages. I didn't answer any of them, as I really prefer to meet women in person before deciding if I want to go out with them or not."

Adeline could swear she saw Dean blushing. She wasn't sure what to say to his admission. Part of her wanted to admonish him for putting up a profile when he had no intention of doing anything with it, but she supposed that happened all the time. She was saved from having to reply when their waitress came by the table with their drinks.

"Water and ice tea. I'm Ruth, I'll be your waitress. Do y'all need more time to look over the menu?"

Dean looked over at Adeline. "You know what you want?"

She nodded. "I might as well get what I'd ordered before I had to leave." She looked up at Ruth. "I'll take a BLT with ranch dressing instead of mayonnaise and extra tomatoes added on, please. Oh, and a side of ranch for my fries as well."

Ruth wrote it all down and looked to Dean.

"I'll just take a bowl of the broccoli cheese soup."

Ruth nodded. "Great. It shouldn't take too long. If you need anything else in the meantime, let me know."

After she'd walked away, Adeline told Dean, "You're gonna make me look like a pig, you know."

Dean looked horrified. "No! I had a sandwich earlier with my friend. It's not...you can get whatever you want...I didn't mean..."

Adeline took pity on the man and let him off the hook. She reached out and put her hand on his arm, still lying on the table. "I was kidding, Dean. Sorry, I have a weird sense of humor. It's fine. And you should know, I'm not the kind of woman who orders a salad and picks at it because she's scared of eating in front of a guy. I've been known to out-eat some of my male friends."

Dean's arm shifted and he immediately laid his free hand over hers. He looked her in the eyes as he smiled and said, "Good. I'm not the kind of man who likes, or wants, a woman who isn't herself in front of me. *Always* be yourself, Adeline. If you're hungry, eat. If you're thirsty, drink. If you're pissed, let me know, especially if it's at me. If you're sleepy, tell me that too. I've always hated the games women play. Maybe that's why I'm still single."

Adeline wasn't sure what to say, so she simply nodded.

Dean sighed and grinned self-deprecatingly at her. "I'm taking this first date into dangerous territory, aren't I? We're supposed to stick to innocuous topics and not get too personal. Sorry, I'll try to be better. Let me tell you the basics about me. I'm Dean Christopherson, and I'm thirty-two. Hopefully not too old or young for you." He smiled, letting her know he was teasing.

"I've been a firefighter for around twelve years, and a paramedic for about six of those years. I've never been married and haven't met anyone yet I'd consider spending the rest of my life with. That's the basics. I'm sure you'll get to know all my nasty habits in time. What about you? I don't think I even know your last name. Where do you work? How old are you? What's your favorite color? You know…all the normal first date things."

Adeline was very aware that Dean hadn't let go of her hand, and she tried not to read too much into it. She liked his no-nonsense approach to trying to get to know her. She appreciated his candor. "My name is Adeline Reynolds. I'm probably not supposed to tell you my age, but if we'd met online, you'd already know it. I'm thirty-four. My job is pretty boring, especially compared to what you do. I'm in marketing. Right now I pretty much hate where I work. Not because of what I do, but because my boss is a jerk. He takes credit for our work and thinks he's all that and a bag of chips."

Adeline took a deep breath. Thinking about Douglas Hill the Third always made her want to scream.

"What is it you do?" Dean asked, running his fingertips lightly over the back of her hand.

Shivers raced down Adeline's arm, but she tried to ignore them. Dean was a healer, he probably had no idea he was even caressing her. She told herself that he probably did it to all his patients.

"I work for a large advertising-slash-public relations firm. We take on clients who are looking to advertise in all media. We put together promotional packets for them, including advertisements for magazines, newspapers, and even online ads. They pay us to get the graphics and details ready, and then once they're up and running, the client takes over managing them. Of course, we've got larger clients who we do everything for, set up the ads and manage for them, but those kinds of portfolios usually go to the employees who've been there longer…or who kiss my boss's ass."

Dean smiled at her. "I take it you don't kiss his ass."

"No, I don't."

"So what's your ideal job?"

"I love marketing," Adeline told him, relaxing as she talked about what she loved most in the world. "It's so interesting to me how much psychology works hand in hand with marketing. From which direction people turn when they're in a store to colors and fonts most are attracted to, even what websites they go to and what catches their eyes as they're surfing. I'd love to work for a midsize company and get full rein to do whatever I wanted with their advertising. To help design it from the ground up, then monitor it. See what works and what doesn't and tweak it as I go. There's so much more to marketing than making a pretty graphic. If the clicks aren't tracked and it's not followed up on, the company might as well be throwing their money into the trash every night for the janitors to take out."

Adeline took a deep breath and realized that she'd been going on and on without letting him get a word in edgewise. She looked sheepishly over at Dean. "Sorry. I tend to get worked up about it. What do you—"

"Don't. Don't brush off your enthusiasm," Dean told her. "Too many people don't give a shit what they do for a living. They hate their job and it shows in the kind of performance they give. I can tell just by listening to you talk that you love marketing, and you're the kind of employee who stays late just to get projects done…without having to be asked to do it. Your dark eyes actually sparkle when you talk about what you love. Your breathing sped up and you gripped my arm so tight I bet you've left marks."

"I'm so sorry—" Adeline started, but was interrupted once again.

"Don't be. Again, I might've thought you were pretty before, but watching you talk about what you love, makes you beautiful."

Adeline had no comeback for that. None. She could count on one hand the number of people who had ever told her she was pretty. Her sister, Alicia, and her husband, Matt, her parents, and a boy in high school who'd done, and said, everything he could think of to get in her pants.

"I didn't say that to embarrass you, Adeline," Dean said in a low, earnest voice. "It's one hundred percent true. I make it a point to try not to lie to people. For example, if they're badly hurt in an accident, I let them know, gently, exactly what's wrong. I'm sorry your boss is a dick. That sucks. He could probably get a lot more out of his employees if he let them do what they were good at rather than trying to be a big man on campus. Have you applied anywhere else? The best time to look for a job is when you *have* a job."

Adeline smiled through her embarrassment. "Now you sound like my sister."

He smiled back. "She must be really smart."

Adeline laughed. "She thinks she is. But to answer your question, I just started the job search process. I'm getting my resume together and researching where I think I might like to work."

"Here in San Antonio though…right?" Dean asked, suddenly looking concerned.

Adeline shrugged. "Probably. My family is here and I've never lived anywhere else. I love it. Why?"

He sighed hugely in relief. "Because I'm just getting to know you. It'd suck to find out that we really like

25

each other only to have you accept a job in Seattle or New York or something."

"Do you have any brothers or sisters?" Adeline knew she was blushing. It was crazy, but she liked Dean already, and wanted to know more about him.

"I have a sister, Laura. She has Down syndrome and lives in Arizona." He shook his head at the look of sympathy he obviously saw on her face. "Don't feel sorry for me. Laura is amazing. I'm five years older than her and always looked after her, but as it turns out, she didn't need much looking after. Yeah, she was bullied, but she has such a cheerful personality, it didn't seem to bother her much."

"Does she live by herself?"

Dean shook his head. "No, she's not quite independent enough to do that, but she's perfectly happy living in a group home with other men and women like her. They have jobs and do everything any able-bodied person would. There are a few caretakers who live in the house and make sure everyone eats healthy meals, and assist in everyday activities."

"That's amazing. And your parents?" Adeline rested her chin on her hand and leaned her elbow on the table, giving Dean her full attention.

"Still alive, healthy, and madly in love," he told her, smiling. "Seriously, I think they're more in love today than they were when they first got married. They're amazing. When they found out about Laura, they didn't even blink. Even with the difficulties of raising a handicapped daughter, they swear they wouldn't have changed one thing about their life."

"They *sound* amazing," Adeline said honestly.

"They are," Dean responded immediately. "And I want what they have. I want to be the first person my wife thinks about when she gets up in the morning. I want to buy her silly gifts to let her know I'm thinking about her, and I want to go to sleep at night holding the woman who understands the kind of man I am, and respects that. That's the kind of relationship my parents have."

Adeline didn't have a response to that, either. It was sappy and extremely romantic—and exactly what she wanted in her own life. Luckily, she was saved once more by Ruth with their food. Moving her arm, which was still stretched over the table with her hand lying beneath Dean's, Adeline sat back in her seat.

"Here we are!" Ruth chirped in a perky tone. "BLT with tomatoes and ranch, fries and a side of ranch, and a bowl of our broccoli cheese soup. Is there anything else I can get for you?"

"No, this looks great," Dean told her.

Adeline folded her napkin in her lap, relieved to have a bit more space between her and Dean. She liked him. Way more than she should for a first date. But there was just something about him that made her immediately feel at ease.

They were quiet for a moment as they dug into their meals. Finally, Adeline broke the silence and asked, "Why a firefighter? Did you always want to do that?"

Dean wiped his mouth with his napkin and shook his head. "Nope. I had no idea what I wanted to do with my life. None. I was a senior in high school and all my friends knew exactly what they were going to major in when they went to college, or they had already signed up for the military. I wasn't sure what it was I wanted to do."

"How'd you get into it then?" Adeline asked, extremely curious, wanting to know everything there was to know about the man sitting across from her.

"Laura. When she was twelve, and I was seventeen, she fell over in a dead faint in the middle of dinner. She just keeled over out of her chair, and I swear I thought she was dead. My mom called nine-one-one and we all just stood around helplessly, having no idea what had happened or what we could do to help her. Then in came the firefighters. There were three of them. One went to my parents and started asking questions about Laura's medical background, and the other two went to work on my sister. They were completely calm and confident in what they were doing. Before the ambulance even arrived, they had her hooked up to an IV and had a heart-rate monitor on her.

"It turns out that because of her DS, she had a cardiac defect. We knew she had a slight heart murmur, but not about how serious it could be. Her blood pressure dropped really low and she passed out. She was fine, but it scared the crap out of all of us. The thing I remember most was those firefighters. They swooped in when we had no idea what to do and they took control. I knew from that moment on that it was what I wanted to do with my life."

"So it's not about fighting fires? I thought that's why people became firefighters," Adeline asked.

"It is and it isn't. It's about taking control of the situation. That could be a sick person, a structure or grass fire, or extracting someone from their wrecked car. It's an adrenaline rush that can't be replicated any other way. I'm not saying that I don't like throwing water on an out-of-control fire," Dean told her with a grin, "but for me, it's more than that. It's the camaraderie with my friends. It's knowing that when push comes to shove, I won't feel helpless ever again like I did when I was seventeen and had no idea how to help my sister."

"Wow."

Dean smiled at her. "Is that wow, good, or wow, bad?"

"Definitely good. I guess I've been lucky and haven't really been in a situation like that. Although I'm sure my sister and parents would say that when I have my seizures they feel just as helpless as you did back when you were a teenager."

"I'm sure they do. You seem to have a good handle on them though."

Adeline appreciated his careful approach to the topic. She typically didn't like to talk about her illness because most people didn't understand and gave her clichéd platitudes. But Dean had the kind of medical background that made it easier to talk to him.

"When I was younger, I used to have grand mal seizures all the time. But, thankfully, I don't have many of those anymore. Now I'm more apt to have a myoclonic episode, which is less stressful on my body, but harder for many people to understand, I think. It looks weird when I jerk and stare into space and people think I'm just ignoring them or whatever."

"Then they're idiots," Dean growled.

Adeline couldn't help but feel good about how irritated he was on her behalf. Most people didn't get it. "Thanks, but I think they just don't know anything about epilepsy or seizures in general. Unfortunately, the doctors also think I've got refractory epilepsy now, as well."

"Damn. They can't find the right drugs to bring it under control?" Dean asked, obviously understanding what refractory epilepsy was.

"Man," Adeline mumbled, "I'd forgotten how nice it was to talk to someone who can comprehend exactly what I'm talking about without me having to dumb it down for them. Yeah, I've been on just about every popular drug, and some not-so-popular ones as well, and none of them have been able to bring my seizures under control. I've got a device under my skin right now that sends signals to my vagus nerve to try to control the seizures, and while it seemed to work pretty well when I first had it implanted, it's lost its effectiveness over the last year or so."

"So what's the next step?"

Adeline shrugged and tried to look nonchalant. "Brain surgery." Just the words scared the hell out of her, but it was getting to a point where she didn't have much choice. She'd tried almost everything else.

"Shit, really?"

"Really."

"Jesus, that sucks," Dean told her, pushing his now empty soup bowl to the side and reaching across the table for her hand.

Without thought, Adeline extended her hand toward him and tried to ignore the tingles that shot up her arm when he grabbed hold of her.

"How do you feel about that?"

The question surprised Adeline, but made her feel good. So many people had *told* her how they thought she should feel about surgery, rather than *asking* what she actually felt. "It completely freaks me out, to be honest," she told Dean candidly. "My sister and mom really want me to consider it, but I'm just not sure I want someone to cut into my brain. I mean, removing a part of my brain to try to reduce the seizures isn't my idea of a good time. What if they take out too much and I'm not me when I wake up? What if I don't remember my sister or her husband, or my parents? What if the knife slips and I'm a vegetable for the rest of my life?

"But just when I've talked myself out of having the surgery altogether, I think about a life where I don't have to worry about when or where I might have an episode. About how nice it would feel to not have to constantly be concerned about seizing as much anymore. The surgery scares the hell out of me, but I'm almost at a point where I'm willing to take the risk if it means that I can live a life without seizing so often."

"I imagine those are all completely normal thoughts," Dean told her in a soft voice.

When he said nothing else, Adeline lifted an eyebrow. "No other commentary?"

He cocked his head in confusion. "What do you mean?"

"It's just that usually people have all sorts of opinions about what I should and shouldn't do."

"Adeline," he said in such an understanding tone it

made her want to cry. "It's *your* body. You've lived with the disease your whole life. I don't have epilepsy and I have no idea what it's like to lose control as you do when you have a seizure. I would no sooner tell you how you should feel or what you should do than I would someone who was contemplating having cosmetic surgery or any other kind of procedure. I might have my own thoughts on the subject, but one, we've only just met, and two, I don't know enough about you or your history of seizures to presume to give you medical advice about it."

Tears sprang to Adeline's eyes and she took a deep breath to try to keep them at bay. The last thing this beautiful man needed was a woman he'd just met bawling in front of him. "Thank you."

"For what?"

"For understanding. For not telling me how I should feel or think. For just…everything."

"You're welcome. Where does your dog fit into everything?" he asked, gesturing to the black Labrador retriever sleeping under the table.

Adeline appreciated his change in subject. "Coco?"

"Yeah. How long have you had him? Did you get him because he was a seizure alert dog?"

She shook her head. "Nope. I was staying home more and more. I was terrified of having seizures in public. They were uncomfortable for me and everyone around me, and dangerous too because I never knew when they'd hit. I got a dog because I was lonely. There's actually quite a controversy about seizure alert dogs in the epileptic world. Some people claim dogs can't be trained, others say they don't actually work at all, and on the other side, proponents claim that this type of service dog absolutely *can* be trained to let people know they're going to have a seizure.

"No one was more surprised than me when Coco seemed to actually start alerting me when I was about to have a seizure. I'd had him a year before the first time he alerted. That first time it happened, I thought it was a fluke. Coco had always been loving and attentive, but when he continued to jump on me before I seized, I finally made the connection.

"I noticed that about ten minutes before I was going to have a seizure Coco would jump up on me, or get in my lap and not give it up. After about the third time he did it, I realized that he really *was* letting me know that I was about to have a seizure."

"Wow," Dean said with a small smile. "That's amazing. Bet he changed your life."

"You have no idea," Adeline told him. "Coco allowed me the confidence to travel more, to be able to drive, to go out on dates…in short, he let me live without fear of embarrassing myself for the first time in my entire life. I applied and was approved to make Coco an official service dog, so now he's allowed to go anywhere I do."

"That's awesome," Dean told her.

"I think so. The only thing it didn't change, unfortunately, was how others treat me. Many people don't understand epilepsy and are embarrassed when I have a seizure, even a small one. I told Bud in one of our online chats about my disease, and he reassured me that it didn't matter. But obviously he didn't understand the severity of my condition, because he acted as if I'd told him I was going to strip off all my clothes and dance naked around the table." Adeline rolled her eyes.

"I probably should've been upset with the way he reacted when he found out I was about to have a seizure, but honestly, I only felt relieved to learn how he really felt now, on our first date, rather than later."

Dean looked her straight in the eyes as he said, "You don't *ever* have to worry about that with me. I learned from my sister that what's most important is the person you are inside. And Adeline, from everything I've learned about you today, I *like* who you are. I hate that you have to go through the seizures, but it doesn't affect how I feel about you."

"Thanks." Adeline wasn't sure exactly what she was supposed to say to his impassioned words, but her response seemed to please him because he continued.

"For the record, just in case my pager goes off before

we're done, I'd love to take you out again…when I'm not on shift and don't have to be worried about rushing out on you. Can I give you my number?"

She must've stared at him in disbelief too long, because Dean said a bit sheepishly, "I figured if I give you my number, then the ball is in your court, so if you're only here because you're still out of it from your seizure or you really think I'm a creeper, you could just delete it the first chance you get." He was teasing…but Adeline saw a bit of insecurity in his eyes as well.

Hating that, she hurried to reassure him. "I'm sorry, yes, of course I want your number. And…I'm happy to give you mine as well…if you want it."

"Yes. I *definitely* want it," he said immediately, and then smiled at her and held out his hand. "Here, give me your phone and I'll put my number in then just text myself, if that's okay. That way I'll have yours too. Easier than both of us having to punch in our numbers."

"Sure." Adeline unlocked her phone and handed it over. Her lips quirked up in a smile when Dean tilted his head in concentration as he punched in his number. She heard his phone ding a moment later.

"There. All done. Now if I get called away, we can still get ahold of each other and I won't have to stalk the restaurant in the hopes that you'd someday show back up." He smiled, then visibly relaxed, changing the subject. "So, you have a sister?"

Adeline relaxed into her seat as well and nodded. "Alicia. She's younger than I am and married her high school sweetheart."

"And your parents?"

"Both alive. Like your parents, they're still very much in love."

They smiled at each other for a beat before Dean said, "It's nice to have good role models, isn't it?"

"Very," Adeline agreed. "But I also know that sometimes people grow apart." She shrugged. "I would never want someone to stay with me because he thought he had to. I'd be happier divorced than married to someone who didn't love me."

"Agreed," Dean said immediately. "I didn't mean to imply that anyone who gets divorced has done something wrong. But after seeing my parents' love for each other, I know that I really want that for myself."

"Me too," Adeline said softly, amazed that she and Dean seemed to have so much in common.

"I want to—"

Adeline wouldn't hear what Dean wanted as the pager clipped to his belt suddenly went off, the loud tones pealing through the semi-quiet restaurant.

"Shit. I gotta go."

Adeline had figured that out as soon as she'd heard the device's loud beeps. She opened her mouth to say something, she wasn't sure what, but didn't get the chance.

Dean stood up, keeping hold of her hand. He took a quick step to her side of the booth and leaned down and kissed her. Not on the cheek. Not on the forehead, but right on the lips. And it wasn't a quick peck, either.

His lips caressed hers and he slanted his head slightly. Adeline felt his tongue swipe across her lips and she gasped. He took the moment and licked inside her mouth once, before capturing her lips with his own once more. It was a bold move. Extremely so, but not out of place either. They'd connected on a level Adeline hadn't with many people.

Dean reluctantly, it seemed, straightened and smiled down at her. "I probably should apologize for that, but I won't. Take your time, finish your sandwich and fries. The bill is already paid; we have a tab and everyone here knows us and won't take your money. So don't even try to pay. I'll be in touch soon, Adeline. It was my pleasure to meet you."

"Be safe," she managed to get out breathlessly.

"I will." As if he couldn't help himself, Dean leaned down and kissed her once more, a brief touch of his lips to hers this time, then he was striding out of the restaurant.

Adeline kept her eyes on Dean's muscular butt as he jogged across the street and disappeared inside the fire station. Within minutes, the big bay doors were opening and a fire truck was pulling out with its lights on and sirens blaring.

Adeline sank back against the plastic booth seat and let out the breath she hadn't realized she'd been holding. Feeling Coco's hot doggy breath against her leg, she looked under the table and murmured to her dog, "Wow."

His tongue lolled out as if he agreed with her breathless statement. Smiling, Adeline absently picked up a french fry. The day hadn't started out that great, but had ended up being one of the most exciting days she'd had in recent history. Who would've thought a seizure could actually bring about something good in her life for once? Not her.

Licking her lips, and remembering how Dean's had felt against her own, Adeline sighed. Good Lord, just the quick taste had her more turned on than she'd been in her entire life, but she refused to get too excited.

Lots of men had said they'd call, and hadn't. Yes, she had Dean's number, but she firmly believed, maybe old-fashionably, that the man should be the one to make the first move.

She sent a silent prayer up into the heavens that Dean "Crash" Christopherson wasn't just messing with her. She wanted nothing more than to get to know the gorgeous firefighter.

Chapter Three

————◆————

Dean: *You get home all right?*

ADELINE STARED DOWN at the text on her phone for a moment, then grinned. Dean. She hadn't really expected to hear from him so soon, but couldn't deny that she liked it.

Adeline: *Yup. Thanks. Your day go okay?*

Putting the phone down, Adeline finished getting Coco's dinner ready. She didn't cook for herself, but she had no problem cooking for her dog. Coco had given Adeline her independence back; there wasn't anything she wouldn't do for him.

Emptying the can of chickpeas into the pot already full with green beans, carrots, chicken, and water, she stirred the mixture together. The only other thing it needed was the rice, which was simmering on the stove. This batch would last for about a week and was full of protein, vegetables, and carbohydrates to keep the Lab happy and healthy. She'd started cooking for Coco when he was younger and they'd had an experience with a tainted bag of dog food. Adeline wasn't willing to take a chance like that again with her beloved dog's life. At least she knew exactly what was going into her baby's body if she made his food.

Her phone vibrated with an incoming text.

Dean: *Had lunch with a woman I can't wait to get to know better. ;)*

Adeline smiled. God, she felt like a teenager again, getting a note from a boy she liked. She wasn't sure how to respond, so she put down the phone and finished cooking and packaging up Coco's food for the week. When she was done, she washed her hands and was drying them when her phone vibrated again.

Picking up the phone, she walked into her living room and plopped herself down on the huge armchair. She had a couch, but much preferred to curl up in the buttery-soft leather chair. It was big enough that she could sit with her feet tucked under her and lean against the large arm. It was one of the first things she'd bought after she'd started working at her first "adult job." It was old, and probably needed replacing, but Adeline wouldn't part with it until the stuffing was coming out and it couldn't possibly be repaired.

Expecting the text to be from Dean, she frowned when she saw it was from her boss.

At one time she might've been interested in Douglas. He was fairly good looking. He had light brown hair that he kept short. He was always well dressed and well groomed. But there was just something that had rubbed her the wrong way from the moment Adeline met him. Something that just seemed off about him. And that was before he'd shown what an asshole he really was.

He'd insisted on getting all of their cell phone numbers when he'd been hired. He wanted to be able to have immediate access to all of them, "just in case there was an emergency."

Adeline shook her head. The only emergencies he'd had were ones of his own making…and they'd all had to deal with the consequences of his actions.

> **Boss:** Meeting tomorrow. 7:30am. Wolfe portfolio needs complete overhaul. Don't be late.

Adeline rolled her eyes and sighed. It wasn't as if she hadn't been expecting it. James Wolfe was a demanding customer—rightfully so. He owned a chain of car dealerships across south Texas. Douglas had acquired the account from the person whose job he'd taken over. Except their old boss had regularly held meetings with all of his employees to get their input and ideas on marketing campaigns in order to keep them fresh and hip. He'd regularly shared some of the profits from those campaigns with his employees as well.

Douglas hadn't once asked anyone for their thoughts, and if the last couple of radio spots and television commercials Adeline had heard and seen were anything to go by, Mr. Wolfe had a right to not be happy. They were awful. Corny and cheesy, they sounded like something a novice would put together, not an award-winning marketing firm like theirs.

She'd been expecting something like this for a few weeks now. And while she might not be happy the reputation of the company was suffering because of Douglas Hill the Third, she felt a bit of excitement that she and her coworkers might get a chance to turn the Wolfe campaign around.

She shot off a quick affirmative reply to her boss— he expected his employees to acknowledge his texts— then sat back with a sigh. She felt okay, a bit dragged out, but she was used to the feeling on days when she had a seizure. Unfortunately, those days were coming more and more frequently.

Not wanting to chat on the phone, but wanting to touch base with her sister, Adeline thumbed a quick note.

Adeline: *Hey sis. Had another seizure today right when I sat down with my blind date. He was an ass, but a firefighter helped me out and let me go to his station across the street to lie down. Nothing out of the ordinary with it though, no worries. Coco was awesome and let me know it was coming. Jerkface* *called us in for an early meeting to fix his mistakes. No surprise there. Hope all is okay with you. I'll call tomorrow night and we can chat. Luv ya.*

Adeline hit send and bit her lip. She really wanted to respond to Dean's message, but wasn't sure what to say. Out of all the men she'd met for a first date from the dating website, no one had inquired as to whether or not she'd made it home all right. Not one. It didn't matter that they hadn't really clicked on their dates; it was a matter of being polite and considerate.

But Dean hadn't wasted any time checking on her and it made her feel good inside. Adeline typed a response to him, smiling all the while.

Adeline: *Anyone I know? :)*

She clicked on the television and turned to the Science Channel. It was her new favorite station. Some of the shows were extremely interesting...thank goodness for the DVR.

Within moments, her phone vibrated.

Dean: *Maybe. She's got black hair, a well-behaved dog, and can make me laugh with only three words.*

Adeline immediately typed out a response. Usually she was a bit more reserved with men. When she chatted with them online, she kept to the basics and didn't let her true self out, figuring she needed to be polite and hold back some of who she was until she really got to know the person. She wasn't sure what it was about Dean that made her want to be completely herself. Maybe it was because he'd been there for her when she'd needed him. Maybe it was how he had put her at ease. Or maybe it was because she was more attracted to him than she'd been to anyone in years. Whatever it was, she felt more energized than she had in a long time. More wired. More…excited.

> **Adeline:** It took three?

His response was immediate.

> **Dean:** Lol. How was the rest of your day?
>
> **Adeline:** Good. Until my jerk of a boss texted to tell me and some of my coworkers that we had to be in thirty minutes early tomorrow for a meeting to discuss how to fix his screw-ups.
>
> **Dean:** Ugh. Sucks. You sent out that resume yet?

Adeline smiled. He wasn't saying anything she hadn't already thought about.

> **Adeline:** It's on my to-do list for tomorrow.
>
> **Dean:** Good. You deserve more than that.
>
> **Adeline:** How do you know? Maybe I'm the trouble-maker in the office. Maybe I'm the bitch and my boss is the one who has to deal with me.
>
> **Dean:** Nope. Not buying it.

Adeline: *Why? You don't know me.*

Dean: *You're right, I don't. Want to go to dinner with me this Friday?*

Adeline looked down at her phone in shock. She really shouldn't be that surprised, he'd flat-out said earlier that he wanted to get to know her. But he'd actually asked her out on a date. It was right there in black and white on her phone.

Did she want to go out with him? Yes. But for some reason she hesitated. Maybe it was because she had a feeling saying yes would completely change her life.

As much as she *wanted* to find a man to love and to love her back, her life was a mess right now. Between her increasing-in-frequency seizures, her work situation being up in the air, and the fact that she was just coming to terms with the realization now might not be the best time to jump into a relationship, it was jarring to have a man like Dean literally pop into her life out of nowhere.

Dean: *Too fast?*

The words blinked back at Adeline as she contemplated what to say. Friday nights she and Alicia usually got together, but that was just an excuse. Her sister wouldn't mind in the least if she canceled on her. She'd been on her case long enough to get back into the dating pool. She'd be ecstatic if she broke off their standing get-together for a man.

As she was about to text back and tell Dean that, yes, it was too fast, and she already had plans with her sister, a message popped up from Alicia.

> **Alicia:** *When do you go to the doctor again to discuss surgery? I hate that you're having to deal with the seizures so much now. And gah, what an ass Douglas is. You need to hurry up and find another job. Oh, and before I forget, I need to cancel for Friday. Matt made plans for us to go to that Brazilian steakhouse. Next week for sure. Love you!*

It was official. Fate was conspiring against her. She shot off a quick return text to Alicia, telling her it was okay about Friday and telling her she was sending resumes out tomorrow. Then she went back to Dean's text.

> **Adeline:** *Yes. And no. It does seem fast, but at the same time, I was more comfortable with you today at lunch than I've been with any guy I've met in a long time. I was going to tell you that I couldn't go because I go out with my sister every Friday, but she just canceled on me. As long as we go somewhere I can take Coco, and I can meet you there…I'd love to go to dinner with you Friday.*

Adeline's thumb hovered over the send button then quickly hit it. She didn't know what it was about Dean that made her want to throw herself into his arms, yet at the same time run as fast as she could away from him. It was ridiculous. She was way too old to feel this up and down about a man.

Dean: Whew. You had me worried there for a bit. Thank you. I promise to be on my best behavior. And I wouldn't have asked you out if I didn't feel the same way about you. Are you sure I can't pick you up?

Adeline: I'm sure.

Dean: Not even if I promise to leave my pager at home and not do anything creepy so you feel the need to get away from me?

Adeline: Lol. Not this time. Maybe next time.

Dean: Deal. And I'm holding you to that.

Adeline: To what?

Dean: To a second date. You just asked me out and I said yes.

Adeline: Wait, what? I didn't ask you out.

Dean: Yup. You said next time we go out I can pick you up.

Adeline laughed out loud. She totally had.

Adeline: I guess I did. So where are we going?

Dean: I'll text ya later. I gotta plan something epic.

Adeline: You mean you didn't already have it planned?

Dean: Nope. I wasn't sure you'd agree. And I don't presume to know the answer to anything I might ask a woman.

Adeline: *Probably a good life plan.*

Dean: *Right? Thank you, Adeline. I can't wait to see you again. I feel extraordinarily lucky I was there at the right time today to not only help you out, but to get to know you a little afterwards too.*

Adeline: **blush**

Dean: *I'm serious.*

Adeline: *I'm glad you were there too. I gotta go. I'll talk to you later.*

Dean: *Sweet dreams, beautiful.*

Adeline stared at the television blankly for a moment before a huge smile crept over her face. Beautiful. She didn't really believe it, but merely imagining the word coming out of Dean's mouth in his deep voice sent warm shivers through her.

She had no idea where they might go, but she hadn't been this excited for a date in a long time. Not even the thought of having to meet with Douglas and hearing exactly what ridiculous thing he had planned for her and the rest of the team could diminish her happy thoughts.

Friday couldn't come soon enough.

THE MAN SAT in the leather chair in his living room, oblivious to the television in the background. He rocked back and forth as he thought about the woman. He hadn't really noticed her until recently. But now that he had, he couldn't stop thinking about her.

She's cute.

I like her.

I want her to be mine.

Tomorrow I'll get to see her again.

I can't wait.

Chapter Four

A S FAR AS he was concerned, Friday couldn't come soon enough.

"What's put that weird-ass look on your ugly mug?" Penelope "Tiger" Turner, the lone female on the squad, asked Crash the next day.

They'd been sitting around watching television, killing time until their shift ended or they got a call, whichever came first.

"Nothin'," Crash told her, not able to keep the small smile off his face.

"Bull. Does it have anything to do with the woman you hid in the back room yesterday, then snuck out of here without letting anyone talk to her?"

Crash turned to her. "I didn't hide her in the back. She was having a seizure. I was giving her some privacy."

"Ha!" Penelope crowed. "I knew it was her. Spill it!"

Crash knew he was grinning like an idiot, but didn't care. Deciding that maybe Penelope was the best person to talk to about Adeline, he said, "Her name is Adeline.

She was on a blind date and when her dog alerted to the fact she was going to have a seizure, the asshole she was with got up and left."

"Christ, what a douche."

"Exactly. So I went over to see what I could do to help, and brought her here. She had her seizure, and we went back over to eat lunch. I asked her out, she said yes, and we're getting together on Friday."

"Somehow I think there's a lot you're leaving out," Penelope said dryly.

"Not really," Crash protested.

"She was cute," Penelope noted.

"Yeah." She was more than cute, but Dean wasn't going to get into it with Penelope. When he was watching over her at the station, he was focused on her health, but later, at lunch, he'd noticed.

She wasn't very tall, probably half a foot shorter than he was. When they'd walked side-by-side to the diner he towered over her. It had made him feel even more protective of her. Adeline's black hair shone in the sunlight and brushed against her shoulders as she walked. Her hair was so dark it almost looked like she had blue highlights in the thick strands. Her lips were full and if she'd been wearing lipstick it had long since been nibbled or wiped off by the time they sat across from each other in the booth at lunch. He recalled her flushed cheeks when he complimented her, as if she wasn't used to them, and her lashes were long and thick when she looked away from him, not able to meet his eyes.

She had been wearing a long, flowery skirt and a white button-down blouse and he'd been able to see a hint of her curves under it. Penelope was right, Adeline was cute, but she was more than that. He enjoyed not only talking with her, but her pragmatic take on her life and illness. He couldn't wait to get to know her better.

"I need to figure out where I want to take her on our date," Crash mused out loud.

Penelope looked at him for a moment with her head tilted. "You like her."

"Uh, yeah."

"No, I mean, you *like* her. This isn't just another date, is it?"

Crash shrugged. "It's too early to know what it is."

"Don't lie about it. There's something about her. Something that's caught your eye."

Crash looked over at Penelope. She was sitting on the couch next to him, her head resting on her hand, her elbow propped up on the back of the couch. She wasn't teasing him; she was completely serious.

"Yeah. Although it's crazy. I just met her."

As much as Crash portrayed the playboy to his friends, in actuality he was anything but. He had a profile on a dating website, but had never entertained the idea of actually meeting anyone in person who messaged him. He dated, but was very picky about the women he took to his bed. He supposed it was sappy. He probably should be happy with playing the field and screwing as many women as he could…but he wasn't.

He once saw a picture on social media that said something to the effect of, "I wish I'd found you sooner so I could've spent more time loving you." It was exactly how he felt. He was only thirty-two, but if he could've met a woman when he was twenty who made his heart speed up just by looking at her, who made him happy simply by hearing her laugh, and who he wanted to wake up to for the rest of his life, he would've married her on the spot.

He couldn't help but thinking about how much time he was losing. Crash knew he wasn't typical in that sense. Most of his buddies enjoyed being single, but he didn't. He only played the game, pretending to be interested in dating as many people as possible. Maybe too well.

"It doesn't matter that you just met her. Sometimes, all it takes is one look at someone and you know." Penelope's voice was low and serious. "It's not necessarily convenient, and it might not be the person you think you should be attracted to. Sometimes you know deep in your heart that it's, in fact, the last person you should be attracted to, but it just is."

Suddenly feeling as if they were no longer talking about him and Adeline, Crash asked, "You felt that before, Tiger?"

The small blonde dynamo nodded.

Protective feelings rose in Crash like a tidal wave. Penelope was one of a core group of friends who worked as firefighters at Station 7. She was Sledge's sister, and she'd busted her ass and proved herself more than capable of holding her own against the taller, heavier, and stronger men she worked with. She didn't quit, no matter what.

When she'd gone over to the Middle East to do a tour with her National Guard unit and had gotten kidnapped, it had nearly killed every one of the firefighters. They'd worked hand in hand with her brother to lobby whoever would listen to rescue her. Luckily, the President had authorized a Special Forces team to go in and get her out.

She was back at work, and most of the time everyone thought she'd been dealing exceptionally well, but every now and then a very vulnerable side of the woman peeked out. Like now. Crash had no idea she might be harboring feelings for someone. He also had no idea who it could be, as the woman volunteered to take shifts for other firefighters all the time...she spent more time here at the station than at her apartment.

But he knew that Moose more than liked the small

spitfire, and it would be ideal if she liked him back. Crash probed for more information.

"Who is he?"

As if his words brought her back to the present, Penelope smiled in a vacant way and Crash knew any chance he had of finding out who she might be pining over was most likely lost. Shaking her head, she said, "Oh, you know, I got to meet Chris Pratt when I went to the White House for that ceremony thing. God, is that man fine."

"Tiger. Be serious. Was it one of the SEALs who rescued you? Or those mysterious Army guys you won't talk about but we all know you see when you go up to Fort Hood for debriefings and your counseling sessions?"

She burst out laughing. "First of all, those SEALs are all happily married. They'd sooner cut off their dicks than even look at me in that way. And secondly, those Army guys are way too alpha for me. Nope, I like a nice malleable guy. Someone I can bend to my will."

Her words said one thing, but the look in her eyes said something else entirely. Crash opened his mouth to say something, but she hurried on, cutting him off.

"Anyway, it doesn't matter. All I'm saying is that if you like this chick, you should go for it. I know you project a manwhore attitude to everyone around here, but you haven't been out on a real date in forever." Her voice got serious once more. "Any woman would be lucky as shit to have you in her life. Don't discount whatever you're feeling about this chick because you just met her. You're not proposing, or asking her to move in…at least you'd better not be, that would be creepy." She smiled to let him know she was teasing, then got serious again.

"Be honest with her. Let her know that you enjoy spending time with her. Get to know her with no pressure. There are way too many assholes out there and it's hard to find a good man. Trust me, I know this, especially after being dubbed the country's 'Army Princess.' You *are* a good man, Crash. A very good man. There's nothing I want more than for all of you guys here at the station to find your own good women."

"Thanks, Tiger."

"You're welcome. Now, what are your plans for your date?"

Crash smiled. "I'm not telling you."

"What? Why not?" Penelope protested, sitting up straight in shock.

"Because."

"What are you, twelve? That's not an answer."

Crash shrugged.

"You suck. Well, I hope it's appropriate for a first date. I mean, most men screw it up. I wouldn't be surprised if you went overboard. You're gonna scare her away if you don't do it right. I'm just trying to help you and—"

Loud tones alerting them to an incoming call pealed through the room, cutting off whatever it was Penelope was going to say. Both Penelope and Crash were on their feet before the voice of the dispatcher came through the speakers telling them they were being called to a multiple-car crash on the Interstate.

Looking over at Crash as they headed to their lockers to put on their bunker gear, Penelope said, "Just tell me one thing, you're not taking her to a country and western bar…are you?"

"All Texan women like a man in boots and a cowboy hat, don't they?"

"Oh Lord. I tried. Don't come cryin' to me when she doesn't want to see you again, Crash."

He merely ducked his head and concentrated on getting dressed and to the fire truck. It was fun to mess with Penelope's head. Even Crash knew better than to take a woman to a bar on their first date. Not only was it usually too loud to really talk, there were way too many other men who might think it was okay to hit on her in a bar setting.

No, he wanted Adeline all to himself.

LATER THAT NIGHT, Crash lay on his bunk at the

firehouse, his arm behind his head. He was tired, they'd been going nonstop all day, and this was the first break they'd gotten. Besides the horrific accident on the Interstate, they'd investigated two fire alarms—which luckily had turned out to be nothing—three medical calls, one car fire, and a small grass fire.

This was the first time he'd had to himself all day. His thoughts turned to Adeline.

Crash hadn't yet come close to finding anyone he wanted to spend the rest of his life with. His parents were happily married, and he wanted what they had. He needed to find a woman who was independent enough to be able to deal with his shift schedule at the station—which meant spending nights alone when he was on duty—but who still needed and wanted him around.

He wanted to be her best friend, and for her to be his. Wanted to see her eyes light up when he came through the door, wanted to be able to talk to her about the highs and lows of his day and have her comfort him when he lost patients. He wanted to be there for her when she needed to bitch about her job or to pick her up when she had too much to drink on girls' night out.

Along with all that, Dean wanted passion. He'd lusted over women before, and had some good times in bed, but he'd never felt the *need* to be with someone. The bone-deep desire to please her, to fuck her brains out, then to make love to her tenderly for hours. It was what had been missing in all of his relationships in the past.

He had no idea if Adeline Reynolds was that person, but for the first time in his life he couldn't stop thinking about a woman. When he'd been holding the head of a lady in her late twenties in a car that afternoon, keeping her vertebrae aligned just in case, he had the horrifying thought that what if it had been Adeline? When he'd been holding the hose and throwing water on the grass fire, his thoughts had turned to Adeline and he'd wondered what she was doing right that moment. When they'd gone to one of the false alarms and he'd heard a dog barking inside the house next door, he thought about Coco and wondered how he and Adeline had gotten together.

It should've annoyed him how she kept creeping into his thoughts, but it didn't. It made him more anxious to see her. To talk to her. To get to know her better.

Scooting up on the bed, Crash leaned back against the headboard and grabbed his phone. He'd held off texting her all day, but couldn't wait anymore. He wanted to know how the meeting with her asshole boss went. Wanted to know if she'd had any more seizures. Hell, he just wanted to talk to her…even if the talking was through text.

Dean: *How was your day, beautiful?*

Crash had never been the kind of man to use endearments with the women he dated. But when he thought about Adeline, the word beautiful just seemed to pop into his brain. Every time.

It took a while—well, five minutes was a while for him right now since he wanted to talk, but finally she responded.

Adeline: *Crappy. Yours?*

Dean: *I'm sorry. I'm guessing the meeting didn't go well?*

Adeline: *You'd guess right.*

Dean: *Want to talk about it?*

It took a couple of minutes, but she finally texted back.

Adeline: *It's too unbelievable and convoluted to type out.*

Dean: *Want me to call?*

When she didn't respond right away, Crash thought about it and hurried to text.

Dean: *Only if you want to. I'm not trying to be a stalker or anything.*

Dean: *Seriously.*

Dean: *Okay, beautiful, I'm not going to push. I'll text later this week with details on our date. I'm sorry you had a bad day.*

Crash sighed and put his head back. Damn. He hadn't meant to rush her, or make her feel uncomfortable. But even just by reading her words he could tell she was upset, and he'd only wanted to make her feel better.

His phone dinged with a text.

Adeline: *If you're not busy, I wouldn't mind talking.*

Without thought, Crash touched the little phone icon next to her name and brought the cell up to his ear.

"Hey, Dean."

Dean. Yeah, he liked his name on her lips.

"Hi, beautiful. I'm sorry you've had a crap day. If you really don't want to talk about it, it's fine. I wouldn't ever want you to do anything you weren't comfortable with."

"Thanks. I…I just usually talk to my sister about my boss from hell, and it threw me for a bit when you offered to talk. I don't—" Adeline abruptly stopped talking.

"You don't what?"

"I don't want you to think I'm a downer. Or that I'm always bitching about my job. I usually don't. But it's been a trying month or so."

"I appreciate that. We don't know each other very well, but even after only being with you for a short lunch, I got that you aren't one to complain about things."

"You did?" she asked in surprise.

"Yeah, beautiful. I did. Now…tell me about the meeting this morning. You said you had to go in early?"

She sighed hugely and Crash could picture her expression pulled down in a frown. It made him want to do anything he could to wipe it off her face.

"Yup. We all had to be in at seven-thirty for a meeting. My boss screwed up an account…again…and needed us to bail him out. You know James Wolfe?"

"The car dealer guy?"

"That's him. Well, our company does his marketing, and it hasn't been going well since Douglas took over the account."

"Ouch. I have to say, I don't watch a lot of television except at the station, but the last few commercials I've seen have looked pretty amateurish. What's with the fake shots of the wolves howling while a car drives by?"

"Right. That's why we had the meeting this morning. Our old boss had been given marketing carte blanche by Mr. Wolfe, so those ads that have been running weren't reviewed and approved by him and he's not happy."

Crash chuckled. "Gotcha."

"Anyway, I was kinda looking forward to the meeting this morning. I mean, I work with some awesomely creative people, and I knew we'd be able to put together a kick-ass campaign for Mr. Wolfe. The meeting started out good. Really good. We talked about new commercials, radio spots, teaming up with the zoo to get some good cross-promo and stuff. Douglas sat quiet the whole time, taking lots of notes, of course. Then he spent the last thirty minutes telling us how everything we'd discussed wouldn't work, and how we were stupid to think it would, and if he was smart he'd fire us all right then and hire an all new staff who knew what they were talking about."

"What an ass," Crash swore. "Seriously, has the guy taken any leadership or management classes?"

"It gets worse," Adeline told him.

"Fuck. Worse?"

"One of his interns, who he treats like shit, later told us that he spent the rest of the morning on the phone with Mr. Wolfe pitching all of our ideas to him. Ideas that he'd told us were crap only an hour before."

"Wow."

"Right?"

"Who does that?"

"Douglas Hill the Third," Adeline said dryly.

"Can't anyone talk to *his* boss?"

"It's complicated. He was hired by the Vice President. And *that* guy is almost untouchable because he's like, San Antonio royalty or something. Basically we could bitch to him about Douglas, but he wouldn't do anything about it. As long as our division is making money, no one cares how it's being done."

"And no one has confronted Douglas about it?"

"Someone did."

"And?"

"He was fired."

"Jesus," Crash breathed. "Please tell me you've sent out resumes. I can't imagine working in a toxic place like that."

"Sent three this afternoon."

"Thank God. I'm really sorry, beautiful. It sounds like you need a glass of wine, a massage, and a day off."

She laughed. "One out of three isn't too bad."

Crash bit his lip to hold back the words he wanted to say. That he'd come over and give her that massage. Too much too soon.

"So, how was *your* day?" she asked, clearly trying to change the topic.

"Busy, as usual." Crash went on to tell her about the many calls they'd had.

"Is it weird not knowing the outcome of the people you help?"

"What do you mean?"

"Like, that accident. You held that woman's head, but you don't know if she's okay or not."

"Ah. Sometimes, but honestly, I don't think about it too much. Ultimately, I do the best I can in each situation. We might learn about what happens to people after they leave the scene, but it's to further analyze the job *we* did. For instance, if we learn that the woman is paralyzed, I would want to try to figure out if it's because of something we did at the scene. But generally, we try not to second guess ourselves or our actions. We make a ton of split-second decisions and we screw up, just like everyone does. It sucks, but it happens. It's why we do so much training, so we don't have to think so much when we get to a scene, we just act."

"Thank you."

"What are you thanking me for, beautiful?"

"For doing what you do. I know you get paid for it, it's a job, but not everyone could do it. I know I couldn't, and I've met enough first responders in my life to know that you're really good at what you do."

Crash chuckled. "You're welcome. Although I have to admit, I didn't really do anything for you."

"Sure you did."

"No, I really didn't."

"You got me to a safe place where I didn't have to worry about being robbed or hurt while I was seizing. I didn't have to worry about Coco and if someone would steal him. Nobody was pointing at me and laughing, or worse, filming me with their damn cell phone cameras. You let me process when I came to, and didn't rush or push me to talk. So yeah, Dean Christopherson, you did a lot. And I appreciate it."

"Damn. Now I want to beat the shit out of anyone who even looks at you sideways. This might not bode well for our relationship."

He closed his eyes and smiled at her small laugh. He could picture her smile in his head almost as clearly as if she was standing in front of him.

"Down, boy."

"Can't help it. I'm a protective kind of man, beautiful, and if I ever see one person with their cell phone pointed at you while you're having a seizure, I can promise you they'll never do it again."

"Dean…"

He tried to tone down the intensity in his voice. "You good otherwise after your shitty day? No seizures today?"

Adeline let out a large breath. "No. I've felt a bit off all afternoon, but no seizures."

"Does stress bring them on?"

"Sometimes. I've noticed that alcohol can do it too. I've pretty much cut it out of my life except for the occasional glass of wine. I really miss being able to have a couple margaritas with my sister when we go out though."

"Maybe getting a new job will help."

"I'm hoping so, but not counting on it."

"Have you decided to have the surgery then?"

"I just don't know. It scares the crap out of me and

I'm not ready yet."

"Then wait until you *are* ready."

"It's not that easy."

"Why not?"

"Well, because."

Crash laughed. "Now you sound like me. I was asked something today and that was the answer I gave. Adeline, give yourself a break. You know your body. Having the surgery isn't an easy decision. I don't think I'd be able to do it for all the reasons you mentioned yesterday. It's simple for a doctor to tell you it's what you should do, but it's not his brain, or his life, that'll be affected. Besides, even if you do go under the knife, there's a chance the seizures won't completely go away, right?"

"Right."

"So there you go. You've got time to fully weigh the pros and cons. Cut yourself some slack."

"You're pretty smart, you know that?"

"Of course."

They both laughed.

"Seriously, thanks for calling. I needed this."

"Anytime. I mean that. I like talking to you, Adeline. You make me feel that there's more to my life than jumping at the sounds of the tones and doing errands on my days off."

"What *do* you do on your days off?"

"The same things you probably do on the weekends," he told her easily. "Grocery shopping, clean the house, sit on my butt and watch football."

"I don't like football."

"Be still my heart," Crash teased. "Not like football?"

"Okay, I do like watching the guys' butts in their uniforms. That better?"

"We won't watch football," he declared immediately.

Adeline giggled. "Why 'Crash'?"

"What?"

"Why is your nickname Crash? Or is that a secret?"

"Nope. No secret. On my very first day on the job, we got nothing but call after call for car crashes. The others dubbed me that. It stuck."

"I thought it might be because of your driving habits."

"No way. I'm the safest driver out of everyone. I promise you'll be safe with me."

"I wasn't—"

"I know you weren't," Crash interrupted, "but I felt it needed to be said anyway. You should know when you're out with me, you'll be safe. If Coco alerts, I'll get you someplace clean and protected to have a seizure. If you're in a car with me, I'll never speed or be unsafe. If we're walking somewhere, you and Coco will be away from the street. I take your safety seriously, beautiful. No matter where we are or what we're doing."

"Okay," Adeline said in a whisper.

Crash took a deep breath. "On that note, I should probably let you go. I wasn't aiming to freak you out, and you sound like I did anyway."

"It's not that, it's just…I generally *never* feel safe. Anywhere."

"You are when you're with me. I know it's not something I can just say and you'll automatically feel it. I hope that you'll come to know it as a fact over time. I'm sorry you had a bad day. I was serious earlier when I said you could always talk to me about it. Anytime you need to talk, just call. If I don't answer, leave a message and I'll call when I can. Okay?"

"Okay."

"Have a good night, beautiful. I'll text tomorrow and let you know where to meet me Friday night."

"Sounds good."

"Good night."

"Good night, Dean."

Crash clicked off the phone and groaned. He hadn't meant to say all that shit about her being safe with him, it'd just popped out. He couldn't be sorry it had, though. No woman should feel uncertain or unsafe when she was with a man. It didn't matter if they'd just started dating or had been together for years. The world was a harsh place, even more so for people who didn't fit societal norms.

Adeline was not only pretty, she also had a disability that was more than evident at times. It couldn't be easy. Crash made a vow right then and there to do whatever he could to make her life easier. He couldn't be with her at work, but he could be there for her after.

Plans for their date swirled in his head and he suddenly knew exactly where he wanted to take her on Friday night. He smiled and scooted back down on the mattress getting comfortable once more.

NO, NO, NO!

Yelling doesn't work. She doesn't like yelling. She scowled and wrinkled her nose. She thought you didn't see, but you did.

She needs to be courted. Treated like gold.

She'll like you if you talk nice to her. Get her to go on a date. Women like that.

Take her to lunch.

Then dinner.

Then she'll be yours.

You can keep her forever and she'll love you.

Chapter Five

ADELINE CHECKED HER phone for what seemed like the hundredth time to make sure she was in the right place. She was.

Dean had told her to meet him at an address in Southtown, an area just south of downtown San Antonio. It was generally known as the creative part of the city. There were a lot of eclectic shops and smaller specialty restaurants. She wasn't really the creative type, even though she worked in marketing, but Dean got points for doing something outside the norm.

The rest of the week at work had been relatively uneventful. There hadn't been any more run-ins with Douglas, thank God. He'd been tied up in meetings or out of the office. Which was fine with her. Adeline had lunch with her sister one day and told her all about the goings on in the office as well as about Dean.

Alicia, of course, had cautioned her to take things slow, picking up on the fact that Adeline really seemed to like Dean. Adeline had reassured her that she actually knew more about Dean than she did some of the men she'd met online.

After Adeline promised that she'd call Saturday morning to let her know how it went, Alicia had finally stopped nagging. But Adeline had a feeling she'd probably get a call or text Friday night from her sister, checking up on her and making sure all was well. Even though Alicia was younger than her by a few years, she was the worrywart of the family. Adeline's health scares didn't help the matter any.

Adeline hadn't spoken with Dean in the last few days, but they'd had a few chatty text conversations. He inquired about her day and health, and Adeline did the same. On Thursday afternoon, she'd received the text asking if she'd be able to meet him around five in Southtown. She'd had to leave work a bit early, but Adeline didn't have any issues with that, considering how Douglas had made them all come in before eight for that meeting earlier in the week.

It was now 5:05 and Adeline nervously made her way with Coco to the address he'd given her. She saw Dean before she realized what the address was, and had to swallow hard. Lord, the man was good looking. Tonight he was wearing a pair of dark jeans, cowboy boots, and a button-down white shirt, the stark white against his tanned arms making him all the more handsome. The sleeves were rolled up to his elbows and

Adeline decided there was nothing sexier than the sight of a well-built man's forearms.

He smiled at her as she neared him and Adeline's knees almost buckled. Somehow she'd forgotten how his smile lit up his face. How it made her want to make him keep smiling, if only to see the joy on his face aimed at her. Laugh lines around his eyes deepened as his lips quirked up. Adeline felt like the most important person in the world as he looked only at her as she approached.

"Hey, Adeline. You look great."

"Thanks. Sorry I'm a bit late." Adeline had changed out of her work clothes before she'd left the office. She wasn't one to get dressed up that often, but she'd made the effort for Dean. She was wearing a knee-length skirt that swished around her legs as she walked. It was purple with white flowers and had several light layers. It made her feel feminine and pretty. She'd paired it with low dark purple heels, knowing better than to attempt to wear anything over a couple of inches. She used to wear heels all the time when she was younger, figuring the extra inches they gave her were a good thing, but after too many sprained ankles to count, not to mention how she used to have seizures without any warning, she'd learned that two inches were now her physical limit.

She was wearing a cute lilac-colored, cap-sleeved knock-off designer blouse, which matched her skirt. It had a scoop neck both in the front and back. It hugged her breasts and even though she wasn't model thin, her lingerie kept all her bits tucked in and pushed up in the right places.

She didn't wear them a lot, but something about wearing a corset made her feel sexy and confident. It held her stomach in and pushed her boobs up…and when paired with a silky tank top couldn't really be noticed under her shirt. Win-win-win in her book.

She'd put a bit of makeup on, lipstick, blush, mascara, and a light dusting of purple eye shadow to round out her look. Her hair she'd left down, but had brushed it out and sprayed some volumizer on to give it a fresh look after the long work day. She could've been more creative if she'd had the time, but she thought she looked pretty good.

Without hesitation, Dean placed his hand on her hip as he leaned into her. He kissed her on the lips gently then pulled his head back, not removing his hand. He looked into her eyes as he said, "Hi."

"Hi."

Dean licked his lips and his eyes darted down to her mouth, before coming back up to meet her eyes again. "You're beautiful."

Adeline knew she was blushing, but tried to be suave. "Thanks. You clean up pretty well yourself."

He squeezed her hip at her words and leaned in again, brushing his lips against her cheek this time and then moving to her ear. "Thank you for agreeing to meet me tonight."

"Thank you for asking me out," Adeline returned.

"You're welcome." And with that, Dean finally let go of her waist and crouched down to greet Coco. "Hey, handsome. How ya doin'?"

Coco's tail wagged in response as he sat at Adeline's side wiggling in excitement.

"Go on," Adeline told her dog, releasing him from duty.

As if he'd been physically held back, her words were the signal he'd been waiting for. Coco leaped up at Dean and the force of his ninety-pound body knocked Dean over onto his butt on the sidewalk.

Adeline would've been horrified, but Dean immediately laughed and shifted to his knees. Taking her dog's face in his hands, Dean play-wrestled with Coco and tried to keep the dog's tongue away from his face. After a couple moments of roughhousing, Dean finally stood up, patting Coco on the head.

"Coco, heel," Adeline ordered, pleased when the dog immediately came back to her side and sat, as if he hadn't been drooling all over the man now standing in front of them.

"God, I miss having a dog around."

"You had one?"

"Yeah. She died last year. A Rottweiler. I got her

from the pound. The staff estimated she was ten years old and told me she'd been dumped by her family. They decided that they just didn't want her anymore." He shrugged. "She was the most gentle, loving dog I'd ever met. All she wanted to do was lie around and sleep…oh, and get pets. She had a level-four heart murmur and her ol' ticker just gave out. I found her one morning in her doggy bed, not breathing; she'd passed away during the night. I miss her."

"I'm sorry." Adeline put her hand on Dean's forearm.

He immediately put his hand overs hers and turned them to head down the sidewalk. "Thanks. You ready for tonight?"

Adeline smiled at him. "Depends on what you have planned. Ready to go skydiving or street race? No. To eat? Yes."

"How about a quick stop first?"

Adeline shrugged. "Sure."

"Good. Here we are." Dean gestured at a small shop they'd stopped in front of.

She looked up and saw a sign that said Garcia Art Glass, Inc. Through the windows, she saw shelves upon shelves of beautiful glasswork. Glasses, plates, vases, and sculptures. All in different vibrant colors. Inside the store, there was an ornate chandelier hanging from the ceiling. She looked up at Dean in confusion.

"It's a hand-blown glass store," he told her. "For some reason, I thought you might enjoy it. They're going to do a demonstration for us."

"Really?"

"Really. Is it okay?"

"It's perfect," Adeline breathed. "I've never seen it done before. How fun!"

The worry lines on Dean's forehead smoothed out. "Good. Come on, they're waiting for us."

Dean held open the door for her and Coco and Adeline gazed around in wonder as she entered. Everywhere she looked was beautiful, colorful handmade glass. Stained-glass windows hung on the walls and row upon row of glasses were displayed as well. She wasn't sure where to start.

"Mr. Christopherson and Ms. Reynolds, yes?" a woman asked from the back of the store.

"That's us," Dean replied.

"I'm Clarice. You're right on time. We're all set up and ready for you."

Dean put his hand on Adeline's lower back and urged her forward.

As if in a daze, she followed the woman through the store to a door in the rear. They entered a room with a few large ovens along the far wall. There were benches set up in a semi-circle in front of them and the woman motioned for them to sit in the middle section in the front.

"This is Andres. He'll be demonstrating how glass-blowing is done for you tonight. It'll take about forty minutes or so, then you'll have some time to browse the store if you'd like. Enjoy."

Adeline nodded, but her eyes were fixed on the His-panic man in front of them.

"*Hola*," he stated in a warm, friendly voice, holding out his hand. Adeline and Dean shook his hand and he got right to it.

Thirty minutes later, with more information than she'd ever need about how to blow glass, Adeline watched as Dean took a shot. The room was warm from the furnace and Adeline knew she was perspiring but didn't care. There was something so erotic about watching Dean manipulate the pipe.

He gathered the melted glass from the furnace, turn-ing the pipe in his hands over and over, the muscles in his arms rippling with his movements.

Andres told him he had enough and Dean moved to a steel table and began rolling it. Andres instructed him on how to blow into the pipe to make a bubble in the molten glass. Dean went back to the furnace and gathered more glass, then returned to the steel table to repeat his earlier steps. Andres then began to shape the hot glass with a piece of soaked newspaper.

Dean and Andres discussed something for a moment

and the instructor took the pipe from him. They nodded at each other and Dean thanked him.

He came back to her side.

"That was cool. Was it hard?"

"Well, let's just say if it was left solely up to me, I'd end up with a blob of glass that didn't resemble anything but a blob of glass."

Adeline laughed. "This was fun. I don't think I've ever even thought about how that works before."

"I agree. I figured I'd try to impress you with something you might not have done. Want to browse a bit before dinner?"

"Yes!" she exclaimed. "I think I saw about ten things I had to have just at first glance on our way back here."

Dean laughed and took her hand in his. "Well, come on then. Far be it from me to keep you away from your treasures."

They walked back into the small storefront and the woman who'd originally greeted them smiled. "Like it?"

"Oh, yes," Adeline told her. "I can't believe everything in here was handmade."

"Yes, it's all been created by artists in the area. They sell it on commission. So take your time and see if anything strikes your fancy."

"Oh, I can tell you right now, all of it does!" Adeline said with a laugh. She walked to the front of the store and told Coco, "Sit. Stay." He did as asked and followed her with his eyes as she wandered around the displays.

Adeline seriously wanted to buy about fourteen things, but limited herself to two small sculptures and a beautiful multi-colored vase. Dean wanted to pay, but she absolutely refused, saying that just because he'd asked her out, didn't mean he had to pay for her baubles.

Surprising her in a good way he didn't argue, simply holding his hands up in a surrender gesture and backing away. Adeline laughed. "Thanks. I get that you're a guy and you want to pay, and it's appreciated, but it's not right."

"I *am* a guy, and I *will* be paying for dinner; as long as you understand that, we're good."

Adeline rolled her eyes and shook her head, smiling. Saying in exasperation to the lovely woman checking them out, "Men."

Clarice chuckled and continued to wrap up the fragile pieces. When she was done, she handed them to Adeline, but didn't let go of the bag when Adeline grabbed hold of it. Leaning forward, she said in a stage whisper, "He's a keeper."

Beaming at the woman, Adeline simply nodded and allowed Dean to take the bag out of her hand once they were on their way to the door. "I'll carry it. You take Coco."

The bell over the door tinkled as they left. When

they were on the sidewalk again, Adeline turned to Dean. "What now? I'm not sure you can top that."

"Dinner, of course."

"Of course."

"How adventurous are you?"

"Um…if we're talking do I want to bungee jump out of a helicopter over the Alamo, no. If you're talking trying new things, then I've been known to do crazy stuff now and then."

Dean laughed. "No bungie jumping, that's for sure. There's a wonderful Belgian Bistro across the street that has delicious *moules frites*. But if you don't eat seafood and don't like mussels, they have other things like chicken and steak as well."

"I've heard great things about that place," Adeline exclaimed. "But I've heard it's hard to get in."

"I have reservations, beautiful," Dean chuckled.

"Oh. Then yes, please. It sounds great."

Dean made them walk down the street to a crosswalk rather than simply jay-walking, and he kept his word, making sure she walked alongside the storefronts rather than on the other side of the sidewalk next to the street. It was a small thing, but the fact that he made a concerted effort to put himself nearest to the cars went a long way toward making this a perfect date.

They were quickly seated when they got inside, and even though it wasn't that crowded at first, by the time they'd received their appetizer, it was packed.

The small restaurant was loud and Dean pulled his chair closer to hers at the table in order to hear her better. Coco lay sleeping at her feet, and Adeline couldn't remember a better date. Dean got the mussels and she got the hanger steak. The *frites* were to die for and they ordered a sampler of dipping sauces so they could try them all.

Feeling replete, Adeline sipped a glass of Rombauer Merlot and relaxed in her seat, wishing the moment could last forever.

"What're you thinking?" Dean asked, putting his hand over hers on the tabletop and idly brushing his thumb over the back of it.

"I've had a good time. You're good company."

"Thanks. But the night's not over."

"It's not?"

"Nope. I have one more surprise up my sleeve."

Adeline eyed him with a smile. "I'm afraid to ask."

Dean laughed. "Nothing bad. Promise. But we have to drive there. I'd like you to ride with me...if that's okay. I'll bring you back here for your car."

Adeline bit her lip. The night had been amazing. Dean was funny, interesting, and surprisingly romantic. She hadn't expected that. Probably stereotypical of her, and rude, but there it was. She would've never guessed the hot fireman would take her to a glass-blowing demonstration then dinner at the small Belgian hole-in-the-wall bistro.

"This isn't where you're gonna take me back to your apartment and show me the hidden closet where you keep the bones of women you've taken out then killed and stashed, is it?"

Dean chuckled and put his free hand on her shoulder, brushing it down her back to rest in the hollow of her spine. "No, beautiful. I told you before, you're safe with me. I wouldn't hurt one hair on your head."

Adeline considered him a moment. Tipping her glass up and finishing the last of her wine, she finally nodded. "Okay. I trust you."

Dean's eyes closed for a moment, then opened, and Adeline almost gasped at the intense look he gave her.

"Thank you," he said. "That means a lot to me. Ready?"

She nodded, and he stood and held the back of the chair, helping to move it out of her way as she got up. As they walked through the restaurant, his hand made its way to the small of her back, and even though she was wearing the corset, Adeline could swear she felt the heat from his fingers seep into her skin.

They leisurely walked to the parking garage where he'd left his car.

"You don't mind a few dog hairs do you?" Adeline asked him. "I brush Coco every day, but I swear the dog grows hair overnight, just to annoy me."

"It's fine. There's probably still a lot of hair in my car from my Rottie."

Adeline didn't ask where they were going, which was probably stupid, but she hadn't lied. She did trust Dean. Besides, he seemed to like surprising her.

They drove for around twenty minutes on the Interstate, and she recognized the area as he turned off. "What are we—"

"Hang on, beautiful. Almost there."

Adeline didn't say a word as Dean pulled into the parking lot next to Station 7. The building was lit up and she saw one of the trucks parked behind it.

Dean cut off the engine and turned to her. "You trust me, right?"

"Yeaaaaaaah?" The word was drawn out in question.

"And you said you can be adventurous, yeah?"

"Again, for the most part, yes."

"Good." With that, Dean opened his door and got out. Adeline sat in her seat in confusion as he came around to her side and opened her door. He held out his hand. She put her hand in his and he pulled her out to stand in front of him. Looking up at him, she waited for an explanation.

"Wanna watch the sunset with me?"

"Sure. I'm not sure how that's adventurous though."

"How about watching it from the bucket at the top

of the ladder?" He gestured to the truck sitting in the lot next to them.

Adeline's eyes got huge as she looked from the fire truck and the ladder safely tucked in the down position, then back to Dean. "Seriously?" she asked.

"Seriously. Unless you're scared of heights, then no, I'm just kidding."

"I'm not afraid of heights," Adeline enthused. "This is so awesome!"

He smiled then, and Adeline realized how nervous he'd been that she'd say no or otherwise freak out.

"Great, let's go in and say hi to whoever's here, then we'll get our butts up there before the sun goes down. I'd hate to have planned for this and then freaking miss the sunset." He turned and opened the back door of his car to let Coco jump out, then took her hand again and excitedly walked them to the side door of the station.

Adeline shook her head as Dean pulled her along. She'd thought several times that night that Dean was the most romantic man she'd ever met. But now she saw the excited little boy who lived inside the man shell. God help her, it was a combination she couldn't resist.

Chapter Six

"**H**EY GUYS!"
        "Crash!"

"Yo!"

"'Bout time you got back. Cuttin' it close!"

The four firemen sitting in the large common area watching a basketball game on the huge television all spoke at once as they entered.

"Whatever," he told his friends. Turning to Adeline, he waved a hand at the guys. "Adeline, meet Moose, Taco, Killer, and Jones."

"Nice to meet you," she said, nodding at each of the men.

"Moose and Taco usually work with me, but they're taking an extra shift for a couple of guys who needed the night off."

The two men in question stood up and came over to where Adeline and Crash were standing.

An older man, tall, built, and good looking, stuck out his hand to Adeline. "I'm Moose. We've heard a lot about you from Crash. It's good to finally meet you."

Adeline's eyes swung to Dean's in surprise, but she quickly looked back at the man in front of her and shook his hand. "Do I want to know how you got your nickname?"

All three of the men laughed. "No."

The other man reached his hand out after she dropped Moose's. "I'm Taco. And yes, I got my name probably for the reason you're thinking. It's my favorite food and I've been known to eat a few in one sitting."

Crash leaned forward and put his mouth next to Adeline's ear and said in a low voice, but not low enough that the man in front of her couldn't hear, "He's been known to eat over ten at a time. Don't ever challenge him to a contest."

He saw Adeline's shiver as his warm breath brushed over the nape of her neck when he spoke and felt his insides clench. He'd had a wonderful time getting to know Adeline tonight. She was funny and interesting, not to mention beautiful. He'd put his hands on her as much as he could get away with and not be a creeper.

Crash wasn't an expert, but he could tell she had some sort of contraption on under her clothes. Whatever it was, it was doing amazing things to her shape. Her tits sat high and perky on her chest, her cleavage playing peek-a-boo in the scoop neck of her shirt. Her waist was hourglass-shaped, but she wasn't skin and bones. She was all woman, and every time she moved, he got a whiff of whatever perfume she'd put on. He'd been half hard all night, and he couldn't wait to get in the bucket and get to know her even better.

Moose and Taco had said they'd help him set it up. They'd made sure the truck was ready and safe for them to be lifted high in the air. They'd sit below in the parking lot as spotters for as long as Crash needed them to be there. While he might want to be completely alone with Adeline, for safety's sake, that wasn't going to happen.

Adeline looked up at him after dropping Taco's hand and grinned. "I'll keep that in mind." She turned back to his friend. "Although the most I've ever eaten in one sitting was four, and that was because I'd just walked a five-K and was starving. I think your record is safe from me."

Taco beamed. "You walked a five-K and were starved and only ate four? Shit, I'd've downed that many as an appetizer."

Everyone laughed.

"You didn't run it?" Moose asked conversationally.

"Do I look like a runner to you?" Without giving him time to answer, Adeline continued, "No. I'm too thick to run. I don't run. Ever. There would have to be zombies, serial killers, and maybe my asshole boss chasing me to want to break into a jog." She shook her head and smiled. "So, no, I didn't run. I only did it because my sister begged me. And when Alicia begs, it's not pretty. So Coco and I walked, she ran it, and we went out to eat afterwards."

Moose leaned forward and said in a deep voice, "Honey, you're not too thick for anything. You don't want to run, don't run. You're perfect just the way you are."

"Okay, that's it. We're done," Crash growled, not liking the way Moose was looking at Adeline. He wrapped his arm around her waist, resting his palm on her belly, and pulled her into him and away from Moose.

The other man laughed, then stepped back, giving them both some room. "It's so much fun to fuck with you."

Crash glared. "Not cool. How would you feel if I said that to Tig—"

"Careful," Moose clipped.

"Not as funny when the shoe's on the other foot, is it?" Crash ground out between clenched teeth.

"Okay, okay, enough. How 'bout we go and get you two set up in the bucket?" Taco said, playing peacemaker.

Crash took a deep breath and tried to calm down. Feeling Adeline's fingernails in his arm, he looked down at her. She was holding onto his forearm with one hand, the other still holding Coco, but instead of being stiff in his arms, as he'd expected, she had relaxed into him. Her back was warm against his chest and he could feel her quick breaths. She was looking at Moose, but somehow Crash knew she was wholly focused on him.

Damn. She was fucking perfect.

He shifted his hand to the left an inch, enclosing her in his embrace a bit more, and her hand pressed against his arm infinitesimally.

"Crash?"

His name coming from Taco brought him back to his senses. He couldn't feel up Adeline standing in the station in front of his friends…no matter how much he wanted to. Reluctantly, he backed away and let his hand fall from her body. "You ready, beautiful?"

She looked up at him and Crash wanted to say "fuck it" and take her back to his car and make out with her for the next few hours. Her eyes were slightly dilated and she licked her lips. Her chest rose and fell each time she breathed and he could see a slight sheen of perspiration on her forehead. If he wasn't mistaken, she was as turned on as he was.

Deciding he needed a fucking gold medal for his restraint and the light tone of his voice, Crash moved his hand to hers and tugged. "Come on. Let's go see a sunset. You ever been up a ladder like this?"

He was pretty sure she hadn't, but asked anyway.

He wasn't surprised when she shook her head. He pulled her toward the door.

"There's not a lot you need to know. The ladder is all hydraulic. We'll strap the safety lines on, and Moose and Taco will do all the work. They'll lift us up until we're high enough. If it gets to be too much, just let me know and we'll stop. You sure you're not afraid of heights?"

She smiled up at him as they headed back out into the warm Texas air. "I'm sure. Now if you took me up in a plane and told me I had to jump without a parachute, I would guarantee that I'd be scared of heights."

He grinned.

"But no, I'm really not. Bring it, Dean."

"All right then. Will you be good leaving Coco down here with my friends?"

"Yeah, he'll be fine."

"No, gorgeous. Will *you* be good?"

She looked down and to the right for a moment, then back up at him. "Yeah. I think I can manage thirty minutes away from my medical alert dog, Dean. If you're afraid I'm going to have a seizure, we can just skip this and you can take me home."

"Damn," Taco murmured from nearby.

Crash looked at Adeline and winced. Taking her hand and taking two steps away from the truck and the two men, he turned his back and used his free hand to tip her chin up to him. "I didn't mean it like that and I'm sorry if it sounded like I did. I can see that this is a sore subject, so instead of beating around the bush and pretending I don't know what you mean, I'm gonna lay it out. I don't give a fuck if you have a seizure when you're around me. It doesn't matter. If you do, I'll take care of you until it passes. I only asked because I know you enough to know that you seem to be more relaxed when Coco is around. I get it; he's allowed you to have your freedom. All I meant was whether you'd be comfortable enough, if you trusted me enough, to leave Coco behind. I wasn't judging. If you're not, he can certainly come up too. There's room in the bucket. But I swear to God, beautiful, warning or not, I can take care of you if you have a seizure. A hundred feet in the air, or both feet on the ground."

Adeline closed her eyes and took a step forward. She laid her forehead on his chest and sighed. Her hand was still in his and her other hand still held Coco's leash. The dog didn't make a sound, but Crash saw him lean against Adeline's leg as if emotionally supporting her.

"I'm an idiot," she mumbled into his shirt.

They weren't hugging, or touching anywhere except where her head met his chest and their clasped hands, but it felt more intimate to Crash than any encounter he'd had with a woman in the past year. He could no more resist touching her than he could drive past a wreck and not stop to see if he could help.

His hand came up and rested on the back of her head. He used his thumb to lightly caress her hair. Her perfume wafted up to his nose along with whatever shampoo she'd used that morning. Inhaling deeply, Crash wanted to bottle her essence so he could bring it out whenever he needed to remember this moment.

"You're not an idiot."

"I'm so used to being defensive about my epilepsy, I didn't even stop to think that you weren't asking if I thought I could go half an hour without having a seizure but were actually just being thoughtful. I'm sorry."

"Apology accepted," Crash said immediately. "And I'll try to make sure I'm more clear in the future. Yeah?"

"Okay."

They stood there for a moment before Crash said dryly, "If we're gonna see any part of this sunset, we should probably get moving. But I'm good with staying right here, just like this, and saying to hell with the damn sun too."

Adeline chuckled and straightened. Crash didn't move his hand from the back of her head, keeping her close.

"You went to a lot of trouble. And when I tell people about the best first date I've ever had in my life, I'd really like it to include not only glass-blowing and Belgian food, but having the opportunity to go up in a fireman's ladder and watching the sunset from the bucket high above his fire station."

"Then by all means, let's get moving so you can have that, beautiful."

"Thanks. Seriously."

"You're welcome. Seriously." Crash leaned forward and kissed Adeline's forehead, leaving his lips on her skin for a moment longer than was situationally appropriate. Then without a word, he turned and walked back to where Taco and Moose were standing next to the truck, grinning widely.

Shaking his head at his friends, but not saying a word, Crash led Adeline to the back of the truck. She held out the leash to Taco. "Will you hold him while we're up there?"

"Of course. Don't worry about us. We'll just hang down here and do manly shit."

Adeline giggled. "If I come back down and find out you've taught my dog to guzzle beer, smoke cigars, and whistle at the ladies, I won't be happy."

"Aw man," Taco mock-whined. "Girls take all the fun out of everything." He winked at her. "No worries, Adeline. I'll take good care of him for you."

"Thanks. Coco, go on."

Again, as if her words were a magic switch, the dog's body wiggled and twisted as he jumped up onto Taco.

Luckily, Taco wasn't upset that he suddenly had a

hyper, almost hundred-pound dog in his face.

"He's, uh, still learning to tone down his enthusiasm when he's not on duty," she explained sheepishly.

"It's fine," Taco told her, laughing at her dog.

"Come on, beautiful," Crash told her, putting his hand on her back. "Time to go."

He carefully watched as Adeline stepped up into the truck and kept his hand on her back as they made their way into the bucket. He held up the chain, letting her duck under it, and he followed right behind her.

Crash vaguely heard Moose and Taco readying the truck as he turned to the beautiful woman next to him. He held up a thick rope.

"Safety line. I'm gonna put on a harness, but that's not gonna work with your pretty outfit. This'll go around your waist and be clipped to the side of the bucket, but also to me. I'll be attached to the bucket as well, so no matter what happens, you're safe. Got it?"

"Of course, Dean. I didn't think otherwise. I know you wouldn't take me up there if it wasn't one hundred percent safe."

Crash bent to step into the harness. He'd done it a thousand times and could clip himself in without thought. "I wouldn't say it's one hundred percent safe," he admitted. "But it's also not exactly dangerous either. There's no wind tonight and the ladder just passed inspection last month. You're safer in this thing with me than you will be driving home tonight. Simply because I know every inch of this machine. I tested it out before dinner to make sure it was operating normally, and I personally inspected the carabiners and ropes we'll be using tonight as well. I can tell you that you're as safe as you can be with me, but I can't vouch for the assholes who'll be driving around you tonight."

Adeline reached out and touched his arm. "Thank you."

Crash felt his dick twitch in his pants. Jesus, he had to get himself under control. If one small touch of her fingers on his arm could make him get hard, he was doomed. But it felt good. Felt good to be so attracted to a woman he knew he'd do anything to keep safe. Felt good to be completely focused on her. It felt good to simply be with a woman who seemed to want to be with him too.

He finished clipping the harness and attached the safety line on the back and both sides to the safety points on the bucket. Satisfied that he was properly clipped in, he held up the rope. "Your turn. Lift your arms."

Adeline did as he requested and Crash put both his arms around her waist, transferring one end of the rope in his right hand to his left. He stood there a moment, loving the feel of his arms around her.

"Dean? Will it fit around me?"

"Yeah, beautiful. It fits just fine. I'm just enjoying being here with you for a moment."

She smiled at him then. "We're gonna miss the sunset if you don't hurry up."

"Right."

He took a step back and brought the ends of the rope together in front of her, clipping them together with a carabiner, and taking another piece of rope and attaching it to the side of the bucket. Lastly, he attached one more line from the harness around his own body to the rope around hers.

"There. Now where you go, I go."

If Crash could've stopped time, taken a photo to remember the exact look in Adeline's eyes, he would've. Her eyes got soft, and the look of yearning, disbelief, and hope seemed to echo everything he was feeling inside. Instead, he merely smiled and held up his hand to signal to Moose that they were ready.

The bucket jerked as the ladder slowly started to unfold and Adeline staggered. Crash put one arm around her waist to steady her and held on to the side of the bucket with the other. "Easy. I've got you. Hold on to the rail. You'll be fine. Let me know if it gets too high."

Adeline nodded and grabbed onto the metal rail with both hands. They slowly rose higher and higher until they reached the top of the ladder's extension.

They were about a hundred feet in the air, way

above the treetops and able to clearly see above all the buildings in the area. The skyline of San Antonio was easily visible in the distance as well.

Adeline sighed. "It's so beautiful."

Crash noticed she hadn't let go of her death grip on the side the bucket. She was enjoying the view, smiling, but it was obvious she wasn't comfortable. It didn't sit well with him.

Moving slowly, knowing he was overstepping the unwritten rules of firstdatedom, he did it anyway.

He came up behind her and wrapped both hands around her waist and pulled her into him. He wasn't as tall as some of his friends, only topping out around six feet, but he was tall enough for Adeline to feel petite in his arms. Her head was about his shoulder height and she fit against him perfectly.

Crash wanted to put one arm around her shoulder to lie between her breasts and the other on her stomach, right below her belly button, but knew that would be too intimate for two people who were still getting to know each other. Instead, he settled for resting both hands at her sides along her waistline. He leaned over until his chin rested on her shoulder and their heads were side by side.

"Hang on to me if you need to. Relax. I've got you."

She slowly lifted her hands from the rail and they fluttered around a moment before settling over his hands. Making a move he never would've guessed she'd do, she pulled his hands off her waist and wrapped them around herself until they were crossed in front of her. She then moved her hands to his waist and hooked her thumbs into the belt loops at his sides.

Damn.

His breathing hitched and Crash closed his eyes for a moment. Yes. He liked this.

He liked it even more when Adeline put her head back and rested it on his shoulder.

"Is this okay?" she asked softly.

"Yeah, beautiful. This is more than okay."

They stood like that without speaking for at least ten minutes. Watching as the sun got lower and lower on the horizon. Cicadas started their mating song in the warm air and lights slowly came on around the city below them. Porch lights, streetlamps, headlights from cars, even the downtown buildings lit up.

As if they were in a world of our own and the slightest sound would break the mood, Adeline whispered, "That was amazing."

"Yeah," Crash responded in the same low voice.

"I needed this after the week I had."

"I'm sorry you had a crap week, beautiful. But I'm glad I could end it on a high note for you."

"Me too." She turned in his arms until they were face to face, chest to chest, legs against legs. Looking up, she licked her lips as if she was nervous, then told him, "Thank you for asking me out."

"Thank you for saying yes," Crash returned, not able to take his eyes off her mouth. It was getting dark, but there was still enough light to see her clearly. Her lipstick had long since disappeared, but her lips were still red and lush. Out of the corner of his eye he could see, and feel, her breasts rising and falling against his chest. He knew if he looked down he'd be able to get quite the eyeful, but he was too fascinated by her lips.

He wanted to taste her. Needed to feel her lips moving under his. To twine his tongue with hers. They had chemistry, there was no denying it, but he wanted to take it a step further, to see if they would be as explosive together as he imagined. But it had to be her choice. He didn't want to make her uncomfortable.

"Do you think your friends can see us?"

The question shocked him for a moment. Crash wasn't sure he liked that Adeline was thinking about Moose and Taco when she was standing so close to him. He shrugged. "Maybe. But they won't be looking at us."

"Why not?"

"Because they're my friends. They might be serving as safety monitors, but they're too good of friends, and men, to make you feel uncomfortable for even one second. And you knowing they were watching us would make you uncomfortable. So they won't do it."

"How can you be so sure?"

"Because I'd do the same thing if it was me down there, and they were up here with a pretty woman they were desperately trying to impress."

"Is that what you're doing?"

Crash smiled sheepishly. "Yeah."

"Well, it's working. I'm impressed."

"Yeah?" This time it was a question.

"Uh huh. Know what would impress me more?"

"What's that?"

They were both still whispering.

"If you'd kiss me."

Crash waited one beat then without a word, dipped his head, just as she went up on her tiptoes.

Their lips met and Crash would swear he saw sparks behind his eyes. At first he lightly brushed his lips across hers, sipping and teasing. But when Adeline let out a small note of impatience…and desire…he couldn't hold back.

One hand came up to the back of her head and the other went to the small of her back, under her shirt, seeking warm skin. His opened his mouth and ran his tongue along the seam of her lips. Without any more coaxing she opened for him. Crash's tongue surged inside her mouth as he pressed his hand to her back and brought her flush against his body.

Without any finesse or thinking about his technique, Crash devoured her, wanting to get closer to her. Their tongues dueled together, and he growled deep in his throat when she sucked on him as if she were devouring his dick.

The thought went from his head straight to his dick, and before he could even think about trying to hold back to keep from freaking Adeline way the hell out, he was pushing her hips against his rock-hard cock. Using his tongue to show her what he really wanted to be doing to her body, he thrust in and out of her at the same time he rocked against her.

Adeline gasped and pulled back an inch, breathing as hard as if she'd run the dreaded 5k race she'd mentioned earlier. Not wanting to lose contact with her, Crash moved his lips to her neck, licking and nipping at her skin, loving how she squirmed against him.

He made his way back up to her mouth and teased her. Licking, but not entering. When she was chasing his lips with her own, he settled back in, letting her take the lead. Her tongue swept into his mouth and he moaned with the carnality of her actions, taking what she wanted and not letting shyness or their location hold her back.

Knowing he had to stop, but not wanting to, Crash ended their kiss by taking her bottom lip between his and sucking lightly. He let it go with a pop and moved his mouth to the sensitive skin below her ear.

His hand stayed behind her head, keeping her tucked into him, and his brain finally kicked in and realized that instead of warm skin, all he felt with the hand at her back was thick material.

Without lifting his head, he whispered, "What is this?"

"Corset." Her voice was shaky and still low.

The word did the one thing he would've sworn he'd never be able to do—made him pull back from her.

"What?"

"It's a corset." Adeline looked embarrassed now. "Not like the ones from the eighteen hundreds or anything, and it's not really all that tight, but I like how it makes me look and feel."

Crash closed his eyes, assailed by a vision of her standing in front of him with nothing on but a sexy-as-fuck corset and a tiny pair of undies. His hand tensed at her back and he tried to bring himself under control.

"You don't like it." It wasn't a question. "I know that men typically like skimpy lingerie on a woman, and I feel good in it, but if you don't—"

"Hush," Crash ordered.

"But—"

"Adeline. I swear to God…I'm hanging on by a thread here." He opened his eyes and looked at her. "I'm trying to be a gentleman, but between the most amazing kiss I've ever had in my life, and the vision of you standing in front of me wearing nothing but a corset and a pair of panties…I just need a minute. Okay?"

She smiled then. A wide smile that he could barely see in the darkness that now surrounded them. "Okay."

Crash took a deep breath and decided he must be a glutton for punishment. "What color?"

"What color what?"

"What color is your corset?"

"Black."

"Damn. And it's got ribbons holding it together?"

She shrugged. "Sorta. There are snaps in the front, which makes it easier to put on by myself, but yeah, if the ribbons are undone in the back it'll come off."

Crash moved the hand that had been on the back of her head and traced her collarbone with his index finger. He *really* wanted to run it over the tops of her breasts, which he could barely see, but knew a first date wasn't the time and this really wasn't the place. "I've never seen a woman in one."

"Really?" She sounded skeptical.

"Really. I've seen actresses wearing them in movies, and I might've seen one in a porn video or two, but I imagine that you'd look very different."

"Yeah," she breathed harshly. "I weigh way more than any of them."

Not liking her tone, Crash leaned over and brushed

his lips over the skin his fingertips had just skimmed. She shivered under him. "I wasn't being derogatory, beautiful. Far from it. I can picture it. Your waist nipped in by the material, your tits spilling over the top, begging to be released. You have no idea the things I want to do to you while you're wearing that corset."

"Dean…"

"Yeah, beautiful. And I have a good imagination. You over me, the first couple of snaps undone so your nipples have popped free, riding me—fuck!" Crash let go of Adeline so quickly she staggered. He stepped away and turned his back to her, holding on to the railing as tightly as she'd done earlier.

"I'm sorry. Jesus, I'm so sorry. I was way out of line. Shit." Crash took a deep breath, then another, trying to get himself under control. The vision of her riding his cock as he watched her tits bouncing up and down had been so vivid he would've sworn it was a memory rather than a fantasy.

Crash knew to the marrow of his bones, when— hopefully not if—he saw her in the corset, she'd be the most beautiful thing he'd ever seen in his life. And he wanted it. Wanted her. More than anything he'd ever wanted before.

"Dean."

He felt her small hand on the middle of his back and he tensed. Fuck. Fuck. Fuck.

"It's okay. You weren't out of line."

"Yeah, I was," he countered, still not turning around.

Adeline's arms wrapped around him from behind and came to rest on his pecs. She laid her cheek on his back. "You weren't out of line, because I imagined your lips moving from my collarbone down my chest, as you licked and sucked your way down."

One of his hands moved from the railing to envelope hers on his chest. He stayed silent and held on.

"Not only that, but I had a sudden vision of dropping to my knees right here, high above the ground, and seeing if you're as big as you feel. Taking you out of your pants and sucking you off right here, right now."

Crash closed his eyes and said a silent prayer of thanks that he hadn't repulsed or turned her off with his earlier words.

He turned in her embrace and pulled her closer. Not trusting himself to kiss her again; now *he* had the image of her in that damn corset on her knees in front of him, his cock between her lips.

"I guess it's safe to say we're attracted to each other," he said dryly.

She giggled and nodded against him. "Yeah."

"When can I see you again, beautiful?"

Adeline looked up at that and shrugged. "Whenever you want."

Crash brought a hand up and smoothed her hair away from her face. It was too dark to really see any details of her face anymore, but he could still picture her clear as day in his mind. "I love that you don't play games. Thank you. Unfortunately, tomorrow I start a seventy-two hour shift. Then I have forty-eight hours off. Then I do it again."

Crash saw a flash of her white teeth as she bit her lip. "I have a new client and next week will be busy for me. It's always tough when I first start with someone new. Lots of phone conferences and back and forth brainstorming about ideas. I'm usually exhausted by the time I get home."

"Fuck. Okay. We'll figure it out. Next Sunday for sure?"

"You'll need to sleep, won't you?"

Crash kissed the top of Adeline's head. She was so sweet. "Not really. We sleep when we're on shift. Yeah, we get calls, but we usually get plenty of shut-eye between them. Besides, I'd rather spend time with you than sleep."

"Then I'd like that," she whispered.

"We'll text and talk on the phone until then though."

"Yeah?"

Crash pulled back a bit. "You think we can go over a week without talking to each other?"

He felt her shrug.

"Well, I can't," he said definitively. "I like you, Adeline. I want to know how your day's been. I want to know if Douglas has been giving you shit. How you're feeling. If you're thinking about me. What your sister thinks about our first date, 'cause I know you're gonna call her tomorrow and talk to her about me and tonight." He smiled, remembering the text Adeline had received earlier that night from Alicia. She'd shown it to him. Her sister had wanted to know if she needed to put into motion "Operation First Date Dud."

Adeline had explained that it was code for her sister calling with a fake emergency, and she'd let him watch as she'd replied to her sister that there was no need for the drastic measures, that she was having a great time and would talk to her tomorrow.

"We're gonna make this work, Adeline. If you think I'm gonna let you go without getting to see you in that corset, you're crazy."

"Okay. Sunday. But this time I get to pick where we go and what we do."

"Deal. You gonna let me pick you up this time?"

"Maybe."

"Adeline," he growled.

She giggled, and Crash knew he'd spend the rest of his life trying to make sure she always sounded as carefree and happy as she did right then.

It was insane. One date and he was already thinking long-term, but he knew a good thing when he saw it, and no way was he letting her slip away. No way in hell.

"Oh all right. You can pick me up."

"Thank you. One more kiss and then we'll head down."

"Okay."

The word was more a breath than an actual word and Crash's head was already moving before it left her mouth.

He couldn't see her very well anymore, could only feel her body against his, her lips against his, and her tongue brushing against his own, but it was as if he'd suddenly woken up from a long coma. He could see his future, with Adeline by his side, as clearly as if they were standing in the middle of a stage with every light focused right on them.

Reluctantly pulling away and licking his lips, getting one last taste of Adeline, Crash told her, "Cover your ears."

She moved her hands up between them and put them over her ears.

Crash turned his head and whistled one long, loud note, and within moments the bucket started descending.

Adeline's hands came down and wrapped around his waist once more, giving him her weight. Trusting him to help her remain balanced as the bucket jerked and bounced as they got closer and closer to the ground.

"Looks like y'all had a good time," Moose drawled when the ladder reached the bottom.

The lights from the building shone on the truck and Crash could see the blush that bloomed on Adeline's face. He ran his thumb over the apple of her cheek and smiled at her. "We did."

"Thanks for letting Coco hang with us," Taco told Adeline. "He's a great dog."

"I know," she returned.

"Arms up," Crash told her softly.

She did as he said and he unhooked the safety line from around her waist, then did the same with his own, removing the harness and storing it in a small metal box at their feet inside the bucket. "Come on, Cinderella. Time to get you home."

Adeline ducked under the chain and took the hand Moose held out to her. He helped her to the ground and she crouched and greeted Coco, who acted like she'd been gone for weeks rather than only an hour or so.

"Thanks for your help," Crash told his friends.

They nodded at him.

"Anytime."

"No problem."

The two men headed back into the fire station and disappeared.

Crash leaned over and helped Adeline to her feet. They walked to his car and he got her and Coco settled. The drive back to the parking garage in Southtown was done in relative silence. It was comfortable, and Crash held Adeline's hand the whole way.

She told him what floor her car was on and he insisted on taking her all the way to it, rather than dropping her off at street level and having her take the elevator up to her car by herself. When she argued, saying it was silly for him to pay to drive up to the third floor, he shook his head.

"I don't care about the couple of bucks it'll cost me," he told her sternly. "Your safety is way more important than saving money. Now hush."

"You're kinda bossy, you know that?" she asked as he grabbed the ticket and entered the garage.

"I am. And I'm sure there will be a lot of other things you find out about me that might irritate you," Crash said easily, not worried in the least. "I'm not perfect. Not by a long shot. I could list a whole litany of things that my friends and ex-girlfriends found annoying about me, but I'd rather you found them out on your own."

"You would?" Adeline asked, her head tilted with curiosity.

"Yup. Because I'm hoping by the time you figure out what they are, there'll be a whole lot of other things about me you *do* like, so they won't seem as bad."

"Do you leave dirty dishes in the sink for days so the food has time to dry on them, making it impossible to clean them in the dishwasher?"

He chuckled. "No."

"Do your feet smell so horribly bad that I'll need to wear a gas mask when you take off your shoes and socks?"

Crash snorted. "No. Although I would recommend you take a few steps back if you ever see me right after a fire. Our turn-out gear can get pretty rank...not to mention the boots we wear trap heat inside."

"Noted," she deadpanned. "Do you kick small animals and sneer at children when you see them in the mall?"

He reached over and tugged on a piece of her hair teasingly. "No and no. Now hush. Stop trying to figure out all my secrets."

"I know you're not perfect, Dean. Neither am I. Aside from the obvious illness I've got, I take off my shoes as soon as I get inside my house so there are shoes everywhere, forget to open my mail for days at a time, I've never dusted a day in my life, and have a weird thing about making sure my toenails are always painted. As long as you don't have any bodies hidden under your house, I'm sure I can deal with any other idiosyncrasies you might have."

He smiled at her. "Good. But I'm going to remind you that you said that the first time I do something stupid."

They continued up the ramps until they reached her car.

Crash got out, grabbed a small bag from the floor at his feet, and met her at the side of her car.

She let Coco into the car, put the bag with the purchases she'd made earlier that night on the floor, shut the door, then turned to him. "Thank you for a wonderful night, Dean."

"You're more than welcome. I can't wait until next Sunday. I have something for you." He held out a small bag with the logo from the glass-blowing shop on it.

Adeline looked up at him. "What's this?"

"Open it and see."

She reached into the bag and pulled out an object swathed in bubble wrap. She slowly unwrapped it, and gasped when she realized what it was.

"Told you it'd turn out to be a glass blob," Crash told her. "But I thought it'd make a fun memento from the night. Not as impressive as the things you bought, that's for sure."

"Dean, I love it," Adeline said, looking up at him with big eyes. "When did you get this?"

"I told Andres I wanted it before we left the store. He dropped it off at the hostess station at the restaurant while we were eating. When you were using the restroom before we left I picked it up."

"How did I not notice you carrying a bag when we went to the car?" she asked, bewildered.

"It's small enough I tucked it into the back of my jeans under my shirt," he told her with a slight flush on his face. "I wanted it to be a surprise."

"Sneaky. But I love it. It was definitely a surprise. It's gonna go in a place of honor for sure. Maybe I'll bring it to work so I can think of how much fun tonight was rather than my asshole boss. Thank you."

"You're welcome. I'm glad you like it. Drive safe. Text me when you get home so I know you got there all right."

"I will." She looked nervous. "Well, thanks again. I'll see you in a week or so."

"Come 'ere, beautiful," Crash said, pulling her into his arms.

Her chin came up at the same time his dropped and their lips met as perfectly as if they'd been practicing it their entire life. Crash tried to keep it short, but it was still several moments before he finally lifted his head. His fingertips had made their way under the tight corset at the small of her back and she was plastered to his front.

He chuckled. "Now *that* was a good-night kiss."

"Yeah."

He kissed her once more, a quick peck on the lips, and removed his hands from her and stepped back. "I'll talk to you soon, beautiful."

"'Bye, Dean."

He went back to his car and backed up, giving her room to get out of her parking space. He followed her out of the garage to the Interstate, where she turned right and he went left.

Crash smiled all the way home. A week ago he was bitching to Hayden that he hadn't had a decent date in way too long. Now he knew he'd found the woman he wanted to spend the rest of his life with. He just had to convince Adeline that she wanted to spend the rest of hers with *him*.

It was funny how life worked out sometimes.

Chapter Seven

"**S**PILL, SIS," ALICIA demanded.

Adeline groaned and fell back on her bed. She squinted at the numbers on the ceiling projected by her clock. She'd bought it on a whim a couple of years ago and now couldn't imagine not having it. It was heaven to only have to open her eyes and look up when she woke, and not have to crane her neck to see the clock.

Seven thirty-three.

"Really? It's Saturday morning and you're calling me this early? Why are you even up?" Adeline grouched at her sister.

"Because my only sister was on a date and didn't need me to start Operation First Date Dud and I want to know more."

Adeline smiled and closed her eyes, remembering. "It went good."

"And?"

"And what?"

"I need details!" Alicia practically screeched. "What'd you do, where'd you go, did he kiss you, what'd you eat, when did you get home…you know…*details*!"

"I met him in Southtown, as you know. We first went to a glass-blowing demonstration. Then we ate at that little Belgian bistro down there. Then he drove me to his fire station and we watched the sunset from the top of one of the ladders on the back of a truck. We kissed. He drove me back to the parking garage so I could get my car, and I came home."

There was silence on the other end of the line for a moment.

"What?"

"I met him in Southtown, then we went to a glass-bl—"

"Shut up, I heard you," Alicia said impatiently. "A glass-blowing demonstration?"

"Yup. He arranged it."

"Then you ate Belgian food?"

"Yes."

"He took you to his fire station and you had to climb up the ladder to see the sunset?"

"No. We got in the bucket thing and his friends raised the ladder."

"And you kissed." It wasn't a question.

"Oh yeah. We kissed."

Alicia was silent for another beat. Then, "You like him."

"I like him," Adeline confirmed.

"If he hurts you, I'm kicking his ass," her sister declared.

"Leesh, stop it."

"No, I'm serious. You've been out on four thousand one hundred and forty-seven first dates and not once have I ever heard the tone of voice you used while talking about this one. If he does one thing to hurt you, I don't care if he's twelve inches taller and an MMA fighter, I'm kicking his ass."

"He's not an MMA fighter. And it was only one date," Adeline protested, pushing herself up so she was sitting. Coco was sleeping at the foot of the mattress. He opened one eye at her movement, but closed it again when he saw she wasn't getting out of bed.

"But you've got a second one planned, don't you?"

Adeline felt herself blush. She wasn't sure why. "Yeah."

"When?"

"Next weekend."

"Next weekend? Why wait so long?"

"He has to work. I have to work. Life, sis. It's not like we can hang out every day. I'm not sure I want to. Yet."

"I'm happy for you." Now Alicia's tone was soft.

"You deserve to be with someone nice."

Adeline smiled. "Well, I'm not sure I'm 'with' him yet, but it's a good start."

"Good. Okay, I'm gonna let you go…I'm going back to sleep."

"You suck," Adeline groused. "You've always been able to sleep anywhere, anytime. And you know once I'm up, I'm up."

"Yup." Alicia didn't sound the least bit sorry. "Glad you had a good time. Later."

"'Bye." Adeline clicked the phone off, but didn't put it down. She thought about it for a second, then clicked on the text icon. She quickly shot off a note to Dean. It might be too soon, and it was definitely too early, but if he was sleeping, he'd get it when he got up.

Adeline: *Had a wonderful time. Thank you.*

She'd put the phone down and swung her feet over the edge of her mattress and was only halfway across the room when she heard her phone vibrate on the table next to the bed. Smiling, Adeline padded back to her phone and picked it up.

Dean: *It was my pleasure, beautiful.*

Adeline sighed with happiness. God. He might insist that he wasn't perfect, but so far she hadn't had even a glimpse of anything that said otherwise.

CRASH'S LIPS QUIRKED up in a smile as he sent a return text to Adeline. He'd told her last night, but it was totally true. She didn't play games, and he loved that. She hadn't hesitated to let him know she'd had a good time. Didn't play coy and wait for him to contact her. Seven forty-five in the morning and she'd reached out to let him know she enjoyed their date.

"That her?" Cade "Sledge" Turner asked.

They were standing around the kitchen at the station.

All of the other men stopped what they were doing to look at Crash.

Moose's hand, holding the spatula he'd been flipping eggs with, was held above the pan, motionless.

Penelope turned from the fridge where she'd been reaching for a carton of orange juice.

Squirrel's eyes were comically huge behind his glasses as he stared at Crash.

Chief and Taco stopped putting plates on the table and looked his way.

And Driftwood rested his hip on the counter, the silverware drawer open next to him, waiting for his friend's response.

Crash could've blown off the question. Could've shrugged and said something sarcastic. He could've deflected and told his friends it had only been a first date and didn't mean anything. But it was Sledge who'd asked. The man had recently found a woman he loved more than being a firefighter. And he'd almost lost her.

"Yeah. She wanted to let me know she had a good time last night."

Smiles broke out on the faces of the men, and the woman, around him.

"I'm glad she's not doing the whole wait-for-the-guy-to-text-first thing," Penelope noted, the first to unfreeze and get back to what she was doing. "I don't know why women in their thirties still feel the need to play high school games with their dates."

"You mean, if they like someone they should just come right out and say it?" Moose asked softly.

Crash saw Penelope wince before turning her back to the room and grabbing some glasses from the cabinet. She didn't respond to Moose's question, simply pretended she hadn't heard him.

"Looked like you guys had a good time last night," Taco noted. "I take it the sunset thing went over well?"

Crash nodded. "I appreciate you and Moose helping out."

"Anytime." Taco waved off his thanks.

"You look happy," Chief commented.

"I am," Crash told his friend. "She's funny, interesting, pretty, is gainfully employed, close to her sister, and considerate. What's not to like?"

"She a good kisser?" Driftwood asked with a grin. "I mean, she might be all those other things, but if she's no good in bed, I'm not sure she'd be a good long-term bet."

"Fuck. You've been dating those online chicks so long I think it's gone to your head," Crash told him.

"Avoiding the question. So you either didn't get in there or she's a lousy kisser," he retorted.

Crash had enough. He stalked toward his friend and didn't stop until they were chest to chest. "You've got a fucked-up sense of women, Driftwood. It was a first date. She's not a hooker I was looking to fuck for the night then never see again. She's way too fucking good for me but for some reason she seems to like me. If you have to know, she's a fuck of a good kisser. So good I wanted nothing more to spend all night with my lips on hers. I wanted to keep on hearing the little moans and sighs she made as I fucked her mouth. If the way she squirmed and rubbed herself against me was any indication, I could've done her in the backseat before I dropped her off at her car. Is that what you wanted to hear?

"But I respect her too much to treat her like that. The first time I 'get in there,' I want her to remember it years later as the most exciting, romantic thing anyone's ever done for her. I want her more than I've ever wanted anything in my life. I want her to meet my friends and think they're good men. I want her to meet Beth and Penelope and to want to hang out and have girls' night out with them. I want to see her ass in the stands when we have a cop versus firefighter softball game, cheering for me. So to answer your insensitive and jackass question, yeah, I kissed her. And she's a fucking great kisser."

The air around the kitchen was electric and tense. Crash gritted his teeth together and his breaths came out in sharp puffs through his nose.

"Sorry, Crash. I didn't mean anything by it," Driftwood said quietly. "I didn't know it was serious."

"It's serious."

"I'm happy for you, man," Driftwood said honestly. "Seriously. Dating sucks. Online dating *really* sucks. Women hear what I do for a living and want to fuck me just to say they've banged a firefighter. She'll get no disrespect from me. Swear."

Crash inhaled a sharp breath and took a step back from his friend. He ran a hand through his hair and closed his eyes for a moment, then opened them and looked at Driftwood. "Sorry. I didn't mean to lose my shit."

"No, *I'm* sorry. I obviously haven't been hanging around the right type of women lately." He held out his hand.

Crash immediately took it and they shook.

"We good?" Driftwood asked.

"We're good," Crash reassured him.

"So…" Penelope asked from a chair at the large table. "When are we gonna meet her? If I'm gonna go out and get drunk with her and have a girls' night out, I need to meet her so we can get on that."

The men around the table chuckled.

Crash helped Moose carry the plates piled high with omelets to the table. When everyone was settled and started serving themselves, Crash turned to Penelope.

"Our schedules aren't gonna mesh until next weekend."

She whistled low. "You're gonna let a whole week go by?"

Crash shrugged. "Before I see her in person again? Yeah. But to talk to her? No."

"What about scheduling a softball game?" Squirrel asked without looking up from his plate of food. "It's low-key and she could meet some of the other girls."

"Yeah, good idea," Sledge agreed. "I'd love to get Beth to one, but she needs reinforcements. Since no one else here is dating anyone, I don't want her sitting with the enemy's women." He smiled to show he was kidding.

"I'm not sure Mack, Corrie, Mickie, or Laine would appreciate being called 'the enemy,'" Penelope said dryly.

"Maybe not," Sledge said, still smiling, "but when it comes to softball, they're just as competitive as their men are."

"God, ain't that the truth?" Chief muttered. "Wasn't it Mack who decided last time to bring air horns and set them off every time we went to hit?"

The men chuckled.

"Good point," Penelope muttered. "So yeah, we need to get your girlfriend to meet Beth so we can have at least two women in the stands when we play."

"You could always sit with them," Moose suggested playfully. "You *are* a girl and all."

Penelope threw a piece of bacon at him. "Whatever. You know you need me to play. Who scored the winning run last time?"

Everyone grinned, enjoying the banter between Moose and Penelope. She might be small, and a woman, but she was as tough a firefighter as any of them had ever met. The couple of months she'd been a prisoner of war over in Turkey had been the worst thing they'd lived through. Thank God she'd been rescued and returned in one piece.

Mostly in one piece. As time went by, the men had noticed she'd been getting more and more with-drawn…so it was good to see some of the old Penelope back.

"True, your boobs are a good distraction," Moose

teased.

He'd said it as a joke, just as they'd all kidded around too many times to count in the past, but Penelope looked as if Moose had struck her before she pushed her chair out from the table and mumbled, "I gotta go check on something," and fled.

"Fuck," Moose swore, running his hand through his hair. "I was kidding. Sledge, you know I was kidding, right?"

Penelope's brother looked at the doorway his sister had disappeared through and nodded. "I know, Moose. We're good. I don't know what's been up with her lately. She's not...she's not the same."

"Did you really expect her to be?" Moose asked quietly. "She went through hell over there."

"I know. I do. But I'd hoped that being back with us, doing what she loves, would help," Sledge said sadly.

"I think it is, but maybe it's not enough," Moose returned. He wiped his mouth with his napkin and stood up. "I'll go talk to her."

"Maybe I should—" Sledge started to say.

"I said I'll go," Moose repeated, his jaw tight.

The six men watched their friend stride out of the room after Penelope.

"Hell of a morning," Squirrel observed. "Crash almost beat the shit out of Driftwood for dissing his woman, Penelope looked like she wanted to either cry or quit, and Taco managed to eat his way through twice as many eggs as the rest of us."

The men laughed. Squirrel was normally quiet. He was tall and skinny where the rest of them were brawny and thick. But the man was observant as hell, and he frequently dropped funny zingers here and there. He might not be as strong as the rest of the group, but he was always the first one to read a scene, or fire, and know exactly the best way to approach it.

Chief stood up and started gathering dishes. The group didn't typically let dishes sit in the sink and they didn't hang out around the table, chatting after eating. They never knew when a call would come in and they much preferred to get the dishes done and put away as soon as they ate, rather than having to deal with it after a call, when they might be tired, dirty, and irritable.

Twenty minutes later, when the dishes were done and the group was dispersing, Driftwood put his hand on Crash's arm, halting him.

"We really good?"

"Yeah."

"I meant what I said. I didn't know she meant something to you. I thought she was just another hookup," Driftwood said.

Crash nodded. "I know. But, bud, you need to stop treating the women you meet as if they're nothing but a roll in the hay. You might miss her."

"Miss who?"

"The woman meant to be yours. If all you expect is a quick fuck, you could let someone special slip through your fingers and not even know it."

Driftwood eyed his friend for a long moment. "How would I know the difference?"

"You'll know."

The two men looked at each other for a long moment before Driftwood nodded. "I'm looking forward to meeting her."

Crash lifted his chin and watched his friend walk away toward the main room to watch TV. Pulling out his phone, he typed a quick note to Adeline, hit send, put his phone back in his pocket, then followed behind Driftwood.

TWENTY MILES AWAY, Adeline looked down at the phone in her hand and smiled. She hadn't ever dated a man who was as considerate as Dean.

> **Dean:** Have a good day, beautiful. Know I'm thinking about you. Be safe. I'll call you tonight if I get the chance.

The glass blob he'd made the night before sat on the windowsill of her kitchen. The sunlight catching it and throwing lines of red. purple, and green all across the small space. Every time she saw it, she remembered little things about him.

How his lips had felt against her own.

How he'd run his hand through his hair when he'd thought he'd offended her.

How his fingers felt at the small of her back.

Yeah, Dean Christopherson was going to be very hard to resist…but she didn't feel even the slightest need to do so.

REMEMBER, NICE.

You want her to like you.

No more yelling.

She likes coffee. She drinks that flavored stuff all the time. Get her some.

Smile at her. If she smiles back, you'll know that she likes you and wants you to keep paying attention to her.

Woo her.

Ladies like to be wooed.

Coffee first. Then lunch. Then dates.

She'll be yours forever and will never leave you. Never.

Chapter Eight

I T WAS FRIDAY night and Adeline was exhausted. She hadn't lied to Dean, she knew the week would be tiring, and it had been. The new client was enthusiastic and excited about new advertising and marketing opportunities, which was great. But dealing with a new account also made for very long days.

Not to mention, the seizures were unrelenting. In fact, they seemed to be increasing in frequency. The thought of surgery in the back of her mind didn't make them any easier to deal with either. It was as if with each seizure it was hammered home even more she'd have to make a decision that much sooner.

She hadn't wanted to believe that brain surgery— having part of her brain cut out, for God's sake—was the answer. She kept hoping that a new drug would come out to miraculously reduce her seizures. But it hadn't, and Coco was working overtime.

She'd had a seizure every day since her date with Dean and she was tired. Tired of feeling stressed about when one might happen. Tired of worrying whether she'd have a seizure at work. Tired of pretending they didn't sap the strength right out of her. Adeline so desperately wanted to be normal, but it was looking like that was nothing but a pipe dream.

Work was good, but it was also not good. Douglas had switched his tactics. Instead of being the standoffish asshole he'd been since he'd been hired, he'd started hanging out with his employees more. He stood in their office doors and chatted. He showed up in the break room and had lunch with them. He smiled at them and even seemed to be listening to their ideas.

Adeline didn't buy his good-guy act for a minute. He was up to something, but no one seemed to know what it was. He'd brought her a cup of coffee that morning, setting it on her desk, proud as he could be.

"What's this?" Adeline had asked.

"Coffee for you. Just the way you like it. Strong. Two creamers, three sugars," he'd said happily, putting his hands behind his back and smiling down at her.

"Uh, thanks. I appreciate it."

"No problem. You look nice today, Adeline."

Now really uncomfortable, she'd merely mumbled, "Thanks."

"I thought we could get together at lunch and discuss the Wolfe account and you can catch me up on the new client you met with this week."

Was he asking her out? He totally was. Eek. "Oh, well, I'm happy to discuss both with you, Douglas, but I can't today."

"You're going to skip lunch? That's not good for you," her boss chided.

"I already had plans to eat with Pam and Twila," Adeline told him, knowing the two women would back her up if asked. They'd had more than one conversation about Douglas and how weird he'd become recently.

"Hmmmm," Douglas muttered. "Maybe some other time."

There would definitely *not* be another time, but Adeline wasn't going to tell him that. "I'll email you the notes I took this week and you can look them over," she'd said instead.

"That'll do for now," her boss said, then straightened. "Enjoy your coffee."

Adeline looked down at the cup of steaming coffee he'd brought her and suddenly wondered if he'd done anything to it.

The thought was ridiculous. Douglas was her boss and they were at work, he wouldn't drug her or anything. At least she didn't think he would.

"Well, I gotta go," Douglas said. "I'll see you later. Have a good day."

"You too."

The entire conversation rubbed her the wrong way,

but Douglas hadn't said or done anything that she could make a complaint to human resources about. He was just being…nice. And Douglas and nice were two words that didn't go together in the least.

She wished for a moment that she'd let it slip she was seeing someone. It really wasn't any of Douglas's business, but maybe if he knew she was off the market, so to speak, he'd go back to his asshole self. It was sad that she'd prefer him to be a jerk than to hit on her.

The only really good parts to the last week were her communications with Dean. They'd been texting a lot. And he'd called almost every night. They'd even started FaceTiming. Adeline was reluctant at first. She was tired from work and hadn't wanted him to see her without any makeup on in her "lay around the house" clothes, but Dean had insisted.

And it was good.

Really good.

It was nice to be able to see his face while they were talking. His smile wide and happy, and his eyes sparkling when she made him laugh. She had no idea what he saw when he looked at her, but supposed the fact that he kept calling meant she wasn't turning him off too badly. She hadn't thought she was, but since she hadn't had the best luck with men lately, the reassurance was nice.

But tonight she was feeling off. She didn't really

want to talk to Dean. Or her sister. Or anyone. She wanted to hibernate in her room, in bed, covers pulled up over her head, and hide from the world. Simply put, she was grumpy.

Not wanting to cook anything, she'd cut up some tomatoes and put salt on them. Then she sliced half a cantaloupe, and then ate two slices of kosher dill pickle right out of the jar. It wasn't a dinner of champions by any means, but it was easy, fast, and hit the spot, as weird as it was.

Adeline sat cross-legged on her bed and pulled up the covers. She'd already cranked down the air; it was beastly hot and humid outside and she'd felt as if she was melting all day. She was blankly flicking through the channels, not finding anything she wanted to watch, when her cell rang.

She thought about ignoring it, but when she saw it was Dean, relented.

"Hi, Dean."

"Hey, beautiful. How are you?"

"Good. You?"

There was a pause before he said, "You don't sound good. Everything okay?"

"It's just been a long week. I'm so happy it's Friday."

"Your conference call go okay with that guy today? Did he like your mockups for the Google ads?"

"Yeah, he was happy with them."

"What about the website proposal you had for him?"

"That too." Adeline knew her voice was flat, but she just wasn't in the mood.

"Then what's really wrong?"

Adeline sighed hugely and put the TV on mute. She curled up on her side, holding the phone to her ear. "I'm just…tired. I don't want to talk about my work, or fucking Douglas, or anything about ads or marketing. Okay?"

"Okay, beautiful. No problem." He didn't even sound like he was the least bit irritated with her tone. "How about I talk about *my* day?"

"Sure."

"You know this was the second of three days of my shift, yeah?"

She did know. He'd told her his schedule last weekend and she'd gone home and put it in her calendar like she was twelve years old, doodling his name and hers in big hearts in a notebook. "Yeah," was all she said.

"You know about the domestic we were called to yesterday?"

"Uh huh." He'd told her all about the call they'd gotten for an "injured person." They'd arrived and had found a woman who'd been beaten by her boyfriend. Her two kids had hidden in a back room and were scared out of their minds.

"Well, we got called back to the same residence to-day. The woman had refused to press charges and had bailed the guy out. He came home today and apparently got drunk and did it again."

"Oh my God. Is the woman okay?"

His voice got soft and Adeline could tell he was less than happy. "Yeah. *She* was fine. Bruised all to hell from yesterday, her eye swollen shut, but fine. He'd taken his anger out on one of the kids this time."

"Shit," Adeline breathed.

"She's five. He hit her in the face, just like he did her mom the day before, then kicked her in the side when she was down. Driftwood talked to a nurse he knows in the emergency room and found out he busted her spleen. She had to go to surgery."

"Was the guy arrested again?"

"Yup. But that's not the worst part."

"Oh fuck," Adeline breathed.

"Her mom refused to press charges again."

Suddenly, Adeline wished she was there with Dean. He sounded pissed and extremely upset at the same time. She wanted to give him a hug. Hell, she wanted him to give *her* a hug. "Please tell me those kids don't have to go back there. It's one thing for a grown woman to make a decision to stay with someone who hurts her, but it's inexcusable for her to put her own kids in a situation like that."

"I agree. And no, the kids aren't going back. We kept the younger girl in our truck until the cops arrived and got everything straightened out. She grabbed hold of Chief and wouldn't let go. He actually ended up going with the cops to the station to meet with child protective services."

"Is he okay?"

Dean chuckled in her ear. A low sound that sent electricity right to her crotch.

"Yeah, beautiful, Chief's okay. He has a soft spot for kids, he'd be the first to tell you that, so don't think I'm telling you anything that's a state secret. Something about growing up on the reservation out in New Mexico and taking care of the little ones in his neighborhood. He said it took a while, but she eventually warmed up to the women who came to meet her. Because of her history, they're placing her with a lesbian couple."

"Wow, um…I don't mean to sound prejudiced, be-cause I'm not, but is that normal?"

"What?"

"That the super-conservative state of Texas approved a lesbian couple to be foster parents?"

"Beautiful, they're two people who have volunteered their home and love to abused kids who need a place to stay to be safe. Foster parents are in short supply. They don't give a fuck."

"Oh, okay."

"And the fact that those kids don't have to be in a house with a man is the best thing for them right now. They can heal and find out what 'normal' is."

"So Chief grew up on a reservation?"

He didn't even falter at her change in subject. "Yup. He's only about a quarter Native American. His mother was born as a result of a one-night stand with someone off the res, and he doesn't know who his dad was, as his mother followed in the same footsteps as *her* mom."

"Only a quarter? I wouldn't have guessed."

"He might not be one hundred percent, but he grew up there, living in poverty along with the rest of his people. Knowing there wasn't much opportunity for him there, he moved to Texas. He worked his butt off to get his fire science degree, and I can tell you, if I was ever in trouble, I'd want him at my back."

"I'm glad you have that. Can I ask something else?"

"Of course, you can ask me anything," Dean told her.

"It's about Chief. I don't want to offend you."

"You're not going to offend me. Well, as long as you don't tell me that you're interested in dating him rather than me. I'll definitely be offended by that."

She chuckled. "No. Definitely not. I like you, Dean."

"Good. 'Cause I like you too."

Knowing she was smiling like an idiot, but not caring, Adeline asked, "Being that Chief is part Native American, his nickname seems kind of…" She paused, searching for the right word. Then finally finished, "Wrong."

"He's not offended by it, beautiful. He'd be the first to tell you that too. In fact, his nickname around the station used to be Gromit. You know, from *Wallace and Gromit*."

"I have no idea what you're talking about," Adeline told him with a small shoulder shrug.

"I can't believe you've never seen *Wallace and Gromit*; we'll have to remedy that. Anyway, Gromit is Wallace's dog, and doesn't ever say a word. But there's no doubt that he communicates. He's got this eyebrow-raise that makes you know exactly what he's thinking. Anyway, Chief got the nickname Gromit early on because he doesn't talk a lot. But one day we were all out drinking and some asshole cowboys started calling him Chief. The rest of us were pissed beyond belief and ready to kick the shit out of the guys, but Chief merely shrugged and said, 'I like it.' So it stuck."

"It's still weird," Adeline pressed.

"Honestly, he doesn't care what others think of him. He grew up on a reservation and has spent his life being proud of who he is and his heritage. Other people stereotyping him and saying insensitive shit doesn't faze him."

"I like him," Adeline blurted.

Dean chuckled. "Me too. He's become like a brother to me in the time we've worked together."

"How was the rest of your day? Did it live up to your nickname?" Adeline tried to lighten the mood as she changed the subject.

"Yup. Three vehicle accidents. Two smoke investigations and one structure fire."

"Are those dangerous?"

"What? Structure fires?"

"Yeah."

"They can be. But this one wasn't. By the time we got there, the mobile home was fully engulfed. Nothing we could do but throw water on it until the flames were out. It was completely destroyed."

"No one was hurt?"

"No one was hurt. Can we FaceTime?"

The question coming out of the blue surprised her and Adeline hesitated. Apparently it was too long, because Dean said quickly, "I need to see you, beautiful. I've had a crap day and it sounds like you have too. There's nothing I'd like more than to lose myself in your eyes."

"I'm in bed, Dean."

She could hear the smile in his voice when he said, "What're you wearing?"

Adeline giggled. She couldn't help it. "Nothing sexy. Sorry."

"Please?"

She sighed. "All right." As if she could deny him anything. She clicked a button and soon his face showed up on the screen of her phone. Suddenly shy, she said, "Hey."

"Hey," he returned with a smile. "You really are in bed."

"Yup."

"Are you sure you're okay?"

"Yeah. Again, it was a long week. I cranked down the air because I've been hot all day. I love snuggling under blankets."

"I'll keep that in mind."

"Dean," she scolded.

"What? My girl likes the air conditioning in the house to be on the chilly side. I can deal with that. I'm out in the heat all day myself. If I get cold, I'll put on sweats. And, just sayin', I'm down with snuggling to keep warm."

"As long as you don't wear socks to bed. That's gross."

He chuckled. "I'm not telling you. Again, you'll have to find out my bad traits without me helping."

Adeline smiled, she couldn't help it.

"I love your smile," Dean told her easily. "Even

when you're not feelin' it, it lights up your face. How's Coco?"

He did that all the time, Adeline realized. Paid her a wonderful compliment, then asked a non-related question right afterwards. "Why do you do that?"

"Do what?"

"Say something nice, then ask a question that has nothing to do with it."

"You really want to know?"

Adeline scrunched up her nose. "Of course. I wouldn't have asked if I didn't."

"That's true. You don't play games. I keep forgetting. I do it, beautiful, because you have a hard time taking compliments. You either try to deny whatever it is that I've said, or you roll your eyes and change the subject. I don't like making you feel uncomfortable, and I really don't like when you put yourself down by denying it, so I change the subject to try to make you feel more at ease…and I hope that if I keep sneaking compliments in, you'll soon come to believe me and not try to deflect when I do it in the future."

"Oh." Adeline wasn't sure what to say. It was true. She wasn't comfortable with all of his compliments, simply because she hadn't really heard anyone say those kinds of things to her before. Sure, when she was dressed up and trying people told her she looked nice, but Dean complimented her all the time. Like when she was lying in her bed, hair mussed, tired from a long week of work and completely stressed out and makeup free. She decided to just ignore it for now. "Coco is good. Tired too. When I work a lot, he does too."

He let her move on from the compliment conversation. "I'm impressed how well he stays on task when he's with you. I noticed that until you told him it was okay, he didn't pay any attention to Taco or Moose."

"Yeah, when I realized he really could tell when I was going to have a seizure, I took him to get official service dog training. They emphasized that when he was working, he needed to be working. And he knows not to get distracted unless I tell him it's okay."

"It's amazing."

"It is. Although people don't seem to get that he's working. They come up all the time to pet and make smooshy faces at him. I mean, I get it, he's cute, but it's just not cool."

"They do it even though he's wearing a vest that says, 'Working dog, do not distract or pet'?"

"Yup."

"Jerks."

Adeline smiled. Dean really looked put out. She could tell he was sitting on a couch and saw half of a picture on the wall behind him.

"What're you looking at?" he asked, noticing her distraction.

"Oh, sorry. I was just trying to figure out where you were."

"I'm at work. Want a tour of the station?"

"What?"

"A tour. Well, a virtual one for now."

"Sure."

Adeline watched the screen intently as Dean stood up and started walking around. He showed her the small room he was currently relaxing in, then walked down the hall to a room with several bunk beds lined up on the walls.

"This is where we get some sleep when we need it."

"You all sleep in the same room?" she asked incredulously.

"Well, yeah. The station isn't big enough for us all to have our own rooms. Why is that weird?"

"I don't know." She smiled at him. "Okay, that's a lie. I do know. It's because you're like, a guy's guy, and I can't see you having a slumber party in a room with a bunch of other guys who are probably just as alpha and male as you."

Crash turned the phone around so she could see him. "It's not like we're giggling and doing our nails together, beautiful. We come in here to sleep. Hell, it probably sounds like a bunch of chainsaws when we're all snoring together. But I'm not admitting that I snore. Nope, again, that's something you'll have to find out yourself. There's absolutely nothing sleepoverish about the sleeping arrangements."

"Gotcha." She was still smiling at him.

Crash just shook his head in amusement and continued on with the tour. He showed her the locker room—after making sure it was empty—then the weight room, the big TV room she'd seen the day she'd been there, the kitchen, and finally the bays with the trucks and engines inside.

"What, no pole?" she teased softly.

"Oh, there's a pole, beautiful," Crash said with a twinkle in his eye.

Adeline laughed. She probably should've been turned off by the obvious sexual innuendo, but couldn't be. He was funny.

"Do you think—" Adeline's words were cut off by Coco jumping up onto the bed and landing on her side.

"Coco! Get off!" She laughed and pushed the large dog to the side, turning on her back and dropping the phone in the process.

She fumbled for the phone and laughed again as Coco pushed his head under her free hand. Adeline petted him absently as she brought the phone back up in front of her face. "Sorry about that. As I was saying, do you think there's a fire station around somewhere that does have a pole? I'd love to experience sliding down it just once."

Expecting Dean to laugh at her and possibly make another innuendo about sliding down a pole, she was surprised to see his brows drawn down over his eyes in concern.

Adeline pushed Coco away again, not wanting to pet him at the moment, and asked, "What? What'd I say?"

"Is Coco alerting?" Dean asked in a quiet, urgent tone.

Oh shit. She'd been so into her conversation with Dean and admiring the station that she hadn't really paid attention to her dog. She looked at him now.

Fuck. Yup. He was alerting. The dog was staring at her in the intense way he had when he could tell she was going to have a seizure. He was lying half on top of her and kept head-butting her hand.

"Shit. I gotta go, Dean."

"Don't. Let me be there with you."

Annoyed, and definitely not wanting him to see her have another seizure, Adeline didn't think about her words before she spat, "You haven't been here for any of the other seven I've had in the last week, why would you want to be here for this one?"

His eyes narrowed. "Seven? You've had seven seizures this week? You haven't told me about any of them."

Knowing she'd screwed up Adeline closed her eyes

for a moment, then looked at the phone. The concern mixed with anger almost made her cry, but she didn't have time for that. "Look, I know you're a paramedic and all, but it's not a big deal."

"Is that more than usual?"

He wasn't even listening to her, and he definitely wasn't letting her blow him off. Adeline knew all she had to do was click off the phone, or put it down so he couldn't see her, but a part of her didn't want to be rude.

"It's been a tough week. I've been stressed. They seem to increase when I'm stressed."

"Prop the phone up on your nightstand, beautiful. Let me be there for you with this one. Please?"

Hating that she felt vulnerable, Adeline hesitated.

"It's nothing to be embarrassed about," Dean said in an understanding tone. "I've already seen you have one. Remember? I just want to be here for you. If something goes wrong, what's your sister's number so I can call for help. I hate thinking about you being there alone. It'd make me feel better."

"Okay, fine," Adeline huffed, not comfortable with it, but giving in because she didn't have time to argue with him. She mentally noted that a bossy Dean could be hot, but also be annoying. She shifted Coco so she could lean over and prop the phone up next to the bed. "Don't blame me if I drool and you can't ever look at me again without picturing that."

"The only thing I see when I think about you is beauty. Now lay back and relax. You got this."

Adeline complied. How did he always seem to say the right thing at the right time?

"I don't like you to see me like this."

"You think I don't know that, Adeline? But trust me, the only thing I see is a beautiful, strong woman lying on her bed, covered by the frilliest, girliest, pinkest comforter I've ever seen in my life. And all I can think of is how much I wish I was lying right there next to her, although afterwards I'd have to go chug a beer, crush the can on my head, scratch my balls, and watch football to get my manhood back."

She chuckled. He was funny. But she felt the need to protest his sexism anyway. "Dean…"

"Shhhhh, relax. I'm here. Coco's there. Just let it happen. You're fine. I remember a time when I was little, I was so sick and my mom let me stay home from school…"

Adeline didn't hear the rest of his story as the seizure took over her body.

Chapter Nine

DEAN CLENCHED HIS teeth as he watched Adeline's body go stiff and saw her stare off into space. The view from the phone's camera wasn't as good as he'd like it to be, but at least he could see her face.

He hated that he wasn't there with her. Hated that she continued to have seizures. And *really* hated that she'd kept them from him. Yeah, they'd only been out on one date, but they'd spoken on the phone every day in the last week. He felt closer to her even after only one date than he had his last girlfriend, who he'd been with for five months.

He kept talking, saying nothing important, just letting her hear the sound of his voice as her body slightly twitched and spasmed on her bed.

Chief stuck his head into the small break room as Crash concentrated on Adeline. He paused in the middle of the story he was telling her and looked up.

"She good?" Chief asked.

"How'd you know?"

The big man shrugged. "I'm next door. I can hear through the wall."

Crash knew the walls were thin, but hadn't thought they were *that* thin. He'd have to remember that in the future. "She's good." His eyes went back to the phone. "Seizure."

"Let me know if you need to get to her. I'll cover for ya."

Crash looked up at Chief. As he'd told Adeline, the man didn't talk a lot, but Crash knew without a doubt that he would bend over backwards to help any one of the men he worked with. He hadn't lied to Adeline earlier. He trusted all his friends at the station, but Chief had an intensity about him that oozed competence and trustworthiness.

"Thanks, I appreciate it. I'll keep ya informed."

Chief nodded and closed the door just as silently as he'd opened it.

Crash shook his head at the easy way Chief prowled around the building. If he didn't want you to know he was there, you wouldn't know he was there. Period.

Turning his attention back to the phone, Crash saw glimpses of Coco as the dog shifted on the bed next to Adeline. He couldn't imagine what life was like for her before Coco started alerting. She'd have had no advance notice of a seizure, which meant she couldn't safely drive anywhere. Or really do anything with the confidence that she wouldn't have a seizure. Eating out, working, walking, sleeping…anything.

Finally, what seemed like hours later, but in reality was only probably ten minutes or so, Adeline blinked.

"Hey, beautiful. Good to see you back. That's it. No worries, you're safe at home with Coco. You're on your bed, it's all good."

"Dean?" she mumbled sleepily.

"Yeah, I'm here. We're FaceTiming. The phone is propped up on the table next to your bed. Take your time. Relax. Take a few deep breaths. That's it. Good girl. Can you turn to your right and look at me?"

Crash relaxed for the first time after he saw recognition in her eyes when she saw his face on her phone screen.

"I'm so tired."

"Then sleep, beautiful."

"Tired of having to worry if I'm going to have to cut a phone call at work short. Tired of worrying about if Douglas is gonna walk in when I'm in the middle of a seizure and freak out and call an ambulance. I'm just tired of being different. I hate having epilepsy. *Hate* it."

"Remember I told you once about my sister?" Crash asked, keeping his voice soft and easy. God. He wanted to be there with her. Wanted to take her in his arms and wrap her up tight and tell her she didn't have to worry about anything ever again. He thought he probably felt more helpless than she did right about now.

"You have a sister?"

Her words here slow, as if she wasn't quite back to herself. He knew he'd told her about Laura when he was explaining how he'd became a firefighter, but she obviously wasn't firing on all cylinders right now. "Yeah. Her name is Laura and she's younger than me by a few years. She was born with Down syndrome."

Adeline made a small humming noise in the back of her throat and turned on her side, facing the phone. "Oh yeah, you did tell me that before. I'm sorry about the DS."

"Don't be," Crash answered immediately. "There's absolutely no reason to feel bad for her, me, or my family. Laura is amazing. She's the most amazing human I've ever met in my life. Nothing gets her down. Nothing. Some people might argue that it's because she doesn't understand much of what's going on around her, but I don't believe that for a second. She just has a beautiful, pure soul and I'm a better person for having her in my life."

Adeline looked more with it now, but she didn't say anything, just kept her eyes on his as he spoke.

"I spent my life looking after her. When boys or girls would make fun of her, I'd be there to protect her and tell them to get lost. When she lost her backpack because she put it down somewhere and couldn't remember where it was, I was there to find it for her. She had no problem telling me how much she loved me, even when we were in the middle of the hallway at school. If she saw me, she'd act like she hadn't seen me in months...running up and hugging me, saying, 'I love you, Dean!' at the top of her lungs. It used to embarrass me . . . until she got really sick."

Crash paused and smiled at the vision in front of him. Adeline had bunched up the covers and was snuggled down into them as if the temperature was below freezing inside her room. He could see most of her face, but her chin was hidden in the pink material. Her eyes were slits and he knew she was fading fast. He needed to wrap this up so she could get some much needed sleep.

"I told you about when she passed out at our table. She ended up having to stay in the hospital as they did tests and tried to figure out how to treat her and make sure it didn't happen again. I missed her enthusiasm. I missed her screeching that she loved me when we both got home from school and I missed her enthusiasm for life."

"Where is she now?" Adeline asked, sleepily.

"Phoenix. My parents sat down with her after she graduated from high school, which in itself is somewhat rare, most kids with DS don't. Anyway, they talked about what she wanted to do with her life. Even though her cognitive ability is different from someone else her age, she knew she wanted to live as independently as possible. My parents knew they wouldn't be around forever to look after her, and wanted to do everything they could to give her the tools she needed to have as much independence as possible. They researched and found a wonderful group home for adults just like her in Arizona. They hate being away from her, but it's amazing how much she's flourished. There are adult helpers who live in the house in shifts with the residents, and they help them with housework and basic necessities. They go grocery and clothes shopping and go to work as well."

"Where do they work?"

"There are a few businesses in the area that take in people with DS. Some stock grocery bags. Others do light cleaning at businesses. Still others greet customers as they enter stores. She's doing amazing. And anytime I see her, she still runs up to me, throws her arms around me in a big hug and tells me that she loves me."

"I'm glad you have that. And that she's happy."

"That's my point, beautiful. She's different, just as you are, but she's happy. Yeah, you have epilepsy, and it sucks, but you've got a wonderful life, great parents, a sister you love who loves you back. And you've got a boyfriend who thinks you're amazing."

He could see she wasn't sure how to process his

statement about being her boyfriend, so she ignored it. He didn't push the issue.

"I know. I'm just scared."

"Of what?"

"Of losing it. I know I need the surgery, but I'm just so scared of never waking up, or at least waking up and not being the same person I am now. What if I don't remember Alicia? Or anything about my job? Or you?" Her voice was low and barely audible.

"I'd be worried if you *weren't* scared," Crash told her honestly. "It's a scary step. But it's not like you're gonna pick a brain surgeon off the street." He paused and smiled at her when she chuckled. Then he continued, "You'll do your research, choose the best doctor out there. Someone you trust, who will do the absolute best job he or she can."

"Yeah." Her eyes were shut now.

"And I'll be right there beside you the whole time."

Her eyes came open at that. "You will?"

"Yeah."

"You can't know that. Why would you say that?"

"Because I like you, Adeline Reynolds. Because the more time I spend talking to you, the more I like you. You're not having that surgery tomorrow, true, but I'm thinking by the time you do have it, I can honestly say I'll most likely be so in love with you it'll take a fuck of a lot for anything to scare or take me away from you.

You won't be alone when you go into the hospital, and you sure as hell won't be alone when you leave it…no matter what you remember and what you don't."

"Hmmmm." Her eyes closed again and she sighed in contentment. "That was so nice of you to say. I wish you were here so I could give you a hug to thank you."

"Me too, beautiful. Now hush. Go to sleep. I want you bright-eyed and bushy-tailed on Sunday when you take me out."

She didn't respond, but Crash sat and watched her sleep for quite a while. She looked so gorgeous. Peaceful. Finally, he whispered, "Good night, beautiful. Sleep well." And clicked off the phone.

He wasn't surprised when, several moments later, Chief opened the door to the small room once more. "All okay?"

"Yeah."

Chief leaned against the doorjamb and crossed his arms over his chest. "We talked about this before, but Sledge really wants to set up a softball game with our cop friends. He wants Beth to be able to go. It's not gonna be official, probably at a park near his house. He wants to keep it low-key and not have a ton of people there. It'd be a great time to introduce your woman to all of us. And have her meet the other ladies as well."

Crash nodded. "I'll talk to her."

Chief didn't say anything for a long moment but

kept his eyes on Crash. Finally, he said, "It's good to see you this way."

"What way?" Crash asked.

"Concerned about a woman."

"I've been concerned about women in the past. What the fuck, Chief?"

"Not like this," he rebutted. "I was there when you almost punched Driftwood. You've been concerned about what *we* think about the women you've taken out. About your reputation as a playboy. You might think you've got us fooled, but you don't. We all know you aren't as casual about hookups as you want us to think. You might be able to pull the wool over some people's eyes, but if you think your friends don't know what's up, you're foolin' yourself. This woman? She's special to you."

It wasn't like he was trying to keep Adeline a secret from his friends, but because their relationship was so new, he didn't want to subject her to his buddies all at once. They were all pretty alpha and could be overwhelming at times. "She is," Crash finally said.

Chief nodded. "Can't wait to officially meet her. I don't consider that first day, when you blew past us taking her to the back room to have a seizure, as 'meeting.' Let us know if you or she needs anything. *Anything*, brother." With that, the large man pushed off the doorjamb and headed back down the hall from where he came.

Crash leaned his head against the back of the couch. He couldn't wait to see Adeline on Sunday. He didn't care what they did together, as long as he got to talk to her. He was quickly becoming addicted. He wanted to talk to her all the time. Wanted to tell her about the calls he'd been on and check in just to see how she was. It killed him that she hadn't told him about the seizures she was still having, but he understood why.

They were new. Hell, they'd only been on one real date. It would take some time for her to get comfortable with him. He hoped after Sunday she'd feel at least a little better about opening up.

Seeing Sledge and Beth together made him realize how precious life was. Witnessing firsthand how frantic Sledge had been when he'd realized his girlfriend was outside his house by herself, and probably suffering from her agoraphobia, and not giving a shit that his friends could see how upset he was about Beth's well-being, went a long way toward making Crash realize that being in a relationship was a give-and-take situation.

He could give Adeline some security and support when she needed it.

And she could give him an ear to listen when he had a tough call.

They could lean on each other, and that was perfectly all right. He wanted that.

Yes, Adeline was strong and tough and could function perfectly fine on her own, *had* been fine on her own…but that didn't mean she should have to.

Crash wanted to be there for Adeline.

Wanted to make sure she was okay after a seizure.

Wanted to have dinner waiting for her when she got home.

Wanted to be the first person she spoke to in the morning and the last person she spoke to before she went to sleep at night.

Watching her have the seizure and not being able to be there made it crystal clear how much he liked her. He wasn't going out with her to simply get off or to tell his parents he had a girlfriend.

Crash wanted to be by Adeline's side when she went in to have her surgery. He wanted to allay her fears and brush away her tears when she was upset or scared. He wanted her to meet Laura and have his sister get to know her in return.

It was a weird feeling; to know he'd met the person he was meant to spend the rest of his life with. Not only that, but to know that he had a hell of a long way to go before he could get on with spending the rest of his life with her.

He had to take it easy, not spook her. He'd take it slow…even if it killed him.

Adeline Reynolds was his. His to protect. His to shelter from the hits life threw at her, and his to love. He just had to convince her.

SHE LIKED THE COFFEE.

She smiled at you. Big. Huge.

And she drank it all. You have the proof.

The man licked the rim of the cardboard coffee cup and closed his eyes, pretending he was kissing her. If he concentrated, he could almost smell her.

He opened his eyes and looked down at the picture in front of him on his kitchen table. He'd gotten it out of his secret hiding place earlier, unable to resist.

He'd taken the picture from behind. She was walking across the parking lot to her car. He ran his finger over her black hair, then down her spine and over her butt. His breathing picked up as he imagined her lying in his bed. Naked. Arms held up as she said his name, encouraging him to come to her. He licked his lips.

Food next. You have to buy her food.

It doesn't matter that she said no last time.

Keep asking. She'll say yes.

Maybe bring her something nice so she'll see you're serious.

Send her a nice note.

She's so small and cute. Her hair reminds me of that cat we had a long time ago. The one who died when it was

sleeping in your bed.
>*But she won't die. No. She'll eat with you.*
>*You can feed her.*
>*Then she'll like you and move in.*
>*Tomorrow. Ask again tomorrow.*

Chapter Ten

————————◆————————

"HEY, DEAN," ADELINE said as she opened her front door.

It was Sunday and she was really, really nervous about their date. Why she'd said it was her turn to wow him, she had no idea. She wasn't really a "wow" kind of person. But he'd gone out of his way to make their first date so amazing, she felt as though she owed it to him to put in the effort making sure he had just as much of a good time as she had the other week.

Not only that, but she was still reeling from Friday night when she'd had another seizure in front of him— well, in front of him on the phone. He'd stayed right there on the phone with her and she vaguely remembered him talking to her while she was out of it. Then she'd fallen asleep on him. Not a very good way to impress him. She just hoped she could manage one day without a seizure. Just one.

"Hi, beautiful," he murmured, then leaned forward and put a hand at her neck and kissed her lightly on the lips. He left his hand on her nape and pulled back only a few inches. Adeline could feel his warm, minty breath on her face as he spoke. "How are you?"

"I'm good. You? You're not too tired?"

"No. Surprisingly, we didn't get any calls last night, so I slept a full night. But back to you. You're really all right? Have any seizures yesterday?"

She wanted to lie, she really did, but blew out a breath and said, "Yeah, one."

"Know what might've caused it?"

"I don't know what causes any of them, Dean. If I did, I'd do whatever it took to make them stop. But, I did have to talk to Douglas yesterday. He called with a question about the Wolfe account, and since he's changed his modus operandi and started being nice, creepily nice, he wanted to pick my brain about one of the things I suggested the other week."

"What do you mean by 'creepily nice'?" Dean asked in a low, hard voice.

Adeline shrugged and suddenly realized she probably shouldn't have described her boss that way. Not to Dean. Over the last week, she'd discovered one of his potential faults…he was über protective and didn't like to hear about anyone being disrespectful or rude to her. She tried to minimize the impact of what she'd said and do damage control. "He's just gone out of his way to be pleasant. Which is so out of the norm for him, it's weird."

"He say anything out of line?"

"Out of line? No. He asked me to go to lunch again to discuss the accounts, but I told him I was busy."

"Again? He asked you out before today?" If anything, Dean's voice got even harder.

"No, no, nothing like that. Not a date. He just thought it would be easier to talk over lunch."

"He asked you out." It wasn't a question this time. "What else?"

How in the world did he always know when she was leaving stuff out? "Nothing important."

"Please don't do that. I know we're newly dating, but I can't stand knowing that you're keeping something about another guy from me. I'm not going to lose my shit. I promise. I just want to make sure you're safe."

"I'm safe," Adeline told him immediately. "Douglas is harmless. I mean, yeah, he's weird, but I can handle him."

"What'd he do?" Dean asked again, crossing his arms over his chest.

"He brought me flowers," Adeline told Dean quietly. "But not as a come-on or anything. They're for nailing the marketing plan with the new client. He also sent me a nice email saying how proud he was of me and that he was honored that I was his employee."

God, when she said it out loud, it sounded bad. But

since she had no interest in Douglas, it hadn't seemed like a big deal at the time. But now she could see that from Dean's standpoint, it wasn't exactly innocent.

"You need to report his ass," Dean bit out, his jaw tensing.

"I'm hoping to be gone soon," Adeline said in an even tone. "I don't want to rock the boat. He'll get the hint and leave me alone."

"Are you a guy?" Dean weirdly asked.

"Uh…no?"

"Right. I am. So when I tell you that he's not going to get the hint and leave you alone, you need to believe me. You're beautiful, Adeline. And smart. And you probably smile at him to downplay your rejection of him, which only makes him more determined to get you to say yes to his not-so-innocent requests for meetings."

"I need this job," Adeline returned immediately. "Trust me, Douglas is harmless. I never see him outside of work, and even if I do have to meet with him, nothing is going to happen."

Dean took a deep breath and gazed up as if looking for divine intervention. Then he returned his eyes to hers and brought his other hand up to rest lightly on her shoulder, practically enfolding her into his large body. "Just be careful, beautiful. Listen to your gut. If something seems off, it's off. I trust you, but I don't trust *him*."

Adeline licked her lips nervously and looked up at Dean. God, he was handsome. He was pissed on her behalf, and a part of her liked that. It meant that he cared. Dean was wearing blue jeans that hugged him in all the right places. He smelled delicious, like he just got out of the shower. She could smell his scented soap, and the calluses on his fingers against her neck were making her nipples tighten in response. She wanted to bury her nose in the crease between his neck and his shoulder, but instead she tried to appease him by deflecting.

"I'll be careful. Promise. Why don't you come in for a minute? I just need to get Coco's harness on and grab my purse, then we can go."

Dean took a step inside her house, forcing her to take a step backwards. He didn't let go of her as he moved. He kicked the door closed behind him then leaned down, moving his hand from her shoulder to the other side of her neck. He tilted her head up to him and looked earnestly into her eyes.

"If he asks you out again, you tell him you have a boyfriend. A boyfriend who wouldn't appreciate another man taking you out to eat. Tell him that if he wants to talk work with you, then he can find you at work during the week, but your weekends are off-limits."

She'd thought they were done talking about her boss, but obviously she was wrong. Dean's declaration that he was her boyfriend made her want to fall to a puddle at his feet. She liked that. No, she freaking *loved* that. Yes, he was high-handed and bossy, but the emotion and meaning behind his bossiness was hot.

Instead of melting where she stood, she said in what she hoped was a nonchalant tone, "I'm a salaried employee, Dean." She wasn't protesting, per se...seeing how irritated Dean was over her asshole boss asking her out was exhilarating, but unnecessary. She didn't *want* to go anywhere or do anything with Douglas Hill the Third. Why in the hell would she when Dean Christopherson was standing in front of her, looking like he did, being all concerned about her and calling himself her boyfriend? She wasn't an idiot.

"I can work on the weekends," she finished somewhat lamely.

"It's inappropriate and could be construed as sexual harassment. Besides, I don't like this sudden change in him. He wants something. And if that something is you, he can't have you. You're already mine."

Again, the ooey-gooey feeling of being wanted zipped through her. But she asked, "Yours? Dean...we've only known each other for a week."

"Figure of speech, beautiful. We're dating. Goin' out. Seein' each other. Boyfriend/girlfriend. However you want to put it. If anyone takes you out to eat, it'll be me."

"Oh. Okay." She had nothing else to say, because

she was one hundred percent down with that.

"Okay." He backed up, smiling at her response, but kept one hand at her nape. "Now…I'm sorry you had another seizure after talking to that asshat. Which is another reason I don't want you anywhere near him. I don't trust him as far as I can throw him. I *especially* don't trust him with your well-being when you're vulnerable in the middle of a seizure. You feel okay to go out today? We can just stay here if you want."

"I'm fine, Dean. I'm used to the seizures."

"I don't care how used to them you are, beautiful. If you'd prefer to stay in, we'll stay in."

"I'm not as good at organizing fun things as you are, but I'm hoping to surprise you with my plans today," she said hesitantly. Staying home did sound nice, but she'd thought long and hard about what Dean might like to do, and thought she'd done a pretty good job. "Although I should probably warn you. I suck at these kinds of things and generally *would* prefer to hang out at home. People are mean. And they only care about doing what they want, and getting service as soon as possible. It's annoying. So not only does staying home mean that I don't have to worry about dealing with that kind of thing, I also don't have to worry about finding a place to sit or lie down if Coco alerts. But I loved what we did so much last week, I wanted to take you out this time."

"Then we'll go out. But, beautiful, in the future, I

have no problem whatsoever staying in. We can watch movies, play cards, roughhouse with Coco, sit and stare at the walls. It doesn't matter. What matters to me is spending time with you. That's what I like. So when we get together, we can do whatever makes you most comfortable and whatever you want."

"Whatever I want, huh?" Adeline smiled at Dean playfully. She knew they were newly dating, but damn…he knew exactly what to say to make her feel squishy inside.

He brought his head close to hers once more and whispered, "Whatever you want, beautiful."

"O-okay then…let me get Coco ready and my purse and we'll go."

It took a moment, but Dean finally dropped his hand and nodded. "No problem. I'll wait here."

"You want a tour?" Her house wasn't anything impressive. It was a smallish home in a fairly nice suburban neighborhood. It had two bedrooms and two baths. She'd only met a couple of the people in her neighborhood, but both were nice enough. She'd bought the house because she figured it was smart to invest rather than continuing to rent. If she ever met a man who she wanted to spend the rest of her life with, and maybe start a family with, they could pick out a bigger house together.

"Later."

Adeline nodded and turned to get Coco situated. Within minutes she was back at the door and ready to go. "Want me to drive?"

Dean gave her such a look of disgust that she burst out laughing and held up her hands in capitulation. "Okay, okay, sorry. You can drive, oh masculine manly man of mine."

The smile that spread over his face was priceless. "I like that."

"What?" Adeline asked with a tilt of her head.

"You calling me your man."

She rolled her eyes. "I wasn't *really* calling you my man. It was a figure of speech."

"You said it, I heard it. You can't take it back."

Her first inclination was to blow it off and continue on their way, but she could see that it meant something to him. "That means something to you."

"Yeah."

He didn't elaborate.

"I know we've just started dating, and I have no idea what's going to happen in the future…but you should know I like you. A lot," she told him.

"Good. Because I like you too."

"But for the record, I'm adding 'not letting me drive' to the list of your imperfections."

He chuckled then shrugged. "Told you I wasn't perfect."

They smiled at each other for a moment before she said, "Okay, then. Enough mushy crap and list-making. We have places to go, people to see, and hopefully assholes to avoid."

"Lead on, woman."

They walked outside and Dean took her keys and locked the door. He handed the keys back and Adeline dropped them into her purse.

He then reached out and took her hand in his as they went down her walkway to his car.

Adeline smiled the whole way.

"YOU CHEATED!" ADELINE grumbled at Dean later that morning. She'd directed him to Cool Crest Miniature Golf. It was a historic landmark in the city that had originally opened during the Great Depression in 1929. It had been renovated a few years ago, but still held the charm of the original course. Banana trees lined the perimeter, their leaves throwing some much needed shade onto the miniature greens.

Dean stepped away from the course and wrapped an arm around her waist, then tickled her. Adeline squirmed in his grasp and giggled. "Interference!"

Coco barely lifted his head from his spot in the shade next to them. At each hole, Adeline told him "down" and "stay" and he did. The dog could certainly be high strung, but he also knew how to nap.

"I need all the help I can get," Dean said, leaning close to her. "I had no idea you were a miniature golf pro."

Adeline laughed again and tried to get out of his grasp, with no luck. "I'm not a professional, I've just played a lot."

Dean turned her in his arms and clasped his hands together at the small of her back and smiled down at her. "It shows."

Adeline bit her lip, suddenly worried he would be honestly upset if she beat him. "Um…I can give you a couple shots if you want…to make it more even."

He threw his head back and laughed.

At first she smiled, then got more and more irritated as he kept on laughing. "Dean!" she exclaimed and tried to pull away from him.

He refused to let her go and was still smiling as he looked down at her. "What, beautiful?"

"I was being serious."

"I know you were. But no way in hell am I gonna take a handicap against you."

"But I might beat you."

Dean smiled again. "Beautiful, I don't give a shit if you do. As long as you're having fun, that's all I care about."

"Really?" Adeline asked with doubt clear in her

voice.

"You don't believe me." Again, it wasn't a question. He did that a lot. Said something that to some people might be a question, but coming from him it was more of a statement.

Since it wasn't exactly a question, Adeline didn't answer, but her look was apparently answer enough.

"Come here." Dean pulled her off to the side so a family could play through. "What are you really concerned about?'

She looked at him for a moment, then decided to be honest. If he really did want a relationship with her, then she needed to be truthful with him. "I don't want to ruin our date if I beat you and you get all huffy about it."

"I'm not gonna get huffy with you, beautiful. First, I'm a man, and men don't get huffy. Second, as I told you before, I don't give a shit if you beat me at mini golf or not. It's not a competition. We're having fun. I take it you've been out with someone who hated to lose to a girl?"

Adeline nodded.

"Seriously, Adeline, I'm secure enough in my manhood to let you beat me at mini golf, checkers, a five-K, or anything else you want to compete with me on."

"Are you sure?"

"Positive."

She smirked. "Good. Although just sayin', I'm not going to enter us in a five-K anytime soon. So don't hold your breath on that. But you should also know, I'm really not that competitive. It just seems to be a waste of energy to compare myself to others. Now, let's get back to the course. You're four strokes behind."

"Four strokes behind?" he repeated cheekily with a gleam in his eye that she could read loud and clear.

Adeline knew she was blushing. "Shut up."

Dean leaned down and kissed her, lingering as he teased her lips with his own, before pulling away just enough to whisper, "Beautiful."

An hour later, when Adeline sank the ball in the last hole, she turned to Dean with a wide smile. "That's it. I win."

"Congrats, beautiful. You beat me fair and square," Dean said, grinning.

"Damn straight."

If possible, his smile got even bigger. "That was fun. I'll tell you right now, I want a rematch at some point."

"Deal." Adeline grinned back, loving that they were freely talking about seeing each other in the future.

"What's next?"

"Lunch with a view."

"Sounds perfect. Hand me your club. I'll take it back to the desk if you want to go to the restroom before we leave."

The more time she spent around Dean, the more she realized how considerate he was. In the past, none of the men she'd dated had ever really paid much attention to what she needed versus what they wanted. She usually had to ask them to wait while she visited the restroom, or she had to flag down a waiter to get a refill. But Dean watched her. He kept note of what she might need, and acted on it. It was gentlemanly and sweet.

Without thought, Adeline stood up on her tiptoes and kissed Dean's cheek. "Thanks. I'll meet you out front."

She went to turn around, but Dean reached out a hand and took hold of her arm. As soon as she stopped and turned back to him, he put his hand under her chin and lifted it at the same time he leaned down. He kissed her long and wet before letting go. "Meet you out front, beautiful."

Bemused, she simply smiled and backed away, Coco at her side as usual. She used the restroom, washed her hands, then stood in front of the sink, looking at herself in the mirror for a long moment. Trying to decide if she looked different than normal, because she certainly *felt* different, Adeline tilted her head and examined herself.

Nope. She was still the same Adeline Reynolds she'd known her entire life. On the short side, carrying a few too many pounds, nice black hair, and perfectly normal. There was no good reason a gorgeous alpha male fireman such as Dean should take a second look at her. But somehow, he had.

Shaking her head, she smiled at her reflection, then took Coco's leash and headed back out to meet up with one of the most amazing men she'd ever met in her life. Time to get the second part of their date going.

"THE TOWER OF the Americas?" Crash asked as they turned into the parking garage near the large tower.

"Yeah. I know, it's totally touristy, but I heard they have a pretty nice restaurant at the top and I thought we could have lunch."

The look of hopeful optimism in Adeline's eyes as she looked at him, wanting him to be pleased with her choice of activity, made Crash smile tenderly at her. "Lunch would be great."

"Have you been here before?"

He pulled into the first parking spot he found, put the car in gear, then turned to her. Crash reached out and brushed a lock of hair behind her ear and nodded. "Yeah, beautiful. This is where the 9/11 Memorial Stair Climb is every year."

"Oh. I didn't realize. Duh, of course it is. It's the highest building in the metro area. Does it bring back bad memories? I didn't even think about it. We can go. We can stop at Chili's or something instead."

Seeing she was working herself up, Crash hurried to reassure her. "Stop. It's fine. Actually, I'm looking forward to being able to take the elevator to the top for once. It's a bitch to climb all those stairs with my gear on."

"I simply can't imagine…"

Adeline's voice trailed off.

"Look at me," Crash ordered, hating to see the happiness fade from her eyes. He waited until she tilted her chin and caught his eyes. "This building is a place that oozes brotherhood for me. It's where I sweat, curse, and swear I'm never going to climb another stair again in my life. By the time I've been up those damn stairs, twice, I'm dripping with sweat, my legs feel like noodles, but I'm so proud of what I do, and what those men and women did on September eleventh, I could burst.

"I feel like it's somehow karma or kismet or something that made you want to eat lunch here with me today. So we'll ride up the elevator like civilized people, eat lunch, maybe take in the movie at the top, if you're up to it. We'll do it knowing that, if required, firefighters, EMS personnel, or police officers wouldn't hesitate to hoof it up all those stairs to get to us if we needed them. Okay?"

"Okay," Adeline whispered back immediately.

"Perfect choice for lunch, beautiful," he told her honestly. "Now, give me a kiss and let's go admire the view and get something to eat."

She smiled at him and leaned forward eagerly.

Crash was still smiling as her lips shyly touched his and her tongue caressed his bottom lip. Using his hand to tilt her head, Crash didn't hesitate to take what she was so eagerly offering. He took the kiss from a pleasant meshing of lips to something carnal in the space of two heartbeats. His free hand rested under her raised arm, his thumb caressing the skin at the side of her breast.

Her hands weren't still. One was clutching him to her at the back of his neck, her fingernails pressing against the base of his skull. The other was low at his side, squeezing as he devoured her mouth.

Knowing he needed to pull back now, or he'd be taking her shirt off right there in the car, Crash eased his mouth off hers, but didn't move either of his hands. She didn't either.

They sat there, both leaning into the center console, breathing hard.

Crash broke the passion-filled silence. "You make me forget everything but how you taste and feel under me."

"Ditto," Adeline murmured, licking her lips unconsciously.

Crash groaned and pulled her forward, brushing his lips over her forehead. "Come on. Lunch."

He sat back and grinned as Adeline tried to get her

wits about her. "Right. Lunch," she murmured.

Pushing open his door, Crash got out and walked around to the other side of the car. Adeline was climbing out and he held out his hand for her. She grabbed hold and together they opened the back door to let Coco jump out. They walked hand in hand to the tower.

Adeline took out her wallet to pay for their tickets to the top, but Crash put his hand over hers. "No. I got it."

"But, Dean. I'm taking you out."

"Beautiful."

He didn't say anything else. Just her name in that exasperated way.

"But I paid for golf. How's that different than this?"

"Because you paid when I wasn't paying attention. I wouldn't have let you pay for it if you hadn't been so sneaky about it."

He saw her blush. He knew she'd deliberately asked him to take Coco out for a quick walk before they went inside to pay. But unfortunately, he didn't figure out why until he'd looked through the window and saw her at the desk, handing over her credit card while he was outside with her dog. "I didn't make a big deal out of it, because honestly it's kinda nice to be out with a woman who doesn't automatically assume I'm gonna pay for everything. But that doesn't mean I'm *not* gonna pay for everything."

"That's not logical," Adeline protested. "And I think this is going on the list of your imperfections too. Dean, I asked you out. I've got a job. This was my choice. I can pay."

Crash leaned in really close to her face and whispered. "I know you have money, beautiful. And I want you to spend that money on yourself. Not on me. You should learn this now. I don't care if it's our second date or our four thousandth. You're not paying."

"Not even if we have a joint account and the money in it is both of ours? How're you gonna separate it and keep me from paying for our dates then?"

"Fuck me," Crash breathed, his face looking weird in an intense but good way.

"What?" Adeline asked. "What'd I say?"

"I like the thought of us being together in a way that we have a joint account. You not caring if your money is mixed up with mine."

She rolled her eyes. "Dean, you're missing the point!"

Crash took her shoulders in his hands and kept his head close to hers. "I'm not missin' anything, beautiful. You are. We're startin' something here. Something I like a fuck of a lot. I like that you're your own woman. I like that you want to take on your share of our date. But it's not happening. Let me take care of you. You can pay for groceries and make me dinner. You can pay for gas, although if I'm with you, you won't. You can pay for Coco's vet bills. You can pay to get your hair and nails done, but you cannot pay for us when we're out together. *Capiche?*"

She sighed hugely, but he saw her lips quirking upward when she huffed, "Fine. But you're gonna get some really kick-ass birthday presents."

He kissed her, lingering a moment too long for it to be a completely chaste public kiss, but he couldn't help it. Anytime he touched her, he wanted nothing more than to inhale her scent, her touch, her essence. "Sounds like a deal to me."

He towed her back to the counter and the woman behind the glass smiled broadly at them. "Twenty-four dollars for two adults," she told him, still smiling, obviously having overheard at least part of their discussion on who would pay for the tickets and seeing their kiss.

Crash liked that Adeline pushed him and didn't automatically say yes to everything he said. It somewhat annoyed him, but he liked it at the same time. She might be smaller and physically weaker than he was, but mentally she was probably stronger. She had to be with her medical history. He hadn't thought he'd be attracted to a woman as independent as Adeline, but he was. He *so* was.

Hooking her arm under his, they walked toward the elevators that would take them to the top of the tower and lunch.

"Do you do the climb every year?" Adeline asked him quietly.

"I have for about three years now. The entire station almost missed it last year, when Penelope was still missing overseas, but we all talked about it and decided that she'd kick our butts if we backed out just because she was a POW. Sledge did a shit-ton of interviews that day, talking about how much his sister loved the stair climb and giving back to her country. We swear to this day it was what finally pushed the powers that be to make the decision to send in the Special Forces to find her."

"I'm sorry you all had to go through that," Adeline told him.

"Don't be sorry for me, beautiful. Be sorry for Penelope. *She's* the one who was kidnapped by those sick fucks. *She's* the one who had to worry every day if she'd be burnt alive or raped. All we did was raise a ruckus here at home. She did the hard part."

Adeline squeezed his arm. "That's not true. Well, okay, the first part is true, but don't ever say 'All you did.' What you guys did was vital in getting her back. I'm guessing you all wanted to hightail it over there and find her yourself, but obviously couldn't. She's your tcammate. You were hurting too, maybe in a different way than she was, but you were still hurting."

"Beautiful, sexy, and compassionate. I can't wait to find out what else is under that tough skin of yours."

Adeline blushed. "Stop it. You're embarrassing me. You're making me out to be some perfect woman, and I'm so not."

"We'll keep practicing on the accepting-a-compliment thing," he told her with a smile.

She just shook her head at him.

The elevator opened and they got in. No one else was around, so they had it to themselves. Coco sat at Adeline's feet, tongue out, panting happily.

"Wow, it's so surreal to be in this elevator," Crash said, looking around. "I'm so used to this being a place of solemn reflection. I love that you're letting me see and remember it in a different way. Thank you," Crash told Adeline seriously. "And I know you're not perfect, no one is, we've had this conversation before. But nothing I've seen so far has given me any reason to have any second thoughts about getting to know you better. Your imperfections make you more real."

"That's how I feel about you too," she told him honestly. She looked up at him with huge brown eyes and smiled.

Crash ran his index finger down her cheek tenderly. He couldn't help but wish the day was going slower. He dreaded saying goodbye to her at the end of the day. Even though he knew in his gut Adeline was meant to be his, he also knew he couldn't push too fast. Their relationship was moving quickly but he wouldn't rush her.

They stood together in silence, enjoying each other's company until the elevator bell rang when they reached the top of the seven hundred and fifty-foot tower.

They stepped out and headed for the hostess stand at the restaurant. "Eat first, then the movie?" Crash asked.

"Sounds good," Adeline replied with a smile.

"The four-D movie isn't going to mess with your epilepsy is it?"

She shook her head. "No, I'll be fine. Thanks for asking and not assuming."

They approached the entrance to the restaurant hand in hand. "Two for lunch," Crash told the tall, slender woman behind the hostess's stand.

She looked at him, then at Adeline and Coco with a frown. "I'm going to have to see your animal's qualification papers."

"His papers?" Adeline asked, surprised by the request.

"This is a public restaurant. We have strict health code standards we have to keep. There have been a few instances where patrons have stuck vests on their pets and pretended they were service dogs. Therefore, we have a new policy where we need to see the qualification papers and know what your disability is and how the animal is needed before you'll be allowed to dine in this establishment."

"I don't think you're allowed to ask for any of that information," Crash said immediately, pulling Adeline into his side.

"She's definitely not," Adeline confirmed and kept her eyes on the woman. "House Bill four eighty-nine states that you can ask me if my dog is required because of a disability and what task he is trained to perform, but that's it. You aren't allowed to ask me to show you proof of certification for my dog"

"Look, I understand it's awkward," the woman said in a fake concerned tone, "but it's also awkward for us when other patrons complain about allergies to dogs or when the supposed service animal makes a nuisance of itself. We're protecting you as well as our other customers."

"Bring the manager up here, now," Crash ordered harshly, not giving Adeline a chance to say anything.

"Now, sir, all I need to know—"

"Manager," he repeated through clenched teeth. "We're done talking to you."

The woman let out an aggravated breath, but turned on her heel without another word and headed into the restaurant.

"Dean, we can just go," Adeline told him, tugging at his arm. "I don't want to make a fuss. This happens more than you know. I'm actually kinda used to it. Remember when I talked about annoying people? This is a part of that."

Crash said nothing, merely shook his head. He was so pissed he couldn't remember the last time he was this angry. But taking it out on Adeline was the last thing he wanted to do. He simply wanted to sit with his girl-friend and have a nice lunch overlooking the city. She'd gone out of her way to try to find someplace special for their second date, and he'd be damned if anyone would keep that from them.

Soon, a middle-age man with a receding hairline and wearing a gray suit jacket, tie, and gray slacks walked toward them, with the hostess at his heels. Neither looked happy.

The man started talking before he even reached them. "I apologize for the inconvenience, sir, ma'am. But we have every right to protect our customers and make sure any animal brought into our establishment is a legitimate service animal."

Adeline was digging into her purse as the man spoke and when he was done, handed him a small card. It was the size of a business card, maybe a bit bigger, and printed on both sides. She took a deep, calming breath before she spoke. Her voice was firm, and she sounded as though she'd made the speech several times in the past.

"I understand, and it's reprehensible that people would choose to falsely claim their pets were service animals. But that is not *my* problem. This card explains my rights, and yours. You cannot ask to see my dog's training papers, nor can you ask what my disability is. But I'll tell you anyway. I'm not ashamed of it. I have epilepsy. My dog alerts me if I'm about to have a seizure. He gives me the extra ten or twenty minutes I need to get someplace safe before it hits. Without him, I could start convulsing right at the table. If I was eating, I could choke on something and possibly die. I'm sure you wouldn't want me to do that in your nice establishment." Adeline paused to let that scenario sink in. When it appeared it had, she continued.

"I am completely responsible for my dog. Not you. Not the state of Texas. Not my dining companion. You can see on the back of the card the law clearly states that you could be fined and I can take you to court if you violate my civil rights. It also states that, by law, an identification card is not required to grant me and my service dog entry to any public place, including restaurants. Now, I'm on a date with a man I'm trying to impress, and you're seriously making me look like a hard-ass bitch when I was going for feminine and lady-like. I'm hungry because I beat the pants off him in miniature golf this morning and now I'd like to sit and enjoy the view, which is my right, and enjoy a large glass of tea.

"I'm perfectly willing to let bygones be bygones, and do that here in your establishment. But if you still deny me, my dog, and my date entry, we'll leave without another word and without making a scene. But you *will* be hearing from my lawyer and from reporters from the *Express-News*, News 4, Fox 29, and any other news station I can get to listen to me about how the restaurant at the top of the Tower of the Americas, which holds the annual 9/11 Memorial Stair Climb and is a large tourist destination, denied me, my service dog, and one of its city's heroes entry. The man standing next to me is a firefighter here in San Antonio. He's participated in the 9/11 stair climb for the last three years, honoring his fellow servicemen and women who died on that day. I don't think it will go over well with the citizens of San Antonio to hear you wouldn't let us eat lunch…would it?"

There was a moment where no one spoke, but Crash noticed both the hostess and the manager looked a little sick.

A man standing behind them leaned toward Adeline with his hand out and said loudly, "Here's my card. You want to sue, I'll happily act as a witness." He turned to

Dean then and said, "And thank you for your service, sir. My mother's life was saved recently because my father called nine-one-one and the firefighters got to his house within five minutes. They provided CPR to my mom and kept her heart pumping long enough for her to get to the hospital and have heart surgery. So thank you."

Adeline looked at him, took his card, and dipped her chin regally. "Thank you. I appreciate it."

Crash was still pissed, but stuck out his hand, shook the man's and nodded. "Just doin' my job, sir."

"Well, it's appreciated nonetheless."

They gave each other manly chin lifts then Crash turned to the manager and the hostess, one eyebrow quirked upwards in a nonverbal question.

Finally, the manager spoke. "Of course. Our mistake. Follow me, please."

Adeline smiled at him as if she hadn't just flayed him alive and nodded. She looked up at Dean, her lips tense despite the grin. "Time for lunch."

Crash moved so his hand was at her back and he pressed against her as he leaned down and whispered, "Fucking perfect, beautiful."

They didn't say another word as the manager led them to a table with an amazing view. It was right next to a large window and faced the Alamo Plaza. He left them with a fake smile, saying their server would be right with them.

Crash held out Adeline's chair as Coco settled under the table, then pulled the chair from the other side and put it right next to hers.

"Um, are you supposed to do that? You're kinda sitting in the middle of the aisle now, Dean," Adeline told him.

"Don't care. And I guarantee they won't say a fucking thing after you wiped the floor with that asshole manager. I bet he's in the back right now telling our server to kiss our ass. Hell, our meal'll probably be free too."

"Good. Since you won't let me pay," Adeline shot back. She was obviously trying to lighten the mood, but Crash could tell she was still bothered by what happened.

He put a hand up to her cheek and forced her to look away from the gorgeous view and to face him. "Talk to me, beautiful."

The waitress chose that moment to come up to their table and, without letting go of Adeline, he turned to her and told her, "Give us a minute."

"Yes, sir. Take your time. I'll be back." And she disappeared.

"Adeline. What's wrong?" Crash asked again.

"That happens more than you know," she said in a soft voice. "I hate it, but it does."

"And?"

"And I hate that it's just one more reminder that I'm different. That I have this black cloud hovering over me. That any minute I could start staring into space or have a fucking grand mal seizure. I love my dog, it's not that, but I wish I could leave him at home like any other normal person. I wish I could go out with a guy and not have to deal with people making me feel like a second-class citizen. I want…" Her voice trailed off.

"You want what? Get it all out, beautiful," Crash told her patiently. He didn't like one fucking word that was coming out of her mouth, but she needed to get it all out before he responded.

"I want you to see me for me. Not a patient you have to worry about. Not a woman with a fucked-up brain. *Me.*"

"I see you, Adeline. I see you just fine. You're the woman who caught my eye the second you walked into that restaurant and you didn't have to say a word to do it. And trust me, I saw *you*, not your dog. You're the woman who's been on my mind every day since we've met. You're the woman whose texts I can't wait to read when I wake up in the morning and who I can't wait to talk to before I go to sleep."

He took one of her hands which had been resting in her lap, and pulled it to his own. He knew he was taking a risk, but he felt like Adeline needed the physical proof that he wasn't blowing smoke up her ass.

Discretely placing her small hand over his rock-hard cock, he said softly, "And as inappropriate as it is, you're the woman who just told off a stuffy old manager and a bitch hostess and made me hard as a rock in the process."

She didn't pull her hand away, but instead relaxed in his hold, molding her hand around his dick. He could feel the heat of her hand through his jeans, and it only made him harder.

Adeline must've felt him twitch under her hand because a smile slowly spread across her face and the darkness receded from her eyes. "You don't think less of me?"

"I have no idea what you're even referring to. Think less of you because you told off that cocksucker when he was being discriminatory? Think less of you for having more class in your little finger than the hostess has in her entire fucking body? Think less of you for sticking up for your rights? Fuck no."

"Okay."

"Okay." Crash smiled at her. He removed his hand from on top of hers and leaned his elbows on the table in front of him. When she didn't move her hand from his crotch, his smile grew. "I like your hand on me."

"I like my hand on you too," she returned, caressing him once more.

The perky waitress reappeared as if out of thin air, but Adeline didn't jerk her hand back immediately as he thought she would. She smiled up at the woman, and rubbed against his cock twice more before finally sliding it along his thigh to his knee and resting it there.

It was going to be a long lunch; Crash knew his erection wasn't going to go down anytime soon. Not with a grinning, more sure of herself Adeline sitting next to him, rubbing her thumb against the inside of his leg. He hoped it went on forever.

Chapter Eleven

"WANT TO COME in and see my house?" Adeline asked Dean nervously.

After the disastrous beginning, lunch had turned out to be wonderful. Their waitress had been extremely attentive, getting refills and making sure they had everything they needed. Adeline enjoyed the looks Dean gave her, as if he really did think her telling off the manager and threatening to sue him was sexy.

And when it came time for the bill to be delivered, their waitress had informed them that lunch was on the house, to apologize for the "misunderstanding" earlier.

Adeline knew it wasn't a misunderstanding, but she let it go. Lunch had been good, she'd enjoyed seeing Dean relax, liked feeling how she affected him, and loved spending time with him.

They'd watched the short 4D movie and now they were standing on her front porch. Adeline had unlocked the door and was standing beside it nervously. She'd let Coco off his leash and released him from duty. He'd bounded into the house, happy as a clam, and now it was just her and Dean.

He smiled at her and put his hand on the side of her neck. God, she loved it when he did that.

"No."

"No?" Adeline asked in surprise. That totally wasn't the answer she was expecting. Especially not after their hot-as-hell kisses and having her hand in his lap. He was more than ready and she had no doubt he could get that way again in a heartbeat.

"Not today," Dean told her with a grin and an intense look in his eyes. "If I follow you inside your house, I'm gonna want to do more than make out. I'm gonna want to find out if your pussy tastes as sweet as your lips. Then I'm gonna want to find out if you're as hot on the inside as you are on the outside."

Adeline could only gape up at him. Did he really just say that?

"Did you really just say that?"

He chuckled. "And that right there is why I'm not coming inside to look at your house. You're not ready. Beautiful, I refuse to rush this. Us. We have all the time in the world."

"But...I thought all guys wanted to have sex."

"Well, I'm not all guys. And let's be clear here. We'll have sex, yes, and we'll fuck, but the first time I take you, we'll be making love. I want to look into your eyes and see more than just lust there. I'm not saying I'm gonna wait until you have my ring on your finger, or that we have to declare our everlasting love for each other before it happens, but I like you, Adeline. I like everything about you. Even the things you think I'm not supposed to like. I don't want to fuck this up before we're solid. Got me?"

"Um…no."

He chuckled and pulled her into his arms.

Adeline wrapped her arms around his waist and laid her cheek on his chest. She could hear the *lub-lub-lub* of his heart beating strongly. She felt his hands splayed wide on her back, one arm low, his fingers flirting with the edge of her jeans, and the other high, between her shoulder blades.

"I'm not gonna rush this, beautiful," Dean stated again softly. "I like this feeling of being on edge around you. Of knowing what you're gonna give me is pure and sweet. The satisfying anticipation of knowing that kisses will lead to me taking off your shirt and paying homage to your sweet tits. Maybe we'll have a few phone calls where we talk about our fantasies and masturbate for each other. Then the next time we're together, we'll take it a bit further, your hands'll be on my bare chest and I'll get you off simply by playing with your tits and rubbing you through your pants. Then the next time, maybe you'll let me do more, and I'll slip my hand

SUSAN STOKER

under your panties and feel your wetness against my fingers."

Adeline gulped, the images his words were bringing forth in her mind making her shift restlessly against him. She felt her nipples scrunch up in tight little buds, wanting his hands and lips on them.

"Then maybe we'll progress to you giving me a hand job and letting me taste that sweet pussy of yours. I'll make you explode simply by sucking on your hard little clit and I'll lose it again merely by watching you come apart in my arms. By the time we get to the point where we both want each other so badly there's no way we can wait another second, it'll be so good, so explosive, you won't have one thought in your head. Not one. You'll never want to leave my bed. Leaving me to go to work will be torture, because you'll know it'll be hours before we can touch each other again. And I'll feel the same way."

He took a deep breath and Adeline was afraid to look up at him. Afraid the lust and want would show in her eyes. He'd been a near-perfect gentleman until now, and hearing this sexual side of him notched up the desire in her body to levels she'd never experienced before. She was afraid to move even one inch, lest she spontaneously combust right in his arms.

"So no, I don't want to come inside. Eventually I'll see your house, beautiful, just as you'll see mine. I've got another seventy-two-hour shift starting on Tuesday and you'll be working. But I'll be free Friday and Saturday. I'm hoping you'll want to get together Friday night after work, and all day Saturday."

"Yes," Adeline said immediately, her voice muffled by his shirt.

"Thank you, beautiful. For not playing hard to get."

She raised her head at that. "You're welcome. I'd be an idiot to play hard to get when I know all you have to do is crook your finger and I'd rip my clothes off so fast it'd make your head spin. I like you. I like spending time with you. I feel safe. Cared for."

"That's because you are. I'm not gonna say this next thing to piss you off, but I'm taking the chance that it might anyway."

Adeline narrowed her eyes at him but he didn't give her a chance to respond before he continued.

"If you're not already doing it, you need to start keeping track of your seizures. How long they last, how long between when Coco alerts and when they start. Look at the clock and try to remember to look at it when you come back to yourself. Pay attention to what you're eating and what you're doing before they happen. Anything you can do to narrow down the triggers can only be helpful to the doc when you go in to discuss surgery and other options."

Adeline put her cheek back on Dean's chest. She

really didn't want to discuss this with him.

"I know you don't want to talk about it…"

Shit, was he a mind reader?

"…but it sounds like you think the surgery is a foregone conclusion. If so, you need to give the doctor all the tools he needs to help make it better. Yeah?"

She nodded. Dean was right. She didn't like it, but he was right. She'd already started doing just what he'd suggested, but she didn't tell him that.

"Yeah. And don't hide that shit from me," he tacked on.

"What?" She lifted her head at that.

"I don't like that you're hiding the fact that you've been having seizures from me. Don't keep doing that. I know you're having them. Let me be there for you. Let me be your sounding board about them. Let me be there even when I *can't* be there."

"I've had them my entire life, Dean. They don't hurt, and I don't even remember them afterwards. I don't want you to be my doctor. I like that you're my boyfriend but I don't like the way your eyes get all squinty and your eyebrows come down in a frown when you hear about them."

One side of his mouth quirked up into a half grin. "I can't promise that hearing about them won't concern me. You can't do anything about that. But I'll do my best to keep my smothering to a minimum. Hell, I'm a paramedic, I might have some insights that your friends or family might not have. All I'm asking is for you not to shut me out. You don't have to call before or even right after, but please don't ever lie and say you didn't have one when you did. When we move in together, I'm gonna get a front row seat to them, so shutting me out now just isn't rational."

"When we move in together?" Adeline asked incredulously.

"Yeah."

"Uh, when is that happening?" she asked a bit snottily. What the hell was he talking about? They'd only been on their second date, but he'd mentally already had sex—no, made love with her—and now they were moving in together? "This whole future relationship you think we're having is moving too fast for me."

He did grin then. In fact, he threw back his head and barked out a laugh. When he had himself under control, he looked at her and said, "Right. So, beautiful...you'll keep track and let me know when you have a seizure."

Knowing he didn't answer her question about moving in, at all, but deciding to ignore it for now—hell, the man wouldn't even step foot in her house because he was enjoying the anticipation of a physical relationship with her—she merely said, "Fine. Yes."

"Good. Now, let's make out on your front step and

give your neighbors a show before I reluctantly pull away and make myself go home and let you go inside your house and do whatever it is you need to do on a Sunday afternoon."

Adeline smiled as his head dropped to hers.

"LET ME GET this straight," Alicia said hours later when they were talking on the phone. "You beat him at putt-putt, you had to threaten to sue the manager of the restaurant at the top of the Tower of the Americas, he calmly walked through how your sexual relationship was going to progress and then said that you would be moving in together, you made out on your porch—and he just *left*?"

"Yup," Adeline confirmed.

"He likes you," Alicia stated firmly.

Adeline barked out a laugh. "Yeah, I think I got that."

"No, seriously, sis. I mean, most guys would totally take you up on that offer to come inside your house. Then they'd pressure you to go further sexually than you were comfortable with. That's *if* they got over the fact that you wiped the floor with them in miniature golf, and *if* they were man enough to stand back and let you fight your own fight with that asshole manager, and *if* they could get over the fact that spending time with you might mean having to deal with you having a seizure at an inopportune time."

"I know, Alicia."

"My big sister found herself a good man," Alicia sniffed.

"Oh good Lord," Adeline huffed. "We've only been out on two dates."

"Did he call you today after he went home?"

"Yeah. What does that have to do with anything?"

"How long did you talk?"

"I don't know. An hour or so maybe. Why?"

"So the man you spent all morning and part of the afternoon with called you, and you spoke for another hour…and you don't think that means anything."

Adeline was silent. It meant something. It meant a *lot*. She hadn't expected Dean to call since they'd spent so much time together, but he had. And they'd talked about nothing, but also about her job. He had a lot of good insight and advice for where she should apply to work and what kinds of jobs she should look for. Adeline knew he didn't like Douglas—hell, *she* didn't like him—but Dean's advice was professional and sound and he didn't pressure her into doing anything rash just because he didn't like her boss.

"Right," Alicia stated firmly. "Just do me a favor…"

"What?"

"Don't elope."

"Leesh!"

"I'm serious. I want to be matron of honor. I want to stand next to my sister when she pledges to love her man through sickness and health and watch him do the same. Besides, you said his friends were hot…I want to drool over hot firefighters and cops in tuxedos."

"I'm hanging up now," Adeline said with a laugh.

"Wait…seriously, sis. He sounds like a good guy. I'm happy for you."

"It's only been a couple of dates."

"All relationships start out that way. And I knew by the end of the first date that I wanted to marry Matt and have his babies. When it's right, it's right."

"I'll keep that in mind. I'll talk to you later."

"Yes, you will. Later."

"'Bye."

"'Bye, Adeline."

Adeline hung up the phone and ran her hand over Coco's head. She felt calm and mellow, and happy. It had been a long time since she'd felt this way. Douglas and her job didn't seem as stressful and dealing with the seizures didn't even seem to be that big of a deal at the moment. Hell, even the surgery was looking more and more like it was a good idea. All because of Dean.

She smiled. Big. And sent a short prayer upward. *Please don't let him turn out to be a douchebag.*

THE MAN PACED back and forth, wringing his hands and rocking as he walked. He was agitated, and not even licking her coffee cup was calming him.

It's not working. She's not agreeing to eat with you.

She has to eat with you before you can move on to the next part of the plan.

Food first, then more dates. Then you can bring her to your house and she'll be happy.

You have to stop letting him yell.

She doesn't like yelling.

Keep control of him, and make sure you're nice to her.

Nice is key.

He closed his eyes, remembering how nice she smelled. She always smelled nice. It wasn't perfume, he couldn't stand that. But whatever shampoo she used made her hair shiny and smooth and smelled like flowers. Every time she moved, he could smell her.

She does it on purpose.

Flips her head around so her hair brushes against your arm and so you can smell her.

She likes you. She's just playing hard to get.

Keep at it.

She'll give in.

She wants you.

She needs you.

Tomorrow.

And if she says no to eating again, that thing is coming up.

You'll have lots of time to get her to like you more.

Lots of time.

Alone time.

The man smiled and relaxed, thinking about all the alone time he'd have with her. He calmly gathered up the pictures he'd taken, happy that there were more now, and carefully stacked them, putting the rubber band around them so they'd not get out of order. He grabbed her coffee cup and walked across the room. He pried up the board in the floor and carefully set the most precious objects in the world to him inside the space. Then he returned the board so the other one wouldn't find his stash.

The other one was mean to her.

Yelled.

It wasn't good.

He had to work harder to keep control.

She liked nice. She liked *him*.

He stood in the middle of the room and smiled. Big.

Chapter Twelve

A LITTLE OVER one month and too many dates to count later, Adeline smiled when she looked down at her phone and saw it was Dean. It was a Wednesday night and it had been a long day. She was sitting on her couch, thinking about getting up for some ice cream, when her phone rang.

Coco was zonked out on his fluffy bed in front of the TV and they'd both finished dinner about an hour ago. She'd changed out of her work clothes and put on a pair of sweatpants and a big T-shirt. She'd confiscated it from Dean's house the last time she was there. It said Station 7 on the front and had a big Maltese cross…the symbol of firefighters.

"Hey."

"Hey, beautiful. How was your day?"

"Good. I heard back from two of the places I sent my resume to. I have a phone interview next Wednesday and one on Thursday."

"Great news," Dean said in a soft voice.

"Yeah."

"Douglas still acting like an ass?"

Adeline hesitated, then mentally shrugged. Douglas was acting weird, and she wanted to talk it through with someone. "He's extremely hot and cold. I can't keep up with his moods."

"What'd he do today?" Dean asked in a reasonable tone.

Adeline appreciated the fact that he hadn't gotten pissed. She really did need someone to talk to about him, and she wanted that someone to be Dean…as long as he didn't fly off the handle. "He was in a bad mood in the morning, not saying hello to anyone, not answering emails, that sort of thing. But after lunch it was like he was a different person. Laughing, walking around and chatting with people. It's just weird."

"He ask you out again?"

"Sort of," Adeline told Dean honestly. "He brought in the first pass at ads for the Wolfe campaign that he wanted me to review. We were in the big meeting room, but he sat right next to me instead of across from me, and I swear to God I heard him smell my hair at one point. I turned to look at him and he was sitting a respectable distance away. It wasn't like I could ask if he was just sniffing me."

"You should turn him in for sexual harassment," Dean said in a flat, hard tone.

"I would if I was going to be there much longer. At this point, I just want to be gone. If I accuse him of anything, it will be my word against his. I have absolutely no proof, Dean. Nothing. What am I going to say…he was smelling my hair and it made me uncomfortable?"

"I hate this for you," Dean said.

"I know. I just have to hang on a little bit longer. Then I'll be gone and Douglass Hill the Third will be a memory."

"Are you scared of him?" Dean suddenly asked.

"Scared? No, not really. He comes off as more desperate than crazy," Adeline told him. "He's weird, and he makes me uncomfortable, but he's too much of a chicken to really *do* anything."

"Don't ever underestimate anyone, beautiful. If he's obsessed with you, and it sounds like he is, then anything could set him off. You could look at him wrong, say something that he doesn't like, or even just wear the wrong thing one day. You just don't know."

"I'll be careful," Adeline promised. "I'll do my best not to be alone with him and I'll make sure security walks me out to my car each afternoon."

"Good. I worry about you."

"I know, and I appreciate it. Enough about him. How was your day? Busy?"

"Unfortunately, yeah. I hate to be bored, but when

it comes to my job, most of the time it's better to be sitting around not doing anything because that means no one is sick, hurting, and there aren't any fires."

"Sorry, hon."

"It's my job. Anything else exciting happen to you today?"

Overall, Adeline found Dean to be fairly easygoing. He wasn't overbearing, even though he could definitely be bossy. He didn't always want to know exactly where she was every minute of the day. He was happy to meet her sister and parents, and of course they loved him. As she teased him, he certainly wasn't perfect, he had some quirks that could be annoying...insisting on driving whenever they went out and not letting her do things she was perfectly able to do—like pick up Coco's poop in the yard and talk to the Internet people when her wi-fi went out at home—but it wasn't as if she was going to complain about either of those things, especially not when she was perfectly happy letting him take care of them.

But Dean did *not* like Douglas. He hadn't ever met the man, but it didn't matter. He thought her boss was an ass. And he was, but Dean didn't have to work with him day in and day out...Adeline did. At first, she'd tried not talking about him at all, but that didn't work, as Dean got all pouty and she'd felt so bad, she blurted out all the smiling, arm touching, and compliments her boss had been throwing her way.

The last time they'd talked about him, and she'd told Dean how she thought Douglas had been looking down her shirt, she'd had to do some really fast talking to keep him from storming out of his house and tracking Douglas down to have a "heart-to-heart" with him. And that "heart-to-heart" would entail Dean laying it out that she was his, and Douglas had better keep his hands, and eyes, to himself. Of course, he most likely wouldn't use words to get his point across, and Adeline didn't feel like spending the evening trying to figure out how bail worked.

Adeline really, *really* didn't want to tell Dean that Douglas had informed her today that in a month there was a conference in Dallas that he wanted her to go to. She'd skipped over that tidbit of news earlier when they were talking about her boss. The conference wouldn't have been a bad thing, except Douglas was attending as well. And the last thing Adeline wanted was to have to explain to her extremely protective boyfriend— protective in a good way, a way that made her feel treasured and cared for, not a creepy, over-the-top, possessive way—that her asshole boss, who'd been hitting on her and acting extremely volatile, would be attending an out-of-town conference with her and most likely wanted to carpool both there and back.

Nope. She really didn't want to tell Dean any of that.

"Adeline…" Dean's tone was drawn out and questioning, as if he knew there was something she wasn't telling him.

So she did what she usually did when she had bad news…or at least news that she didn't think Dean would take very well. She tried to hide it in the middle of other stuff. "Hey, did I tell you that it's been two days since I've had a seizure? I don't really know why except I've cut out caffeine from my diet…you know that, of course you do, I've only been complaining about it for the last two weeks. But I think it's making a difference. Of course, when I go up to Dallas for the conference next month, I might have to make an exception because the last thing I want to do is sleep through a presentation. Are you coming over—"

"Conference?"

Shit. Adeline didn't know why she even bothered trying to slip anything by him. Dean was way too quick. She sighed and didn't even pretend to not know what he'd asked. "Yeah, there's a conference up in Dallas at the end of next month that I've been asked to attend."

Dean was silent for a moment before he asked in a tone that Adeline knew meant he was on the edge of losing his shit. "With him?"

"Well, Douglas will be there, yeah, but it's not like I'll be rooming with him or anything. It's not a big deal, Dean."

"How long?"

"How long is the conference? I think it starts on a Sunday and ends on Wednesday afternoon."

"So you'll be in a hotel with this ass for three nights?"

"Honey," Adeline soothed, "it's fine. I see him every day at work; this isn't going to be any different. I'll try to make sure we're on separate floors if that would make you feel better. I won't even have to talk to him much once we get there."

"You are not going to ride with him."

"You're right, I'm not. I can drive myself, but I was going to ask if you wanted to come up and stay with me if your schedule allowed it."

"Oh, my schedule's gonna allow it. It's about time I met this boss of yours."

"Dean, seriously."

"Look. This isn't a conversation I wanted to have on the phone. But here it is. You know I don't like him nor trust him. You're beautiful, Adeline. Fuckin' *beautiful*. Not only that, but you're smart and a good person to boot. And you're *mine*. I don't want him thinkin' if he takes you up to some conference, he can get in there."

"He's not getting in anywhere. Gross," Adeline said, getting pissed now. This was the reaction she thought she'd get earlier when she told Dean about how Douglas had been acting.

"Who made you come so hard it took you five

minutes to stop shaking, beautiful? Him? Fuck no. Me. And just because I haven't touched your hot, wet pussy yet, doesn't mean you're not mine. Giving you an orgasm by touchin' you through your pants and suckin' on your tit means that you liked it a fuck of a lot. I love that you gave that to me. To *me*. And because I'm a guy, I know *he* wants in there. He wouldn't have stopped being a dick and started trying to impress you if he didn't. I know you still aren't really getting this, and that's okay, because it's really fucking cute how you introduce me to people as your boyfriend and you blush every fucking time, but Douglas Hill the fucking Third isn't gonna even *think* about making a Douglas Hill the Fourth with you if I have anything to say about it. He needs to know you're off-limits. You're so off-limits you're in a different damn zip code."

Adeline knew she had to switch tactics. As much as his words made her feel good, they also kinda pissed her off.

"So you don't trust me?"

"Don't put words in my mouth. I trust you, beautiful. I know you don't have a devious bone in your body, it's that asshole I don't trust. I don't like that his moods have been erratic and that you're not comfortable with him."

"Can we talk about this later?" Adeline figured she'd better shut down the conversation before she really got pissed off and said something she'd regret.

"Yeah. But we *will* be talking about it again."

"I don't know what else there is to talk about. It's my job. I have to go. Hell, I *want* to go. It's a great opportunity for me to network and maybe make a connection that will get me out of my current workplace, and away from Douglas, all that much faster. It's not like I'm going on an out-of-town date with him," Adeline groused, not dropping it even though she'd been the one to suggest talking about it later.

"Adeline, you're an adult. You can do whatever the fuck you want. I'll always support your career. I'm proud of you and what you do. But I'm *worried* about you, beautiful. As much as I love the fact that you take no notice of men checking you out every time we go out, that concerns me too."

"Men don't check me out."

"They do. And that's okay. When you're with me, I can keep that shit checked. But the fact that you won't even admit that your boss has been coming on to you worries me. And it concerns me even more that it's just the two of you goin'. Unless I misunderstood and Georgia or Robert from your office are attending the conference with you?"

"No," Adeline admitted grumpily. "Just me and Douglas."

"Right. So yeah, this convention shit with your boss

worries me."

He sighed hugely and Adeline could picture him running a hand through his hair in agitation. "Okay, we'll talk about it later. I'm gonna hope like hell you impress the fuck out of those people in your interviews next week and they hurry the fuck up and make a hiring decision. Maybe you'll leave your current job before the damn conference comes around and it won't even be an issue."

His voice got softer as he changed the subject. Adeline could tell he was making an effort to tone down his irritation. "Douchebag boss aside, I'm glad the no caffeine is helping with your seizures, beautiful. You talked to your doctor about it?"

Relieved he'd changed the subject, Adeline nodded as she spoke. "Yeah. He's pleased and wants to see me in a few weeks. He's been pushing for me to make a decision about the surgery."

"I know, sweetheart. Okay, you were gonna ask me if I was coming over tomorrow night, right?"

"Right."

"I want you over here instead."

"But I have to work Friday," Adeline said in confusion. "It's a long drive to get back to my place, and if I have to leave earlier in the evening to get home at a decent time, that's less time I get to spend with you."

"I love that you want to spend time with me. And I

know we haven't done this before, but I want you to stay all night. Call in sick to work. You have a ton of time saved up that you'll never use, especially if you take another job. It won't kill you to take a mental health day."

"You're off Friday, right?" Adeline asked.

"Yup. Friday and Saturday. Will you spend them with me? All night and all day?"

Adeline swallowed wrong and almost choked. Spend the night with Dean? She'd wanted to ask him to stay so many times over the last month, but chickened out every time. Even after he'd given her the most amazing orgasm the other night, she hadn't asked him to stay the night, and he hadn't hinted at it either.

"Is this because of Douglas?" she asked skeptically.

"Fuck no. Adeline. That fuckwad has nothing to do with me wanting you in my house and bed. But there's no pressure here. I have a guest room. If you're uneasy, you can sleep there, you can trust—"

"No," she blurted, interrupting him. "I mean…shit."

Dean chuckled low and it made her squirm in her seat. She tried again.

"I trust you. I want to stay with you…I'm just nervous about it."

"No need. If anything, *I'm* the one who should be nervous."

"You? Why in the world would *you* be nervous?"

"I'm a guy. Because this is the first time you'll be in my bed and I want to do it right. I want to make sure you have not one moment of anxiety or fear. I want you to overlook all my weird quirks I don't know I have and I want you to enjoy yourself so much that you never want to leave."

"We'll have to eat sometime."

"Let me rephrase."

Adeline could tell he was smiling.

"That you'll never want to leave my house."

She took a deep breath. "Dean."

"Fuck yeah. I want to hear you say my name just like that when I'm inside you."

"Okay, you need to stop. It's not fair."

"You coming over tomorrow night and staying until Sunday?"

"Yeah. If you really want me to."

"Oh, I really want you, beautiful."

Adeline chuckled.

"I went out and bought a bed for Coco and some bowls. I figure you can bring over his food and next time I'll help you make it for him so you don't have to lug it back and forth. Anything else you or he need?"

"Um, no."

"Good. I'm cookin' for you tomorrow night. Then we'll keep it laid-back. Watch a movie or something.

Stay in so we don't risk running into any assholes. Sound okay?"

"Sounds perfect. I can't wait."

"Me either. Be safe, and I'll talk to you sometime tomorrow before you come over."

"Okay, Dean."

"Oh, one more thing."

"Yeah?"

"As much as I'd like to stay in my house all weekend lovin' you, we might need to take a break. There's a softball game on Saturday. It's kind of a long-standing tradition. It's the guys and Penelope from my station, and a bunch of local cops. I'll tell you more when you're over here, but I was hoping you'd like to go and watch."

"You're playing?" Adeline asked.

"Yeah."

"Then I'll be there to watch."

"Perfect," Dean murmured.

"Not even close," Adeline shot back. It had become their thing.

"Get some sleep. I'll see you tomorrow."

"Okay. Bye."

"Bye, beautiful."

Adeline clicked off the phone and closed her eyes. It was becoming harder and harder not to say "I love you" when she hung up or left Dean. A month and a half was way too soon to fall in love with someone…wasn't it?

Chapter Thirteen

ADELINE WAITED IMPATIENTLY at her house for Dean to arrive. She'd called him during her lunch hour and he told her that he'd pick up her and Coco around six after he got off shift. She had a bag packed and it was sitting by the door, with enough food for Coco through Sunday morning.

It was one thing to know she was going to be spending the night with Dean, it was another thing altogether to pack for the trip, deciding on what she would be putting on after showering and being naked with him.

Over the last month, they'd gotten very comfortable with each other. They'd touched and done everything he'd said they'd do…except make love. She'd touched him through his pants and he'd done the same, but she hadn't seen him, and he hadn't seen her.

She was ready.

Still nervous, but ready. She wanted Dean. Every time they kissed she got wet so fast, it was almost embarrassing. Her body was readying itself for him and it was starting to really suck every time he pulled back with a tender kiss on her forehead.

Dean wanted to make love, but Adeline was ready to fuck. She was so horny, and ready to feel him between her legs, she just knew she was going to embarrass herself. But Dean always said that he loved how she was so open and didn't play games…so she wouldn't.

At 6:02, Adeline saw Dean coming up her walk. She opened the door and didn't even say hello, just threw herself into his arms and brought her lips to his.

Dean didn't seem to mind, opening his mouth and claiming hers in return.

God she loved the way he kissed.

As if he couldn't get enough of her.

As if it was the last kiss he'd ever have in his entire life.

She drew back and licked her lips, which tasted like the mint hc must've popped in his mouth on the way to her house.

"You ready, beautiful?"

"I'm ready," she returned, meaning it in more ways than one.

He obviously got that as she saw his pupils dilate. Fuck, she liked that.

"Come on, let's get Coco and get out of here."

Adeline backed up and he kept hold of her hand as she led them back into her house. She had to let go when Coco greeted Dean by jumping up on him. She didn't even scold her dog, knowing Dean had no problem with his enthusiasm. It was just one more thing in a long line of things that she liked about him.

Without fanfare he picked up her bag and Coco's food. "You ready?"

Adeline nodded. She was so ready.

He smirked as if he could read her mind.

Trying not to blush, Adeline grabbed Coco's vest and told him to sit. As he'd done hundreds of times before, he sat still and let her strap on the harness and vest. As she did almost every time she got him ready, Adeline felt amazed that the simple act of strapping Coco into his "work uniform" switched something inside him, turning him from the happy-go-lucky, bouncy, hyper Lab into a focused and ready-to-work service dog.

Even though Coco was always ready to alert if a seizure was imminent, he seemed to be even more so when they were out of the house and he was wearing his vest.

The three of them walked to the front door and Dean held out his hand for her keys as he always did. Without comment—she'd learned to just let him do his thing—Adeline put them in his hand. He locked the door, making sure the knob wouldn't turn, and handed the keys back to her.

Then he put the tips of his fingers on the small of

her back and led her to his car.

God, she'd never get tired of that. He never pushed her, just gently guided, walking close, letting her know he was there. Once she'd tripped over nothing, as she was sometimes wont to do, but he was right there, grabbing hold of her waist, making sure she didn't face plant on the sidewalk. It was the absolute conviction that he'd protect her, even from her own clumsiness, that made goosebumps break out on her arms every time she felt his fingers on her back.

He opened the back door and Coco jumped in as if he'd been doing it his entire life. Dean put her bag and Coco's food on the floor in the backseat and closed the door. Adeline had opened the passenger door by then and was sitting in the seat. He held out her seat belt, another thing that made her weak in the knees, and waited for her to grab it before shutting her door and striding around the front of his car.

He didn't insist on opening her door, but anytime he was near, he'd hold out her seat belt so she didn't have to twist around to grab it. It was a small thing, and something she would've thought was odd before dating Dean. But now? She loved it. It was another way he took care of her and looked out for her.

They drove to his condo making small talk. Even as she smiled and spoke about nothing important, Adeline could feel her heart beating heavily in her chest. The anticipation of where they were going and what they were going to do making it hard to stay stoic and unaffected.

She thought she'd been keeping a pretty good handle on it until Dean took her hand in his and said softly, "Relax, beautiful."

He thought she was nervous.

"I'm not nervous, Dean," she told him.

He lifted a skeptical eyebrow.

"Okay, not *that* nervous," she insisted. "I'm more excited."

"You want me."

Again, it wasn't a question. She treated it as if it was anyway.

"Yeah, I want you."

"Thank Christ," Dean muttered, then squeezed her hand. "You hungry?"

"No. I ate when I got home from work."

He looked at her then. It was a quick glance, as they were on the Interstate, but it was full of lust…for her.

"When we get there, you take care of Coco. I'll bring in your things."

That sounded like what they usually did.

"Okay."

"Then when Coco's settled, we'll go up to my room. I'll strip you naked and finally get to see what I've dreamed about since that first afternoon we met. I want you bare for me. That work for you?"

Oh yeah. That totally worked for her.

"As long as I get to see you too."

"You'll see me, beautiful."

"Okay."

He smiled again. "Perfect."

"Not hardly."

"Perfect for me."

She grinned back. Then she pretended not to notice he pressed a bit harder on the accelerator until he was going five miles an hour faster than he usually drove.

Luckily, they didn't get pulled over and made it back to his house in record time. Without a word, just a small squeeze to her hand, Dean got out of his car and grabbed the bags from the backseat while Adeline collected Coco.

They entered his condo and Adeline immediately got to work unbuckling Coco and getting him comfortable. She put down a bowl of water and smiled at the brand new dog bed in the corner. She showed Coco the bed before letting him out to do his business.

When she was satisfied that the dog was good to go, she turned to Dean. He was standing by the stairs that led up to his room, leaning against the wall. His arms were crossed over his chest, his legs at the ankles, and he was smiling at her.

Adeline would've thought he was completely relaxed

if it hadn't been for the way his jaw flexed as he ground his teeth together. Seeing him impatient, but banking it, made her melt.

She walked up to him, and when he immediately stood up straight and dropped his arms, she snuggled into his embrace, sighing when his arms wrapped around her without hesitation. She tipped her head back and looked up at him.

"I can't wait to feel your naked body against mine. Inside mine. Making love to me, then fucking me."

She'd surprised him. The look of shock on his face was priceless. Adeline didn't get one up on Dean that often, so this pleased her.

"Where'd my shy Adeline go?" he murmured.

"You killed her when you made her come the other night. Poof. Gone. You left impatient and horny Adeline in her wake."

The devilish smile that crept over his lips made her shiver in anticipation.

"Did I? Hmmmm, maybe I should do something about that."

"Maybe you should," Adeline happily agreed.

He put his hands on her waist and took hold of her shirt and slowly began to ease it up her body. "Lift."

Without hesitation, Adeline put her arms over her head, allowing Dean to whisk her shirt off. It dropped somewhere behind her, she didn't care where. She had eyes only for the man in front of her.

His gaze moved from her face down to her chest and Adeline could feel her nipples peak at the look of intense lust in his eyes. She'd worn a T-shirt he'd seen before, one that was a bit large and boxy. But she'd very carefully chosen her underwear.

Alicia had taken her shopping after hearing about one of their more intense make-out sessions on the couch and listening to Adeline complain that Dean had way too much self-control. She'd worried that her basic black bra hadn't been sexy enough to entice him.

So Alicia had fixed that. She'd convinced her to buy a bra and panty set that would make a dead man sit up and take notice. The bra was fire engine red, which she thought was appropriate, and lacy. It did nothing to give her boobs any support, but that wasn't really the goal of the scrap of material. The lace was wide, and when she'd put it on, her nipples were clearly visible under it. Adeline hadn't been turned on when she'd put on the bra, but now that she was, her nipples were sticking through the holes in the lace.

Glancing down, and seeing how almost obscene the garment was, Adeline blushed and brought her eyes back to up Dean. "I, uh…I thought for our first time, I might go out of my way to—"

Dean didn't let her finish her thought. He leaned down with a groan and took one nipple into his mouth, and his fingers came up to pinch and tease the other.

Adeline's head fell back as she brought one hand to rest on the back of his head, encouraging him, and the other clutched at the shirt at his waist.

The feel of his lips and teeth playing with her nipple as it stuck through the material of the bra was almost too much. She felt hot, then cold, then hot again. Nothing had ever felt like this. Absolutely nothing.

Adeline arched her back, pushing her breast harder into his mouth. She felt his smile form around her, but soon forgot everything but the feel of his fingers tugging and his mouth sucking on first one nipple, then the other.

She staggered in his grip as her knees wobbled, breaking his concentration. He wrapped his arm around her, bringing her hips flush against him. He was hard as a rock and Adeline wiggled, wanting more.

"I can't fucking wait to see the underwear that goes with this bra," Dean murmured as he bent and nuzzled the sensitive skin between her neck and shoulder.

"Upstairs," Adeline told him absently.

"I could take you right here," he returned, not moving an inch.

"Yeah. And I'd let you. I think I'd let you do whatever you wanted, wherever you wanted, but Coco's watching. Can we ease into the audience thing?"

He chuckled and drew back by lifting his head.

"Yeah, beautiful. We can do that. I want you the first time in my bed anyway. Can you walk?"

"No clue. Maybe if you took off your shirt it would help motivate me."

He smiled at her again, letting go altogether. Not expecting that, Adeline stumbled, but quickly righted herself when Dean reached behind his head and grabbed the collar of his shirt and pulled it up and off.

"Do guys have classes on how to do that?" she asked absently.

"What?"

"How to hot-guy-remove your shirt."

He grinned again. "Nope. Comes naturally."

"Figures."

Dean stepped backward onto the first step. Then he did it again, reaching for the button on his jeans. He went up another step as he undid it.

Adeline smiled up at him and stepped to the first stair.

He slowly unzipped his jeans as he continued upward. Adeline followed as if he was the Pied Piper and she was a mouse in his thrall. And she was. She was totally in his thrall. Her gaze going from his fingers at his crotch, up to his smiling dark eyes, and back down. Deciding she could tease him as well, her own hands dropped to the fastenings at her waist.

They played a weird game of show and tell as they

climbed the stairs and then made their way down the short hall to the master bedroom. By the time they reached the doorway, Adeline could see the head of Dean's cock over the top of his boxer briefs and her pants were all the way undone, showing off the bits of red lace covering her mound.

Dean stopped moving just inside his door but crooked his finger at Adeline. She kept moving until they stood no more than a couple inches apart.

"Take off your pants, but leave the panties on. I want to see the whole package."

"I'll show you mine if you show me yours," Adeline retorted, loving their banter.

Without a word of protest, Dean toed off his shoes and shoved his jeans down his legs. He took off his socks then stood in front of her. His underwear did nothing to hide how excited he was for her.

Swallowing hard and glancing at the floor, suddenly embarrassed as well as turned on, Adeline hurried to take off her own shoes and socks and remove her pants. When they were pooled around her ankles, she stepped out and straightened. Trying to suck in her less-than-flat belly and hoping Dean would be too interested in what the red lace was covering and would overlook the small love handles and the way her thighs touched and the hundred other not-so-model-like aspects of her body, Adeline waited.

"Fuck. Me," he breathed. "Put your hands behind your neck for me, beautiful."

Thinking it was weird, she did it anyway, and then realized why he wanted her to. Putting her hands up by her head arched her back and made her breasts lift. It also gave him unfettered access to her entire body.

He used one finger and ran it over the tops of her breasts, then her nipples, which were still sticking out through the lace of the bra. He ran it under each globe, then up and over her collarbone. Still using that one finger, he moved it down to her belly button, and before she felt uncomfortable, he moved it to the top of her panties. Her now soaking-wet panties. He dipped that finger just under the elastic and ran it all the way from one hip bone across to the other. Adeline shivered.

Leaving his finger under her panties, he slowly walked around her. And gasped. The underwear she was wearing was a skimpy thong. The small piece of lace was between the globes of her ass, leaving her butt completely bare.

Dean kneeled down behind her and Adeline unlaced her fingers and brought them down in front of her. Unsure.

"Arms back up, beautiful. Please."

She reluctantly did as he asked, saying, "I think thongs are better in theory than real life. I've had a wedgie all night and with my size butt, I'm not sure it's all that—"

Her words stopped abruptly as the finger that had been still at her hip moved. It followed the line of the thong to the small of her back, then down. Adeline felt Dean's touch all along her butt until it reached her folds and pulled the crotch of her undies away from her soaking-wet slit.

"Jesus, beautiful. Perfect."

Adeline couldn't even get out her usual response. She could only stand in front of him, arms laced behind her neck, and moan in lust. She could picture in her mind his finger moving from the gusset of the thong up and inside her. Fucking her. Her legs shifted apart an inch.

"You want me to touch you?" Dean asked, leaning forward and nuzzling her right butt cheek.

"Mmmmm."

With his free hand, Dean pushed her left thigh out until she moved her foot, giving him more room between her legs. HIs hand moved up to her front and rested on her mons, his palm on her clit and his fingers reaching up to almost her belly button. He held her firmly as his other finger brushed back and forth over her drenched pussy lips.

"You smell delicious. Fuck, you're soaked, beautiful. Every night I jerked off thinking about this. Every time I woke up with a hard-on. Every time I said good night to your beautiful face and spent the rest of the night tossing and turning with the most erotic fantasies of you in my bed, of my cock inside you. It was all worth it for this moment right here. Feeling how much you want me. How excited you are to have me. For me to have you."

He kissed each ass cheek again.

"This is why I took things as slow as I did. I wanted you to want me as much as I wanted you. To be so worked up you'd literally be dripping for me." He pushed the small line of material covering her to the side and leaned down. "And make no mistake, beautiful. You. Are. Dripping."

"Dean," Adeline moaned. "You're embarrassing me."

"No," he admonished immediately. "This is not embarrassing. Not in the least. Me waking up in a station full of men and Penelope, trying to put my gear on over a hard-on, is embarrassing. Me groaning out my release as I lay on my bunk after waking up and remembering my dream where you were going down on me, and knowing the walls in the station are thin as fuck and not even caring who heard me…that's embarrassing. But your body, so fucking ready for me your pussy is dripping in anticipation, is not one fucking bit embarrassing. It's hot as hell. I could sit here all night and watch you."

"I'd prefer you didn't," Adeline managed to grit out between her clenched teeth. Her arms started shaking and she pleaded, "Dean. Please."

At that, he moved his hands to her waist and pulled the lace thong down her hips to her ankles. He held her steady as she kicked them to the side even as Dean stood. He moved in front of her and took her wrists in his, bringing them down to the waistband of his own underwear.

"Take 'em off."

Without hesitation, Adeline did as he requested, pushing the cotton over his hips and down his thighs. His heavy erection bobbed, now free from the confining material. It curved up toward his belly and was definitely bigger than that of any man she'd slept with in her life. Granted, that number of men wasn't huge, but she'd thought of herself as pretty experienced. But one look at Dean's cock and she suddenly wasn't so sure.

He didn't give her a chance to do anything more than look, before he reached behind her and unhooked her bra. Adeline immediately dropped her arms and shrugged her shoulders, letting the lace bra easily fall to the carpet at their feet.

She felt his dick brush up against her, and pre-come smear over her belly as he moved. Feeling and seeing the evidence that he was just as aroused as she was went a long way toward calming the jitters she'd had.

Dean took both her hands in his, intertwining their fingers and bringing them together to rest at the small of his back. He then took a step, forcing her to do the same. He walked them, him going forward, her walking backwards, to his mattress. When the backs of her knees hit it, he let go, saying in a guttural tone, "Climb up, beautiful. I want to see you spread out on my sheets."

Without losing eye contact, she did as he asked, putting her butt on the edge and scooting backward. She pushed the comforter down with her legs and settled in the middle of the big bed. Not knowing where her inner shameless hussy was coming from, she fluffed out her hair and spread it wide on his pillow. Then she lifted one leg and put her foot flat on the mattress. One hand went to her nipple and played with it, and she reached out to Dean with the other.

"Make love to me, Dean."

Chapter Fourteen

CRASH LOOKED DOWN at the woman splayed on his bed and curled his hands into fists. He would not, *could* not, pounce on her as if he was a starving man presented with a feast. Even if that's what he felt like.

Adeline on his bed was more erotic, more beautiful, than anything he'd pictured in his head. And he'd imagined it a lot in the last month or so. Her black hair spread out on his pillow, her legs open and glistening with her excitement for him, and her hand out in invitation, letting him know she wanted him, was almost more than he could take.

He moved a hand to his cock and squeezed the base, hard. Good God, he'd almost lost it without even touching her. The last month had been hell on his libido, but he'd wanted to make sure she was ready. Because he knew deep in his gut that once he had her, she was his. If she decided she didn't want him back, he'd never find another woman who made him feel like this.

Like he was put on this earth to protect her.

Like he could do anything, *be* anyone.

He needed her.

And thank fuck, it looked like she needed him too. At least for this. He'd do everything in his power to make her understand she was the center of his world. That he would always put her first in his life and he'd be there no matter what happened with her health. But first she'd understand that she came first when it came to pleasure. He'd make sure she came first, and second, and last. Her needs would always come before his. She was that important to him.

Her standing in front of him in nothing but those blood-red pieces of lingerie had tested his control. But seeing her juices drip from her swollen and eager pussy lips had done him in.

Slowly, in an effort to try to control himself, Dean put one knee on the mattress, then the other. He crawled to her and crouched over her.

Adeline turned full on her back as he put his knees inside hers and inched upward, spreading her legs around his hips as he moved. Her hands came to his thighs and gripped him tightly.

She looked nervous and excited at the same time. She was spread open under him, her pussy glistening in excitement, her nipples hard, a flush on her chest and cheeks.

"Dean," she whispered.

"Yeah, beautiful?"

She bit her lip. "This is…weird."

"What is?"

"The lights are on. You're…looking at me."

"Fuck yeah I am. You're the most beautiful thing I've ever seen. And you're finally here. In my bed. Under me. Open for me. I wish I could take a picture and memorialize it forever."

He saw the panic flare in her eyes and hurried to reassure her.

"Relax, Adeline. No cameras are allowed in our bedroom. It's just you and me and will always be just you and me. No way in hell I'm gonna allow even a smidgeon of a chance for someone else to see what's mine."

She smiled up at him. "I'm ready."

One side of his lips quirked up. "You are."

"Well?" she demanded, digging her fingernails lightly into his thighs. "Get on with it."

Fuck she was cute.

"Right. Get on with it. Yes, ma'am," Crash told her, still grinning. Knowing she expected him to fill her with his cock, he held back the chuckle that wanted to escape. He'd get to that, but he had more important things to do first. Namely, making her come on his fingers, then his tongue. Then he'd get around to making her explode around his dick.

Crash leaned forward, making sure his cock brushed against her clit, but not giving her the pressure she'd need to get off. He braced himself over her, only touching her with his cock and his lips. He pulled a nipple between his lips, pushing it up against the roof of his mouth and sucking.

She bucked against him, throwing her head back and grabbing onto his sides and moaning. He kept up the sensual torture, switching from sucking, to licking, to flicking his tongue roughly over her tight bud. Letting go with a loud pop, he then blew on the wet tip, watching in fascination as it tightened even further. Adeline's hips bucked again, searching for something to fill her, and Crash pulled back, refusing to give her more than a light touch of his cock.

"Dean," she whined, pulling at him. "I need you."

"And you'll get me, beautiful. Let me play first."

She grumbled, but settled under him.

Crash proceeded to drive her other nipple crazy the same way he had the first, until she was squirming again. Loving that he could make her lose her mind, and knowing it was only the beginning, he settled on his side next to her. He wrapped one of his legs around hers at the ankle, pulling it toward him, immobilizing it. He used his other leg to keep her open to him, propping his knee against her inner thigh.

His cock lay stiff and hard against her thigh, but he ignored it for now. He held himself up on one elbow, using his fingers to tease the nipple closest to him, and his free hand to brush up and down her body.

"Keep your eyes closed, beautiful. Just feel."

Of course, at his words, her eyes popped open. "What are you gonna do?"

"Remember how I told you I was gonna make you come with just my fingers?"

"Yeah," she said in a long, drawn-out drawl.

"That's what I'm gonna do. Then I'm gonna do it again, but with my tongue. Then when you're still trembling from your second orgasm, I'm gonna make love to you. Long and slow, and hopefully make you come one more time, around my cock."

"Oh."

He smiled and ran his fingertip over her brows. "Yeah, oh. Close your eyes. You're gonna like this."

She smiled at him then, lifting her head off his pillow to kiss him. Crash allowed it, wanting to feel her lips on his. He'd never deny her that. Ever.

"Okay. Get to it then. I've waited a long time for this moment."

"Me too, beautiful. Me too." Crash knew he was talking about more than getting her in bed. He'd waited a hell of a long time to find a woman like her. A woman who completed him. He'd waited a long time for *her*.

The moment she closed her eyes, Crash moved his hand down her body. Not stopping at her taut nipple, not stopping to play with her belly button. He didn't even stop at her clit this first time. No, he wanted inside her.

His finger brushed between her lips and pushed inside her without preamble. He felt her squeeze him with her Kegel muscles and groaned deep in his throat, imaging exactly how that would feel when she did it around his cock.

He pulled his finger out slowly, then pushed back in. He did it again and again, loving how she squirmed and gasped at his touch. His other hand played with her nipple as he pushed another finger inside. Her back arched at that, and Crash felt his mouth water. He couldn't wait to taste her. But he wanted her first orgasm out of the way before he made her come with his lips and tongue.

"You're so beautiful," he whispered, using his words as much as his fingers to push her over the edge. He twisted his hand, using his thumb to push against her clit every time his fingers bottomed out inside her. He kept his movements slow and gentle, getting her used to his touch.

"You're soaked, dripping. I wish you could see this. How you open to my fingers and how you're clenching against me. You want something bigger inside you, beautiful? You need more?"

She whimpered, and he increased his pace.

"I'll remember this moment for the rest of my life. The first time I saw your pink, beautiful cunt. The first time you came all over me. The first time I smelled how turned on you are as I finger you. Yeah, that's it, fuck my fingers, Adeline. God, that's so fucking hot."

And it was. Her hips dropped as he withdrew his fingers, but canted upward as he pushed them back in. She was desperately pressing against him, her fingers gripping the sheets next to her, not verbally urging him to hurry; the movement of her hips was doing the begging for her.

Crash began to pinch her nipple harder, in time to the actions of his hand between her thighs. Every time he pushed inside, he squeezed; when he moved his fingers out of her cunt, he'd let go of her nipple. Over and over he continued the sexual torment, continuing to praise her as he did.

When she moaned and pleaded, "Dean…God…yeah…I'm almost there," he increased the speed of his fingers and put more pressure on her clit with each thrust.

The watery sounds of his fingers sliding in and out of her body were loud in the room, and Crash knew Adeline would be embarrassed if she was coherent enough to understand what they were.

"That's it, beautiful. Let go. Come for me. Show me how good this feels."

Her hips lifted and she stayed that way, suspended, as her legs and belly shuddered. Finally, with a wail, she burst. Crash kept up the pace of his fingers as she shook and shuddered around him. Her body tried to hold his fingers inside, but he ruthlessly pulled them out, then pushed them back in through her spasming tightness. Her body's lubrication allowed him to easily slide in and out even as she squeezed him.

Letting her ease down from the orgasm, Crash shifted until he was lying between her legs. He pushed her thighs farther apart, until she was completely spread open in front of him. Her juices ran down her body to her ass and dripped onto his sheets.

Crash smiled, loving that his bed would smell like her long after he was done. Adeline was breathing hard and still hadn't opened her eyes. Her hands had come up and were caressing his head though, so she knew he was there.

He leaned down and ran his tongue lightly from her ass up between her pussy lips and farther, to her clit. He gathered up the copious amounts of fluid leaking from her body and groaned at the taste.

"Jesus, beautiful. You taste so fucking good."

There was so much more he wanted to say, but the words would have to wait. He had heaven in front of him and Crash couldn't wait to get another taste. He opened his mouth wide and placed it over her opening and kept his eyes on her face as he feasted. His tongue pushed inside her as far as it could go and he sucked.

Adeline's eyes popped open and she lifted her head to look down at him in shock.

"What are you… Oh God, Dean." Her head fell back on his pillow with a thump and her hands dug into his scalp.

Oh yeah, she liked this.

It was a good thing because he fucking loved it.

In the past, he'd done this because it was expected. He didn't hate it, but he didn't get off on it either. But with Adeline he knew he could spend the rest of his life doing this, and only this, and he'd be satisfied. Even now he could feel the pre-come oozing out the tip of his cock. But he wasn't ready to give it up yet. His dick would just have to wait.

He broke the seal over her opening and licked again. From bottom to top. Once there, he paid attention to her clit. It was fully engorged, poking out of its protective hood, hard and pink. He flicked it once and Adeline twitched in his grip.

Crash smiled. Fuck this was fun.

He eased one hand from her thigh up to her opening and pushed two fingers inside her slowly. At the same time, he sealed his mouth over her clit and sucked gently. Her hips jolted that time, bucking up against him. Moving his other hand to her belly, he used it to hold her still. As still as he could.

As he continued to fuck her with his finger and suck on her clit gently, she writhed and twisted in his grasp. Crash felt her juices start flowing again. It was almost unnatural how much he wanted her scent all over his bed.

Recognizing the signs that she was close to coming, and ready to make love to her, Crash moved his finger faster and sucked harder on her clit. As he sucked, he quickly flicked his tongue faster and faster over her clit, loving how it got harder and swelled under his ministrations.

Finally, Adeline let out a wail and, gripping his head so hard Crash wasn't sure she didn't pull out some of his hair, she came. He kept licking at her and she kept coming. The juices literally pouring from inside her. His entire hand was wet and all he could smell was her arousal.

Almost blind with lust, Crash pulled back, watching as Adeline still twitched and spasmed. He came to his knees, reached over to the table next to his bed and grabbed the condom he'd put there earlier. It was ripped open and rolled down his cock even as Adeline continued to whimper under him.

He notched the head of his cock against her opening

and braced himself on his arms over her.

"Look at me, Adeline."

Her eyes slowly opened and he felt her hands grip his biceps tightly.

"I want to look into your eyes as I take you for the first time."

He pushed into her an inch and stopped.

"You're mine."

Adeline didn't say anything, but her mouth opened and closed as she gasped for breath and her hands tightened on him.

"Mine," Crash repeated as he pushed in another inch. He was gritting his own teeth now to keep from sinking into her balls deep.

"And you're mine," Adeline said, even as he pushed in farther.

Crash grinned. He had no problem with that. "Damn straight." He pulled out then pushed in again, trying to go slow. To let her adjust to him.

"You're so hot and wet," he told her.

"Yeah, well, you made me that way."

"Fuck yeah I did. You're so beautiful when you come apart. I want you to do it again when I'm inside you. I want to feel all those muscles clamp down on my cock and squeeze."

"I'm not sure it's gonna happen again, honey," she told him, biting her lip. "I haven't…haven't come like this before."

"Then I'll be your first."

"Dean…"

Her voice trailed off as he sank all the way inside her. Pushing past muscles that weren't used to being penetrated. He pulled out halfway, then pushed in again, pressing his balls up against her ass.

"Lift your knees," he ordered.

She did, and groaned as he gained even more ground.

"You're primed, beautiful. You can come this way. It might take more than my cock moving inside you, but I promise you'll come."

"Okay, Dean."

He liked that easy acquiescence.

Knowing he was on the verge of coming—it'd been a long time, and he'd been imagining how perfect it would feel when he got inside Adeline for too many weeks now—Crash knew he had to move this along.

"In the future, I'll be able to stretch this out. But not this first time. I want to keep it slow and easy for as long as I can, but I'm gonna need your help."

"Anything," Adeline said immediately.

Fuck, he loved that too.

"Touch yourself."

"What?"

"Reach a hand between us and touch your clit,

beautiful. You've masturbated before, right?"

"Of course, but not…"

"Not with a man. Good. I'll be your first with that too. Adeline, I promise, this isn't going to take long. Touch yourself like you do when you're in bed by yourself. It'll be better with me inside you. If it's not, you don't have to do it again."

With that, he felt her right hand unclench from his arm and ease down their bodies. He lifted up, giving her room, and then sat up straight. He eased back on his heels and lifted her ass until it was resting on his thighs. She was open, and now that he could watch his cock disappear inside her pussy, the control he'd been holding on to waned.

"Fuck, you have no idea how perfect this looks. You takin' my cock as if it was meant to be in there."

She touched her index and middle finger to her clit and he felt her jerk as she made contact.

"Oh yeah, you like that. Don't close your eyes. Look at me. Keep your eyes on my face. Watch my face as I make love to you. Watch how much I love it."

Crash knew he should look up into Adeline's eyes, but he was too mesmerized by her fingers caressing her own body, and how she sucked his cock back into her every time he pulled out. Her juices glistened on his dick and he could feel her soaking his thighs under her ass.

"Faster, Adeline. I can't hold back and I want to feel you orgasm around me first."

She did as he ordered, rubbing frantically now. Her fingers moving fast and hard over her clit. He knew when she was about to lose it as, once again, her hips bucked upward and hung there, suspended as every muscle in her lower body squeezed tight and froze.

His eyes whipped up to her face, and as she climaxed for the third time, he saw what looked like love flash in her eyes before she tilted her head back and moaned.

Pushing her legs up and catching her knees in the crooks of his elbows, Crash came over her, slamming his cock inside her pussy. She was hot and wet and the final ripples of her orgasm washed over his dick. He pushed into her hard once. Then again. Then again and again. Finally, he felt the come wash up from his balls, through his cock, and explode out the tip. He held himself still inside Adeline as he orgasmed. Kept his eyes on hers, showing her everything he was, and everything he was feeling in his face.

Even though her knees were up by her ears, she skimmed her hands between them and took his face in her palms. She lifted her head and reached for his lips.

Without hesitation, Crash lowered his head and kissed her with all the built-up love and passion he had within him. He devoured her mouth as if he was adrift at sea and she was the only thing between him and certain death.

He sipped and drank from her mouth, all the while cognizant of the way her body hugged his from the inside out. After a long moment, he lifted his head and moved his arms, letting her legs ease back to the mattress. He leaned down and put his forehead against hers.

"I've never. Not once in my life. Felt anything as amazing as what we just did," Crash told her. "It was perfect."

"It was," Adeline said in a soft, sated voice. Her eyes were half closed and she looked like she wouldn't move even if one of his fire alarms suddenly started ringing in the other room. He liked the look on her.

"Stay put. I have to get rid of the condom," Crash told her softly.

He waited until she nodded then eased out of her body with a groan.

"The worst part," she complained.

"Definitely. If I could stay inside you forever, I would."

"I don't think that'd be possible."

"Probably not. But it'd be fun to try."

She grinned up at him.

"Don't move, beautiful," he repeated, not waiting for a response before sitting and putting both legs over the side of the mattress. He quickly walked to the bathroom and got rid of the condom. Then he cleaned himself up with a warm washcloth, threw it on the counter, and made his way back to Adeline.

He straightened the covers and climbed in next to her, pulling her into him and covering them back up.

"Aren't you supposed to bring me a washcloth and clean me up?"

"What?"

"In all the romance books I read, that's what the guy does. He tenderly cleans up the heroine and they snuggle the rest of the night."

Crash chuckled. "No way in hell, beautiful."

She pushed up to an elbow and glared down at him. "What? Why not?"

He pulled her back down so her head was resting on his shoulder and wrapped his arm tightly around her, keeping her still and flush against him.

His other hand moved down her body and covered her pussy. His fingers brushed back and forth in her wet slit as he spoke. "Don't get pissed. It's because I don't want to wash away one drop of your beautiful scent. I want it on you, and me, all night." He matched his words to his actions and ran his hand, damp with her juices, over his belly and cock, then returned it to her body. His fingers lightly played with her as he continued. "I want to be able to wake up in the middle of the night and know you're here next to me. I want to smell you on my sheets, on my pillow, on my hands. We'll shower in the morning and get clean. We can change the sheets if it grosses you out. But, beautiful, I've waited a fuck of a long time to have you right where you are, feeling like you do, smelling like you do. I'm not gonna wash away one bit of it. Don't ask me too."

"Oh…okay then."

Crash smiled. "Okay then."

A moment or two passed before Adeline said, "Those were the most amazing orgasms I've ever had too. I just…I wanted you to know."

The words "I love you" were on the tip of his tongue, but Crash held them back. He didn't want to flip her out or make this weird. "Sleep well, beautiful."

"You too, Dean."

Crash fell asleep long after Adeline did. He was memorizing the feel of her in his arms in minute detail. Finally, when he couldn't keep his eyes open any longer, and when he knew she was deeply asleep, he whispered, "I love you, Adeline Reynolds. In sickness and in health. You're mine."

Chapter Fifteen

SATURDAY MORNING, AND after another wonderful night of mind-blowing sex with Dean, Adeline woke up cuddled next to him…and sweating her ass off. She wasn't used to sleeping with someone else and the extra heat he brought to the bed was almost unbearable.

She'd thrown back the covers and had her legs over the side of the mattress before she was hauled back by an arm around her waist.

Dean had gone on to show her the joys of morning sex…and getting sweatier.

Then they'd showered together, which was another new thing for her, and he'd made her a simple breakfast of scrambled eggs with cheese and some sliced fruit.

"Tell me more about this game we're going to today," Adeline stated between bites.

She was seated next to Dean at his kitchen table, as if he couldn't bear for her to be more than a few feet away.

"You've met Sledge. His girlfriend, Beth, has agoraphobia…she doesn't like to be outside. It has to do with being kidnapped a few years ago."

Adeline gasped and blurted, "Kidnapped?"

Dean put his hand on the back of her shoulder and squeezed lightly. "She's okay. I'm sure you'll hear the whole story sooner or later, but the bottom line is that she moved to Texas to try to deal with it, and wasn't doing so well. She got some help from a specialized clinic up in the northeast and she's doing much better with therapy and medication. It's sometimes still hard for her to be around large crowds, but she really wants to see one of our games. So Sledge set up a low-key thing with our law enforcement friends. It's at a park near his house, so if Beth gets uncomfortable, she can easily get back home."

"It sounds fun."

"Oh, it's fun all right," Dean told her, his eyes dancing. "Although the cops cheat, so we have to be on our toes."

Adeline laughed, getting the feeling the game wasn't going to be anything like what she'd imagined. "I'm suuuuure they do," she teased. "Who else will be there?"

"Well, all of the guys from the station, and Penelope. She usually plays, and can kick all our butts…even if she is a girl."

Adeline punched him lightly on the shoulder. "That's not nice."

He caught her hand in his and kissed her knuckles. "Penelope isn't always nice either."

They both laughed.

"Who else?" Adeline asked.

"Playing for the cops should be Dax, Quint, Cruz, TJ, Hayden the only female in their tight-knit group, Conor, and hopefully Calder. They're all in law enforcement of some type but not with the same agency. Oh, and maybe Westin King. He's kinda new to the group, but he's good friends with Dax."

"I'll never keep them straight," Adeline muttered. Then raised her voice to ask, "And any women…other than Hayden, Penelope, and Beth?"

"Probably. Dax's girlfriend, Mackenzie, and if Mack is there, her best friend, Laine, will be too. She's with the newcomer, Wes. Also hopefully Mickie, who's with Cruz, and Corrie. Corrie is blind, but you'd never know it. I saw her at one of our games and I swear she seemed to be able to follow the movements on the field with uncanny accuracy. She's dating Quint."

"Sounds fun," Adeline told him honestly. She didn't hang out with a lot of people other than her sister. She was usually tired from working, and also a bit nervous about having a seizure in front of others, so she kept to herself more than she probably should. It sounded like fun to get out and meet others…especially if they were friends with Dean.

"We always have a good time," Dean told her, smiling. "We see the guys on the force a lot on scenes, and it's nice to blow off some steam and hang out when they're not working. But they're cheaters…don't let the fact that they wear uniforms and carry guns fool you."

Adeline laughed. "I wouldn't dream of it."

He lifted a hand and stroked a finger down her cheek in a barely there caress. "Thank you."

His tone seemed all wrong for what they'd been discussing.

"For what?"

"For this. For being you. For being willing to hang with me and a bunch of people you don't know. For blowing my mind last night…and this morning in the shower, blowing something else." He grinned and pulled her into him so he could kiss her forehead. He kept her there for a long moment then pulled back. "For giving me a chance. And lastly…for being so awesome and beautiful."

His last sentence chased the tears from her eyes and she was thankful. "You're welcome." She totally thought *she* should be thanking *him*, but she'd let it go for now.

"It looks like we have an hour before we need to be there, so we have some time to kill…whatever should we do?" Dean asked, smirking.

Adeline recognized the look in his eye. "Dean, we've already showered!" she protested.

"Then we'll have to be quick so we have time to shower again," he returned easily. He pushed back his chair and stood, grabbing her hand and taking her with him in the process.

Adeline stumbled after him, giggling, as he towed her back up the stairs to his room.

"Eventually I'll get more creative and we'll christen all of the rooms in my house as well as the furniture, but I love seeing you on my bed, so for now we'll stick with that."

Adeline opened her mouth to agree, but before she could say a word, he was there. His mouth on hers, gently pushing her back onto his mussed sheets. Any thought of anything other than Dean and the way he made her feel was pushed far from her mind.

TWO HOURS LATER, Adeline sat on a hard metal bleacher between Mackenzie and Laine. Mickie, Corrie, and Beth sat behind them. They were the only ones at the small baseball park, and the laughter and good-natured taunts flew back and forth between the firefighters and cops as they played.

Laine had brought her dog along, a pit bull mix named Chance. She was a little rough looking around the edges, but was extremely friendly. She and Coco had hit it off very well and were currently lying side by side on the ground in front of the bleachers.

"I can't believe all the crap you guys went through," Adeline said, shaking her head. "Serious-ly…kidnappings, being stuffed in a coffin, being in the middle of a motorcycle gang war…it's crazy!"

"Don't forget a break-in and falling into an abandoned well," Mack said, cheerily waving her arm in the air toward Beth and Laine respectively. "But I don't think any one of us would say that we'd have it any other way."

Adeline opened her mouth in shock as her eyebrows went up, and she wanted to say something but Mackenzie just continued talking, not giving her a chance.

"I mean, yeah, I wasn't very happy in that stupid coffin, and I know Mickie misses her sister like crazy, even if she was mean to her, but we met our guys as a result. Well, maybe not as a result, but as a part of it all. If it didn't happen, we might not be with them, and that would totally suck. So I can't speak for everyone else, but I know for me, I'd totally do it again, hopefully knowing this time that it would turn out okay and I wouldn't actually *die*, die, if it meant I'd end up with the sexiest Texas Ranger out there…no offense, Laine, Wes is hot too, but I don't want him that way…but that calendar is hot. Swear to God I'm gonna frame it when the year is up because all the pictures are so freaking hot. Oh, and Beth and Adeline, you guys need to start talking to your guys because next up is a firefighter calendar. The cop one did so well, our nonprofit wants to move on to hot firefighters…and I just happen to know a few!" She giggled when she was done speaking.

"Take a breath," Laine teased when Mack did just that. "Lord, I swear you can talk." The other woman turned to Adeline. "You get used to her and learn that sometimes you just have to butt in if you want to get a word in edgewise."

Adeline saw Mackenzie blush, but she laughed. "Yeah, sorry. I have a tendency to ramble."

All of the women around them chuckled.

Beth muttered, "Understatement of the century," and set them all off laughing again.

"So, how'd you meet, Crash?" Corrie asked when the laughter had died down.

"I was on a blind date at the restaurant across the street from the fire station and my date ditched me when I told him I was going to have a seizure, and Crash came over and asked what was wrong, and that was that."

Adeline had told the women about her epilepsy when she'd been introduced to them. It was obvious Coco was a service dog of some sort and she wanted to get it out of the way. The last thing she wanted was for everyone to be sitting around wondering what was wrong with her and why she needed Coco. She'd found over the years it was easier to explain it up front.

"I noticed you call him Dean," Beth observed. "Is that how he introduced himself to you?"

Adeline thought the question was odd, but she half turned in her seat to look at the other woman. "Yeah, why?"

If possible, Beth smiled even wider. "Oh, it was just a conversation I had with him a while ago. I told him that Crash was a silly name, and if he really wanted to impress a woman he needed to tell her his real name from the get-go. He's always been Crash. Glad to see he took my advice."

Adeline wasn't sure what to say about that.

Corrie suddenly stood up and yelled, "Run, Quint! Go, go, go!"

They all turned and saw that Quint had hit the soft-ball way out in the outfield and was sprinting around the bases.

"How in the world did you know it was Quint who hit that?" Mickie asked incredulously.

"I heard him talking. And Calder called out 'Get it, Quint,' right before he hit the ball."

"I swear she's totally spooky sometimes," Beth stage whispered to nobody in particular, which had all of the women giggling again. "Ears like a bat!"

Quint made it all the way around the bases…but

only because Hayden shoved Taco just as he went to catch the ball Driftwood had thrown from the outfield. As a result, the ball went sailing past third base, allowing Quint to keep going without being tagged.

Squirrel chased after the errant ball, trying to get to it to throw to home base to Moose before Quint got there, but Conor somehow managed to get to it first and "accidentally" kick it farther into the outfield.

Everyone was laughing as the blatant cheating continued, but honestly, no one seemed to care.

"What's the score now?" Laine asked.

"I think that makes it thirty-seven to forty-three," Mack said.

All the women laughed again. There wasn't one moment in the game that either side hadn't cheated, thus the hugely inflated scores.

"This is nice," Beth said suddenly. "Thanks for being here."

Mackenzie turned and put her hand on Beth's knee and Corrie put her arm around the woman's shoulders. "You know anytime you need us, we're here for you," Mickie told Beth.

"I know. I'm getting better at being outside the house…but I'm not quite up to a full-blown crowd yet. As it was, I took extra meds to get here today. I want to be able to get to a real game, and maybe the stair climb someday, but I also don't want to be totally out of it from the drugs."

"Maybe you need an assistance dog," Adeline blurted, then kinda regretted it as all five women turned to her in unison. "I mean…well…dogs have been proven to reduce blood pressure in veterans with PTSD and soothe them in social situations, and it might work for you too."

"Oh my God, that's a great idea!" Mackenzie exclaimed. She turned to Laine. "You haven't found homes for all of Chance's puppies yet, have you?"

"No. There are still two left. There was a guy who wanted one, but I couldn't bear to part with either of them yet," Laine said. Then explained to Adeline, "Chance was the reason Wes found me when I was down in that abandoned well. She was a stray and was sitting by the edge of the hole in the middle of a field. She had puppies with her, but stayed with me anyway. We adopted her and took in her puppies too." Laine spun back to Beth. "I'd love it if you took Second."

"That's a weird name," Beth muttered, but Adeline could tell she looked intrigued by the idea. "I'm not sure Cade even wants a dog."

"If a dog helped you, he wouldn't care," Corrie said resolutely. "I don't have a Seeing Eye dog, but I seriously considered it a while back. They really can help, Beth."

"Don't I have to get a specialized dog or something?" Beth asked Adeline.

"Not necessarily. Breed doesn't matter. If the dog can be trained, and if it can pass the qualification tests, then it can be a service dog. You just register it and you're good to go. Coco was my pet first, and I had no idea he could even be a service dog...but one day he pawed me and wouldn't quit, ten minutes later I had a seizure. I thought it was a coincidence, but it kept happening. I guess he was so in tune with me that he figured it out and smelled the chemicals in my body or something," Adeline explained.

"She'd be able to go everywhere with me?" Beth asked, leaning forward in excitement.

Adeline grimaced. "In theory, yes. In practice, people are sometimes assholes about it." She went on to explain her and Dean's lunch at the Tower of the Americas. "I carry the explanation cards so people know it's against the law to discriminate against me or my dog. A pit bull might make it even more difficult for you, but if it helps you, and Second can pass the test, fuck what other people think. Oh and by the way, Second is a great name for a dog...Second Chance, right?"

"Exactly," Laine beamed. "Not many people get it."

"I like you," Mack blurted out with a big grin on her face, putting her hand on Adeline's shoulder. "You're smart, you like Crash, you're pretty but don't act like it, and you like dogs. All pluses in my eyes."

Adeline smiled back. She liked these people too. Was fitting in. And was having a good time. She hoped she could continue to get to know all of them.

Down at the bottom of the bleachers, Coco lifted her head suddenly and sniffed the air. She turned to look up at Adeline, then quickly stood up and ran toward the field.

"Coco. Come!" Adeline shouted sternly, but her dog ignored her.

"What's he doing?" Corrie asked.

"Being a pest," Adeline told her. "He's never ignored my commands like that before."

The group of women watched as Coco ran up to Crash on the field. He was standing next to first base and waiting to see if Hayden was going to be able to hit the curve balls Chief was lobbing her way. The dog head-butted his leg. Crash reached down, smiled, petted Coco's head absently, then turned his attention back to the game.

But Coco wasn't to be denied. He jumped up onto Crash, almost knocking him over.

"Oh my God, I'm so embarrassed," Adeline moaned, putting her head in her hand. "Here I was advocating you getting a service dog and mine has completely lost his mind."

A few of the cops called out things like, "Good distraction, dog!" and "Nice first-base coach!" Crash laughed and pushed Coco off him, pointing toward the bleachers, obviously telling the dog to go back to the women.

Adeline watched in disbelief as Coco sat next to Dean and pawed his leg. Just like he did to her when—

"Oh, shit," she said in a low voice.

"What?" Mackenzie asked, confused.

"Shit, what?" Laine asked at the same time as her friend.

Dean obviously understood what was happening at the same time Adeline did, because he turned and caught her eye before sprinting toward the bleachers where the women were sitting.

Adeline vaguely heard his teammates asking where he was going and the cops cheering because now first base didn't have anyone there to guard it, but she kept her eyes on Dean and her dog running toward her.

Before she could explain what was going on to her new friends, Dean was in front of her, holding out his hand.

"Come on, beautiful, let's get you down from there."

"Crash, what's going on?" Beth asked in a worried tone.

"Coco alerted," he told her shortly. "Come on, Adeline." Not waiting for her to grab hold of him anymore,

Dean stepped up to where she was sitting and pulled her to her feet, keeping one hand around her waist.

"Why did he do that?" Adeline asked, her brows drawn down in confusion, gaze flicking between Dean and her dog.

Knowing exactly what she was talking about, Dean said evenly, "Because he knows I'll take care of you."

"But I was right there. He should've come up to me," Adeline protested.

"Doesn't matter right now, beautiful," Dean reassured her, helping her step down from the bleachers.

"What's up?" Chief asked, appearing next to them as if out of nowhere.

"Coco alerted," Crash explained quickly.

"Not here," Adeline begged, tears in her eyes, looking up at Dean.

"Adeline, you're safe. It's fine."

"I don't want—"

"Did you hear me?" Dean interrupted. "You're safe here with me and our friends. It's not a big deal."

Adeline really didn't want to have a seizure in front of the women she'd met only an hour before. And she really, *really* didn't want to have a seizure in front of the dozen or so hot men now standing around staring at her.

"Give her some space, guys," Mack suddenly called out. She was standing on the bleacher with her hands on her hips. "Stop staring at her. Jeez. I thought you were here to play a game or something?"

Her words did what they were meant to—snapped everyone out of it. Most of the men turned back to the field to retake their places. The men with girlfriends kissed their women before moving. Chief and Sledge hung back.

"You need anything?" Chief asked.

Crash shook his head. "No. I think we're good. She just needs a flat place to lie down."

Coco had crept up to Adeline and was now alerting her to the impending seizure. Adeline looked down at her dog in exasperation. "Oh, so now you let *me* know. When did I become second fiddle in your eyes, bud?" Coco whined and pawed her leg just as he'd done to Dean out on the baseball field.

"Here," Mickie said, "Use this towel. I've been sitting on it because the bleachers hurt my butt." She handed Crash a large beach towel that had been folded into a pad.

"Awesome, thanks," Adeline muttered, not meeting her new friend's eyes, still embarrassed. Figures she'd have a seizure now. It couldn't wait another hour or two when she was home alone with Dean.

Chief took the towel from Mickie and followed Crash and Adeline behind the bleachers. The women all sat back down and only glanced behind them occasionally.

Sledge put his hand on Crash's shoulder. "Let us know if you need anything." Then he turned to Adeline and winked before saying, "Thanks for the distraction, Adeline. With the cops wondering what the hell is going on and worrying about you, they'll be paying less attention. We'll be caught up in no time."

Adeline couldn't hold back the chuckle. He'd surprised her. She thought the men would hover and be über concerned. But it seemed as though her having a seizure was a normal thing—which it kinda was, but they didn't necessarily know that. It was weird…she appreciated it, but it was still weird.

Dean helped her sit a bit away from the bleachers in a grassy spot in the shade, then lay down on the towel Chief had spread out. Coco settled into his usual spot at her feet and laid his head on her legs. Adeline looked up at Dean. "I don't like this."

Dean leaned down and kissed her on the forehead and said simply, "I know."

She wanted to say more. To talk to Dean about why Coco had done what he'd done, but the last thing she remembered was the tender look on her boyfriend's face as the seizure took control of her body.

CRASH WAS GLAD Chief stayed. It wasn't that he was

worried about Adeline, per se, it was more that the other man could run interference with the women or the other men if needed. All of Crash's attention was on Adeline. Her eyes were open and she stared off into space as her body twitched as the seizure continued.

He was also glad the other man didn't try to make conversation—not that he would, Chief didn't talk much, and never engaged in small talk. He was a quiet man. Which Crash appreciated right about now.

He could hear the women talking in low voices in the bleachers behind him, but kept his attention on Adeline. Glancing at Coco, Crash reached out a hand and petted the dog's head. "Good boy," he murmured.

He was as shocked as Adeline had been that her dog had alerted him rather than her. It had taken a moment to truly understand what was happening, but the split second between when he'd understood the dog's action and when he'd turned to find Adeline had seemed like eons. He'd been afraid she'd fallen off the bleachers or was somehow otherwise incapacitated, and that was why Coco had come to him.

But she'd been sitting on the bleachers looking as confused as he'd felt. He'd reached her in moments, but he'd never forget the panic he'd felt when he'd thought she'd been hurt.

He reached up and put his hand on Adeline's forehead as she continued to jerk. He hated that she had to

SUSAN STOKER

go through the seizures. He was all for having the brain surgery to lessen the frequency of them, but could also admit that it scared him as much as it did her.

The last thing he wanted was to lose her now. Not when he'd just found her. The thought of her not knowing who he was, or not really understanding the world around her, made him feel sick. But even knowing the risk, knowing she might not remember him or how she felt about him, Crash would be by her side for the rest of her life. Even if she never remembered him, he wouldn't give up on her. In sickness and in health. They might not be married, but he took the words to heart.

"Looks like she's coming back," Chief noted softly.

Crash nodded and kept his eyes on her face. He brushed her hair back from her forehead, and continued the light caress as her eyes closed then opened again.

As was typical for her, she came back to herself slowly. She blinked up at Crash.

"Dean?"

Thank fuck. Every time she had a seizure, he was half afraid her brain would be damaged and she wouldn't remember him. He loved that the first word out of her mouth was his name.

"I'm here, beautiful. Just relax, you're good."

She sighed and closed her eyes again. Crash could see every muscle in her body relax.

"I'll leave you to it," Chief stated easily, and before Crash could say anything, the man was gone.

Coco whined and crawled on his belly up Adeline's body between her spread legs until his head was lying on her stomach. Her hand came up to pet his head. Crash knew this was a part of their routine as well. She lay quiet for a couple of minutes before taking a deep breath and opening her eyes again.

"Help me sit up, please."

Crash wanted her to stay down for a bit longer, but didn't treat her like a child, doing as she asked, putting a hand behind her back and easing her to a sitting position, letting her lean against him for support.

She looked around then said dryly, "It's not the worst place I've woken up after a seizure."

His lips didn't quite make it up into a grin. "Where's the worst?"

"The floor of the restroom in a bar." She wrinkled her nose. "Have you ever *seen* the floor of a bathroom in a bar? It's absolutely disgusting. I can imagine that the men's room is probably worse, but still. It wasn't fun. I took a thirty-minute shower when I got home and washed my clothes twice."

Crash wasn't amused in the least, but he tried to tamp it down. Just the *thought* of her going through that made him want to hit something. "You feel all right?"

As if realizing he was changing the subject, Adeline

didn't complain. "I'm okay. Just tired as usual."

"Can you stand?"

"Yeah." She said it, but it was obvious she wasn't sure she could by the way she didn't even make a move to try.

"I'll help you. Come on. Up you go." Crash lifted her to her feet and kept his arm around her waist as she swayed and tried to get her bearings. He helped her shuffle back to the bleachers and sit on the bottom row. Coco followed close behind, sitting at her feet next to the row of seats.

Crash looked up to the other women, who were looking down at them anxiously. "Tell the others we're headed home, okay? I'm gonna go get my car."

"Sure, go," Mackenzie told him, moving down the bleachers to sit near Adeline. "We'll keep watch over her until you get back."

"Appreciate it." Crash turned to jog off toward his car. He wanted to get Adeline home and in bed. She could take a nap while he made them something to eat.

The other women moved down the bleachers until they were all sitting close to Adeline.

"Hey, I thought I'd be the first one to leave. I appreciate you letting me outlast you," Beth teased.

Adeline smiled weakly. "Any time."

Mickie put her hand on Adeline's shoulder. "Don't be embarrassed. Seriously."

"Yeah," Mackenzie agreed. "When they found me in that coffin, I was so scared that I'd peed all over myself. I'm sure it smelled horrible, and all of Dax's friends were there. I wasn't at my best at all."

Adeline looked over at the other woman, appreciating what she was trying to do.

Laine piped up next. "And you should've seen *me*. Lord, I was a mess. After spending all that time in a dirty hole, I don't think there was an inch of my skin that wasn't caked with mud."

"And seriously, Adeline," Mickie added, "you looked like you were napping. Do *not* be embarrassed."

"And I swear to God, the way Crash looked at you," Beth said with a sigh. "If I didn't have my own man and didn't see that same look on his face every night, I might be jealous. Adeline, in case you didn't know it, that man is so in love with you."

"I don't think so," Adeline said shaking her head for emphasis. "We just started dating. It's just the rush of a new relationship."

"No, it's not," Beth argued firmly. "I know it's hard to believe. I was right where you are not too long ago. I couldn't believe a man as good looking as Cade would ever take a second look at me. Especially when I was so messed up in the head and couldn't even leave my apartment without holding on to Penelope's hand like an eight-year-old. But he did. And taking a chance and accepting that love, and returning it, is the best thing that ever happened to me." She looked Adeline right in the eye and stated, "Grab hold, Adeline. And don't let go. It'll change your life...for the better. Seizures or not."

Adeline nodded and opened her mouth to say something, but Dean had returned. He'd parked his car as close to the bleachers as he could, ignoring the fact he'd driven over the grass and put ruts in it.

He came over to her and, without a word, took her hand and helped her to her feet, giving the women a chin lift but not wasting any time. He led her to the car and got her settled into the front seat. Then he opened the back door to let Coco jump in.

Turning and waving at the men still on the baseball field, and getting "Laters" and "See yas" in return, he climbed into the driver's seat.

Crash knew he should probably stop and say thank you to the women for looking after Adeline while he got the car, and for not making her seizure a spectacle, but all he wanted to do was get Adeline back to his house and comfortable. They'd understand though, so he put it out of his mind.

Adeline fell asleep on the way back to his house even though it was only a fifteen minute drive. Crash pulled into his parking space and reached out a hand to smooth back the hair from Adeline's face. God, she really was beautiful.

He got out silently and went around to the other side of the car. He let Coco out of the backseat and opened Adeline's door. She'd awakened with the sound of the back door shutting and moved to undo her seat belt.

"I got it, beautiful."

He reached in and helped Adeline stand, then picked her up. It was the first time he'd carried her, and Crash knew he'd be doing it a lot more. She snuggled into his embrace trustingly, as if she had no doubt she was safe in his arms.

He had to put her down to unlock his front door, but as soon as the door was open, he picked her up again and went straight up the stairs to his bedroom. He gently put her down and kissed her forehead. "I'll be right back."

He got some water and brought it back to her. While she sipped, he took off her shoes and laid them on the floor next to the bed. Adeline smiled up at him, eyes heavy.

"Thank you for taking care of me."

"Always, beautiful. Now nap. I'll wake you up in about an hour and we'll eat something, okay?"

"Okay." She snuggled down into his bed and Crash pulled the comforter up and over her, smiling as she hugged it to her chest. Making a mental note to always keep his house on the chilly side so she could snuggle, he patted the bed, inviting Coco to jump up next to his mistress.

He kissed Adeline once more on the side of her head, but she was already out, breathing deep in the throes of a healing sleep.

Pausing at the doorway, Crash looked back at the woman in his bed. He loved her so much, and vowed to do whatever he needed to do to make her happy, healthy, and safe.

She needed that surgery. It was obvious to him with the number of seizures she'd been having, and he knew it was to her too. They needed to talk about that, and her job, and their future. But it could all wait until she was rested.

Crash closed the door behind him and headed down to the kitchen. She'd be hungry when she woke up. He needed to get on that.

"FEEL BETTER?" CRASH asked later that evening. He'd gotten Adeline up and helped her settle on the couch. Then he'd brought in dinner: cheese and beef enchiladas covered in more gooey melted cheese. It was his go-to meal when he was hungry, but didn't want to spend a lot of time in the kitchen.

As they ate, Adeline said, "I have no idea why Coco

alerted you today instead of me. It's weird. I'm not sure I like it."

Crash considered his words carefully, then said, "I think maybe he recognizes me as a part of his pack. I know we haven't spent a ton of time together, but the time we have spent has always been with him too. He's a smart dog, beautiful."

"I know," Adeline said, waving her fork around as she spoke. "But he's never done that with my sister. Or her husband, or even my parents. And he's alerted when I've been around them, and I've had plenty of seizures with them near me."

"Again, I don't know for sure. I'm not an expert on this," Crash told her calmly, "but this was the first time you guys stayed all night here. He has his own bed here. I fed him. I took him out to do his business. I took him out this morning. And don't get weirded out, but he saw us sleeping together in the same bed. I think he somehow realizes that I'm with you. And since you're his alpha, I, in turn, am too. When he realized you were going to have a seizure, it was just as easy to come to me as it was to you."

"Hmmmm." The sound was neither agreement nor disagreement, but it was obvious by her furrowed brow and the concerned look she was giving her dog that she wasn't exactly happy about his actions.

"He knew, intuitively, that I'd protect you. That I'd

let you know."

"I guess."

It was gonna kill him to say it, but he needed to. "Do you want to call a trainer, maybe where he got his certification, and see what they think?"

Adeline put down her fork and leaned on her elbow, which was propped on her knee. "No. I don't think so. I guess it doesn't matter if he alerts to you or me when we're together, as long as you immediately let me know. If he stops alerting to me when you aren't around, then I'll get concerned."

"Adeline," Crash said sternly, his voice deep and commanding, "look at me."

He waited until her wide, surprised eyes met his before continuing.

"I don't think the fact that Coco alerted to me today means he won't alert to you in the future. He loves you. He adores you. But if it becomes an issue, we'll deal with it. Consult with a trainer or something. Okay?

She nodded immediately, which made him feel better.

"And so you know, if we're together and Coco alerts to me instead of you again, there is nothing that I could be doing that would be more important than getting to you to let you know. Nothing. I don't care what it is. I'll always drop it and go to you."

"Thank you," Adeline said, nodding as she did.

"You done eating?"

"I am."

Crash didn't bother taking the dishes to the sink. He took her into his arms, leaned into the corner of the couch, and settled in. "Wanna watch some TV for a while?" At her nod, he turned it on and felt her relax into him as they watched a show on veterinarians.

When the show was over, not wanting to kill the mellow mood but knowing they needed to talk, he said softly, "It took you a while to recover from that today."

She sighed and tightened her arms around his waist. "Yeah."

"I'm thinking that isn't good."

Adeline merely shook her head.

Crash waited her out.

Finally, she took a deep breath and looked up at him. "I'll call my doctor soon. I don't like how tired I've been feeling when I come out of the seizures. It didn't used to be that way. I'd have one then could bounce right back."

When she didn't say anything else, Crash murmured, "Let me know when your appointment is, and I'll go with you."

"I'm not sure—"

"I know we've moved fast," Crash interrupted, knowing exactly what she was going to say, "but being with you like this feels more right than any other relationship I've ever had. I'd like to say that by this time next year we'll be married, though I have no idea what the future will bring. But I will say that if we *are* married by this time next year, I'd be the fucking happiest man on the planet to be sitting here with you just like this, seeing my ring on your finger, and knowing every time I woke up and every time I went to sleep, you'd be there next to me. I'm just telling you that so you know I'm serious about you, Adeline. Really serious. So if you don't feel well, or if you have a doctor's appointment where you might discuss something as important as maybe scheduling a time to have your brain operated on...I'd like to be there to support you, to help you understand any medical terms you might not understand, and so we can comfort each other when it's over."

Crash knew he was talking too fast, and was even more aware that Adeline had stiffened in his embrace, but he wanted to clear the air and make sure she knew exactly where he was coming from and what he was feeling. He shifted until he was lying on the cushions, his head on the armrest, and Adeline was lying over him. Hip to hip, belly to belly, and her tits pressing against his chest.

"I realize you're an adult and that you've been taking care of yourself for a long time. But I'm here now. Let me carry some of the burden you've struggled with.

Let me be the one who holds your hand as you schedule the surgery that can make your life easier. Let *me* be the one who stands by your side and will hold you when you cry, celebrate with you when good things happen, and will shelter you when shit rolls your way."

He saw the tears in her eyes, and hoped like hell they were the good kind. Raising a hand to tenderly brush them away with his thumb, Crash pressed his lips against hers in a tender, closed-mouth kiss.

"How'd I get lucky enough to find you?" Adeline asked, blinking fast, trying to keep any more tears from falling, and failing. "Seriously. I want to know. Because I've been looking a long time. I'd almost given up hope. But then, there you were. Standing next to my table at that restaurant, holding out your hand. I had no idea you were the man I'd searched for so desperately. None. I'm scared, Dean. So scared that this isn't real. That if I let you in, let you stand next to me, and in front of me, that you'll eventually decide I'm not enough. That you want someone without medical issues. I…I can't let you in and have you step away when I've already come to rely on you being there."

Crash felt his own eyes well up with tears and didn't even try to hide them from Adeline. His voice cracked with emotion as he said simply, "You're enough, beautiful. I swear to Christ, you're enough."

Adeline nodded once, sucked both lips in, licked

them, then said simply, "I'll let you know when my appointment is."

"Thank you," Crash whispered, then put his hand on the back of her head and tugged her down. She nestled into him, laying her head on his shoulder, and bringing her hand up to rest on his chest next to her face.

They were quiet for a long moment before Crash took a deep breath and cleared his throat. "Now that we've settled that…tell me about the phone interviews you have next week. The sooner you get away from your asshole boss, the happier we'll both be."

Adeline lifted her head far enough to kiss his jaw, then laid it back down.

They spent the rest of the evening discussing her upcoming interviews. Then, after she reassured him for the tenth time that she felt fine, Crash took her upstairs and showed her the difference between making love and fucking.

An hour later, when Adeline was sound asleep in his arms and Coco was snoring in his bed on the floor against the wall, Crash plotted on how soon was too soon to convince Adeline to move in with him. He couldn't imagine not falling asleep with her weight against him, her naked body soft and warm against his own. Couldn't imagine not waking up to her smiling face and easygoing nature.

WHY WOULDN'T SHE SAY YES?

It was food.

She needed to say yes.

He couldn't move on if she didn't.

The man twitched and grabbed his head. No, the other one wasn't allowed to come back yet. He had to think. Had to figure this out.

Besides, the other one was mean. He still yelled. It needed to stop.

She's mine.

She smiled at me.

She wants me but is playing hard-to-get.

Soon. When we're alone she'll say yes and we can move forward.

The man lay down on the bed and felt the other one taking over. It was okay. His time with her was coming. The other one wanted to bc in charge, but soon he'd know who was really in control.

Chapter Sixteen

"**H**AVE YOU HEARD anything about your interview?"

Adeline sighed and shook her head. "No, Dean. And I'll tell you the second I do. Promise." She knew he was on edge. A lot had happened since the softball game.

She'd had the two phone interviews, and gotten called back for an in-person meeting for one of them. That had taken place four days ago. She'd tried to explain to Dean that it could be weeks before a decision was made, it all depended on the organization's processes and who was interviewing, but he wanted her away from Douglas Hill, and it was killing him every day she wasn't.

Douglas had gotten more unstable. One second he'd be yelling at everyone, telling them they were worthless and that he was going to fire them all, and the next he was smiling and acting as if he hadn't just lost his shit.

He hadn't stopped asking her out, using the pretense that they needed to talk about work, but at least he hadn't given her any problems when she turned him down. But…there were times when Adeline thought he was following her. Every time she left the office, she'd see him.

When she used the restroom, he'd be drinking from the water fountain across the hall. When she went to lunch, Douglas just happened to be leaving his office at the same time. In the evening, when she was being escorted to her car, she'd see him sitting in his own vehicle. Sometimes he waved at her, other times he didn't. Adeline hadn't ever seen him driving behind her when she left, but the feeling of being watched was always there.

She'd told Dean most of what was going on, but some things, she hadn't bothered. She couldn't prove he was purposely following her around. And being a weirdo wasn't exactly a punishable offense.

"You're still going to the conference, aren't you?" Dean asked warily, pacing in agitation in front of her.

As she considered what to tell Dean about her boss, she began to think about their relationship. Somehow Adeline had sorta moved in with Dean. It had just kind of happened. When he was on shift, she went back to her place, but every night he'd been off work, he'd asked her to stay with him. It didn't matter if it was a weekend or a work night for her, he wanted her with him.

And since she wanted the same thing, it wasn't a

hard sacrifice to make. So now she had both professional work clothes and lay-around-the-house clothes at his house, in his drawers and closet. Her shampoo and conditioner were in his shower, and she had a permanent toothbrush and tube of toothpaste sitting alongside his on the bathroom counter.

The first few times she'd carried an overnight bag, and he'd suggested, completely reasonably, that it would be easier if she just "brought some shit over" and kept it there. So she had.

Now she and Coco spent as much time at his place as they did at hers. And she liked it. A lot. Living with Dean had made them even closer. He'd realized that she was an early-bird. Usually rising, even on the weekends, before seven. Sometimes before six. And Adeline continued to find little things that bugged her, but at the same time they made him less "perfect," which weirdly made her like him even more.

Dean hated doing dishes. Would let them sit around—on the table, on the counter, in the sink—until he absolutely had to wash them because there were no more plates, bowls, or silverware clean. He said that because they always did the dishes immediately at the station, it was a relief not to feel the pressure to do that at home.

He also tended to wear a lot of clothes. Adeline could wear the same thing all weekend and be totally fine, it wasn't like she was getting them dirty, but somehow Dean came home from the station after every shift with a full bag of dirty clothes. Even if he only worked three days, he'd have four pairs of jeans, two pairs of cargo pants, eight T-shirts, and around eight pairs of socks and underwear that needed to be cleaned. She realized that if he had a call and got dirty or sweaty, he'd need to change clothes, but he brought as many clothes home to be washed when he was extremely busy at work as he did when he admitted they'd only had a medical call or two.

Ultimately, however, it didn't matter. All the good stuff about Dean way overrode the small annoyances about his clothes and the dishes.

The other thing that had happened was that Adeline had made an appointment with her doctor and Dean had gone with her.

The doctor hadn't been pleased to hear that her seizures were increasing in frequency, and about how it was taking longer and longer for her to come back to herself when they were over.

After much discussion—between Adeline and her doctor, her doctor and Dean, Dean and Adeline, and Adeline with her sister and parents—the agreement to have the surgery had been made.

It was hard trying to come up with the best time for the surgery to be scheduled. If she had it immediately, and if she did get the job with a new company, she'd have to take time off before she even really got started, which wasn't the way she wanted to begin her employment with a new boss and coworkers. But on the other hand, if the surgery was successful, then she'd most likely have to take less time off and there would hopefully be fewer seizures to work around, both of which were good things for her and for whatever company chose to hire her.

She was thinking to schedule it a month or two after the marketing conference. Adeline hadn't told Douglas that she needed to take time off for the surgery yet, but was planning on doing so as soon as she had a firm date. Her boss knew she had a medical issue, of course he did, having Coco in the office was a clear indicator, but he hadn't ever asked what her issue was, and she hadn't volunteered that information. She was protected under federal laws and didn't have to disclose the nature of her disability to anyone other than human resources when she filed the appropriate paperwork.

The last crazy thing that had happened was that Beth and Adeline had grown close. Beth had called after the softball game to check on her and they'd ended up talking for close to an hour. Beth was happy that there was another girlfriend to a firefighter and they spent a lot of time chatting, both electronically and on the phone, when their boyfriends were on shift.

She and Dean had dinner with Adeline's parents a few times, and Matt and Alicia had come over for dinner at Dean's condo one night as well.

Basically, all was well in Adeline's life. Except for the upcoming surgery, increased seizures, and the little fact that Dean was not happy about the conference she was scheduled to attend with her asshole boss. He'd planned to go with her, but his shift at the fire station got switched and he wasn't able to get off for the entire length of the conference.

"Yes, I'm going to the conference," Adeline told Dean. She elaborated, telling him things he already knew, but apparently wanted confirmation on. "I leave Sunday morning and I'll be back next Wednesday night."

"I really wish you weren't driving up there with him," Dean said, every muscle in his body tight with his displeasure.

Adeline sighed. "I know. Me too. I have zero desire to spend five hours in a car with him."

"He still hitting on you?"

He was. She tried to downplay it so Dean wouldn't lose his shit. "Not really."

"Which means he is. Fuck." He came around to where Adeline was sitting and crouched down next to her chair. "If I arranged for alternate transportation for you to get up to Dallas, would you take it?"

Adeline eyed her boyfriend. They'd talked about this in the past. She wasn't comfortable driving herself, her seizures had become too unpredictable for that, even with Coco's alerts, and the stress of driving would most likely ensure that she wouldn't make the entire trip without one.

Douglas was driving up to Dallas, and had indicated he expected her to go with him, but neither Adeline nor Dean wanted her to have a seizure when she was with him. She'd be vulnerable during and after, and Adeline really didn't want her boss seeing her like that anyway.

But Dallas was five hours away. If someone drove her, it would be a ten-hour round-trip for them. Not exactly something you could really ask someone to do and not feel like an asshole about. Alicia and Matt were out of town and Adeline didn't want to ask her parents.

Dean was working until Monday at noon, and he planned on coming up after he got off shift, so he wasn't available to drive her up either.

"What kind of arrangements?" Adeline asked. "We've been over this for the most part already."

"If I arranged for alternate transportation for you to get up there, would you take it?" Dean repeated firmly.

"Yes, Dean. Of course I would," Adeline told him in exasperation. "You know I have no desire to be stuck in a car with Douglas for five hours."

"Then I'll arrange it."

Adeline smiled then and scooted her chair back. Dean was still crouched next to her, but she held out her hand to him when she stood. She had no idea what Dean would do about the transportation issue, but if he said he'd take care of it, he would. The relief she felt was immense. "Now that that's settled…want to take a bath with me?"

Dean smiled, huge. "Is that even a question?"

"Well, I've been drooling over that fantastic tub ever since the moment I saw it." The bathtub was huge. Seriously massive. It looked like it could easily hold four people. There were jets all around it and a large window next to it. The window would've been weird, but it faced west. There was some sort of forest or nature preserve behind his place because there were no buildings, only trees.

The condo wasn't too impressive other than the master bathroom. The people who lived there before him must've been total bathroom snobs, because while the kitchen was nice, the bathroom was *nice*.

Dean had said he only owned a condo rather than a house because at the time he'd bought it, he didn't want to deal with the upkeep needed when owning a house. The management company mowed the grass and dealt with the fire ants.

He was a typical guy when it came to his place. Before Adeline had practically moved in, the living area consisted of a large television mounted on the wall with a complicated-looking stereo system and cable box hooked up to it. A sliding glass door led out to a small fenced yard area, which was perfect for Coco to do his business. There was a dark couch, a recliner, and a low coffee table. A small half bath and the functional, but not overly impressive, kitchen completed the downstairs area. It was pretty bare bones and efficient.

Upstairs there were two guestrooms, a guest bath, and the master bedroom. The master had Dean's king-size bed—no headboard—a dresser, a bedside table, and another large TV. All in all, it was perfectly bland. Until the bathroom.

Besides the amazing tub, there was a long counter with two sinks. There were large mirrors over each sink with plenty of space between them for stuff. Tile floor, alcove with a toilet, and a separate shower with two showerheads rounded it out.

Over time, Dean had begun to pick up small things to brighten up his condo when they shopped together. The first time they'd been out running errands together, he'd stopped at Bed Bath & Beyond, saying he had to pick something up.

He'd asked her opinion on comforters and sheets and even towels, and had bought every single item that Adeline had said looked nice.

It didn't stop there. Over the weeks he'd acquired,

both from shopping and from Adeline bringing them over from her house, brightly colored pillows, throw blankets, area rugs, picture frames—which Adeline helped him fill with pictures of his sister, parents, and of the two of them—and even a couple pictures for the walls.

His place now looked lived in, comfortable…and perhaps most importantly to Adeline, homey.

"I'll take care of Coco," Dean told her, lust clear in his eyes as they roamed up and down her body. "You go start the bath."

"I kinda wanted to try that new bath bomb I got the other day…but it smells a bit girly," Adeline warned him.

"Don't care," was Dean's response.

"But you have to work tomorrow. You might work out and start sweating and then the guys'll make fun of you for smelling like oranges."

Dean leaned in and lifted Adeline's chin. He kissed her hard, deep, and way too quickly before lifting his head. "I could smell like roses and I still wouldn't give a shit. Wanna know why?"

"Why?" Adeline asked, breathlessly.

"Because it means I got that way by sharing a bath with my girlfriend. And to share a bath, we both had to be naked. And when we're naked, good things happen. And every single one of my friends knows exactly what it means when I come into the station smelling like girly orange, and they might not say it, but they're equally jealous as hell and happy as fuck for me. So yeah, bomb the hell out of the water, beautiful. Bring it."

Adeline beamed from ear to ear. God, she loved this man.

She froze. *Wait, what?*

"What was that thought?" Dean asked, his brow furrowing.

"Uh…I just…" Adeline looked anywhere but at Dean. Did she want to do this now?

If not, when?

Dean looked over at Coco who was sleeping in his fluffy bed in front of the TV. On his back, legs splayed, totally unconcerned and not at all giving any indication that he was about to alert.

"I was thinking about how much I loved that you didn't care that the guys at the station knew you'd spent the night with me, and how much I liked the thought of you smelling like me, then I thought about how much I just love you." Adeline blurted it out, breathing fast and still not looking Dean in the eye. She did. She loved him. Totally loved him. And figured he should know.

"Change of plans. We'll both let Coco out, then we'll go up together to start the bath."

Adeline blinked up at Dean. Well, okay. That wasn't quite the response she'd hoped for. "Uh…all right."

He leaned in, wrapping one of his large arms around her waist and plastering her to his chest, then palming the side of her face with his hand tenderly. "If you think for one second I'm gonna let the love of my life walk up the stairs away from me after she tells me she loves me for the first time, you're out of your mind. I want you right here. In my arms. Next to me. I can't bear to let you out of my sight for even the couple of minutes it'll take for Coco to take care of business and to get back upstairs."

It was an unconventional way of saying that he loved her, but Adeline would take it. Being the love of his life was way better than a simple "I love you, too."

She beamed up at him, flushed, happy, content. "Okay, Dean."

He kissed her then. Longer, harder, and much more erotically than the last kiss. They were both breathing heavy when he finally pulled back. "Thank you, beautiful. For loving me. For being here with me. For letting me in. I won't ever let you regret it."

"I know," she told him.

"Now come on. Let's take care of Coco so I can take you upstairs to that monster of a tub and more appropriately show you how much I love you, and how happy I am that you love me back."

Adeline's mind spun with the possibilities. She and

Dean had done a lot—*a lot*—when it came to sex, but he still never failed to surprise her…in good ways.

"Coco, time to go out," Adeline called, not looking away from Dean and not moving.

He chuckled and pulled back enough so she could walk next to him. His hand pushed down into the waistband of her pants and Adeline felt his fingers caressing her butt as they walked. Oh yeah, she loved it when Dean surprised her.

HOW COULD YOU BE SO STUPID?

No wonder she didn't want to eat with you.

She's fucking someone else.

Letting him *touch her hair.*

Letting him *kiss her.*

Letting him *into her body.*

Letting him *feed her.*

Bitch.

She'd been stringing him along the entire time.

She'd pay for that.

Yes…she was definitely going to pay.

Chapter Seventeen

━━━━━━ •◆• ━━━━━━

"ARE YOU SURE Chief doesn't mind driving me?" Adeline asked Dean for what seemed like the hundredth time on Sunday morning. He'd called to make sure she was good to go for the trip before Chief came by to pick her up.

"I'm sure, beautiful. He said he had something to do up in Dallas and he was happy to shift his work schedule and do it today so he could drive you. Stop worrying."

"He won't freak if I have a seizure, right?" Adeline asked, biting her lip worriedly.

"No. Not at all. He stood right behind me at the ballgame last month to watch over you and make sure we didn't need anything. He's stoic. He probably won't say much, so don't take it personally, it's just the way he is. But, Adeline, he absolutely won't freak if you have a seizure in the car with him. Okay? He'll take care of you, swear."

"All right. I just feel bad."

"Did Douglas call you again?"

It was an abrupt change of topic, but Adeline didn't call him on it because she knew he wasn't happy, at all, that she was attending the conference with her boss.

She sighed. "No, Dean."

"I don't like that the prick tried to strong-arm you into riding up with him yesterday, even after you told him you already had a ride."

Adeline didn't have anything to say to that. Her boss *had* tried to strong-arm her into riding with him. Even going so far as to hint that her upcoming annual review might suffer if she didn't. But she'd held firm, not even caring that he might be an asshole and lie about her dedication to her job on the review. She'd hopefully not be there much longer so it wouldn't matter.

There was a beat of silence on the phone for a moment, then Dean said, "I'm sorry. I know, I know…I just don't like him."

Yeah, Adeline got that. She didn't like him either. "You're coming up tomorrow afternoon still though, right?" she asked.

"Absolutely. I get off around noon, an hour or so earlier if I can swing it. I'll be there anywhere from four to five depending on traffic. I'll text and let you know for sure."

"I put your name on the reservation. If I'm in a

meeting or taking a break in the room, you can just grab the key at the front desk without any hassle and come on up."

Dean's voice dropped to the sexy rumble that Adeline loved so much. "Sounds perfect. You know…we haven't had hotel sex yet. I'll have to see what I can do to keep you from screaming when you orgasm like you do here at home."

"I do not scream!" Adeline protested hotly.

"Beautiful…"

One word, and it said so much. "Okay, sometimes I do, but that's because you're so good with your tongue. And mouth. And fingers. And cock."

He laughed then said softly, "Just hearing you say 'cock' has me hard as a rock."

Adeline sighed. "I missed you last night."

"Yeah, I missed you too," Dean replied immediately. "The bed here at the station leaves a lot to be desired, but even more so because you're not in it. I've gotten used to you sleeping next to me. Be safe for me, yeah? Stay away from Douglas and hide out in the room if you have to."

"I'm not going to hide out, Dean. I need to net-work. But I promise I'll do everything I can to stay away from Douglas. I have no desire to breathe the same air as him. Oh, and the person who interviewed me last week is supposed to be at the conference. Even though it's a little soon, I'm hoping she'll have good news for me."

"God, me too. That would be the best gift ever. I'd love to be there and see that asshole's face when you tell him you're quitting."

"Drive safe, Dean." Adeline changed the subject. It made her nervous to talk about giving notice when she didn't even have the job. Although, she'd love to be able to have Dean by her side when she told Douglas she was leaving. It wasn't that she was scared of the man, he could just be unpredictable. He'd been a dick, then he'd tried seducing her, and lately he'd gone back to being a dick when she hadn't fallen in line with his seduction routine. So telling him she was leaving the company wouldn't make him happy, and she had no idea how he'd react.

"I will. Text me when you're on your way, okay?" Dean said.

"I will. Love you."

"Love you too, beautiful. I'll talk to you later."

"Okay. 'Bye."

"'Bye."

Adeline clicked off the phone and tucked it into her back pocket. It was good timing, because just then she saw Chief's gray Ford Explorer pull into a space outside Dean's condo.

"Coco, come."

The dog bounded over and Adeline put on his harness and vest. "Be good, okay, boy? No drooling on Chief's seat, and try not to shed so much. The last thing I want is him getting irritated because your black hair is all over his seat." She knew she was being ridiculous, not only talking to Coco as if he could understand her, but telling him not to shed. She was still kind of nervous to spend five hours with Chief.

It wasn't that she didn't like him, she did, but Dean hadn't lied when he'd said the man didn't talk much.

He knocked on the door with two short raps, and Adeline immediately opened it. "Hey, Chief. I'm ready, just let me grab my stuff."

"I've got it," Chief returned, striding into the foyer and stepping toward her suitcases. She had one larger one with all of her clothes for the conference, then another smaller one with Coco's food, bowls, a toy, a blanket, and an extra sheet to throw over the hotel comforter to protect it from Coco's shedding.

"Okay. Thanks."

Chief nodded his head in reply even as he was reaching for the bags. He was back at the door before Adeline could blink. "You okay to lock up?"

"Yeah. Why wouldn't I be?"

Chief's shoulder went up in a barely perceptible shrug. "Just checking. See you at the car."

Okay then. Adeline couldn't help but smile. She couldn't wait to tell Beth about this. The other woman had been full of questions when she'd heard Chief would be driving her up to Dallas. Mainly because she didn't know anything about the man other than he was part Native American and was incredibly close-lipped. She'd even admitted that she'd tried to find something about him online, as she was some kind of computer expert, but hadn't been able to find much beyond his name, Roman Proudfit.

Adeline picked up Coco's leash and shut and locked the door to Dean's condo. She walked down the path to the SUV and headed over to the passenger side. Chief was there to open the back door for Coco. The dog hopped up easily and settled on the seat.

Chief shut the door and opened Adeline's for her.

"Thanks."

"You're welcome."

He closed the door when she was all the way in and strode around the front.

Adeline took the time to examine him. He was good looking; all of Dean's friends were. But Chief had the whole silent, brooding, sexy-as-hell thing going on. His hair was as black as hers but longer. He'd worn it loose and Adeline could see it came down just below his shoulders. He usually had it back in a simple ponytail at the base of his neck.

Beth had wanted her to ask him if he ever wore it in a man-bun, but Adeline knew even without having to ask that there was no way in hell Roman "Chief" Proudfit *ever* put his hair up in anything resembling a man-bun. Even with that long hair, he was as masculine a man as she'd ever seen.

He wasn't overly muscular. He was lean and sleek. That didn't mean he didn't have muscles, he did, but they weren't bulging out of the edges of his T-shirt. His skin was light brown, as befitted his heritage, and his long nose and soulful eyes made his Native American ancestry easy to see.

All in all, Chief was hot and mysterious...which made him even hotter. Frankly, Adeline was surprised he wasn't already involved with a woman. The women he knew must either already be taken or incredibly stupid, because all it took was one glance and anyone could tell if this man focused on you, really focused, that you'd be the only thing on his mind. And boy was that a turn-on.

Adeline turned her head away as he sat in the driver's seat and turned the engine. They backed out and headed for the Interstate, all without a word.

She struggled for something to say. "So...how long have—"

"You don't have to make idle chit-chat," Chief broke in and said, not unkindly. "I'm sure Crash told you I'm not one for chatting. If you got work to do, go for it. If you wanna read, that's cool too. You can even take a nap. I won't *not* talk to you, but I don't got a lot to say."

Adeline tried to hold back her smile. She liked blunt speak. "Okay. I get that. If you honestly don't mind, there is some stuff I could be doing." She paused for a moment, then decided that if Chief could be blunt, so could she.

"Um…you're okay if I have a seizure, right? And I'm only asking because I've been having them more and more frequently, and unfortunately, I'm due. It's been almost eighteen hours since my last one and that's pushing it for me lately."

"I'm good, Adeline. Don't worry."

God, she loved how he said her name. He somehow made it four syllables instead of three.

"Okay. And just…I'll be out of it, and usually when it stops, I'm still disoriented. I have some water just in case, but if you could maybe help me get to it afterwards, that would be helpful."

"Sure."

"I apologize in advance, I—"

"Don't apologize," he interrupted. "It's not something you can control. Just relax. Work until you get tired. You can nap before and after if necessary. I'll get you up to Dallas safely."

"Great. Thanks. Seriously, Chief, you saved me from a fate worse than death in volunteering to drive me up there," she joked.

He smiled a bit at that, turning his head to meet her eyes for the first time. His black eyes piercing in their intensity. "Just because you're dating Crash doesn't mean the rest of us don't care about you. He's a brother, therefore you're family. I'm happy to save you from a fate worse than death."

Adeline chuckled. He was kinda funny under that serious exterior. "Well, I appreciate it. And I'm glad you had a thing you needed to do up there so you could take me today."

He didn't respond, and Adeline squinted her eyes at him when the corner of his mouth twitched up as if he was holding back a smile.

"You *did* have a thing, right?"

He shrugged and immediately admitted, "Nope."

"What? But Dean said you did. That's why you said you would drive me!" Adeline cried out in disbelief.

"Crash needed you to have a ride, I had some time I needed to use. It worked out."

"But—"

"Thought you had work to do," Chief interrupted.

"Well, shit," Adeline muttered. "Does Dean know?"

Chief's lip curled up before settling again. "He will as soon as you tell him."

"Yeah, he will. He should know how good of a friend he has in you," Adeline said firmly.

"As I said, he's my brother. He'd do the same for me."

Yeah, that was most likely true. "Well, I appreciate it. Doubly now."

"Good."

It was a strange conversation. Chief didn't waste words. He said what he meant and meant what he said. "All right, I'm going to get some work done then."

Chief merely nodded.

Taking a deep breath, and trying to push down the warm and fuzzy feeling she had in her chest—not just because Chief was doing her a huge favor, but because Dean meant enough for him to do it—she took out her laptop. She could work on the latest design for her client. If she got it finished, she could email it tonight at the hotel. That would be one more thing off her plate before resigning. She didn't look forward to telling her douche boss she was leaving the company, if she got the other job, but such was life.

FIVE AND A half hours later, Chief pulled up to the hotel in downtown Dallas and Adeline sighed in relief. It wasn't that the trip had been bad, but she *did* have a seizure, and it had been a rough one.

Right after Coco alerted, Chief pulled off on the first exit they'd come to. He'd parked alongside a random country road in the middle of nowhere and they'd waited. Adeline didn't remember any of it, but Chief informed her that he thought she'd had a complex partial seizure…meaning it had started out as usual, but had evolved into a generalized convulsive seizure.

In other words, she'd had a grand mal seizure, when she hadn't had one of those in months.

Adeline knew Chief wasn't an expert, but he did have medical training, and if he thought she'd had a grand mal, she probably had. It had been tough to come out of it. She felt extremely groggy and out of sorts, and wanted nothing more than to crawl into bed, Dean's bed, and have him hold her.

But she was in Dallas. At a conference. She had to pull it together.

"Stay put. I'll come around," Chief ordered as he turned off his engine. The valet took his keys, which confused Adeline, but she didn't say anything. He helped her out, then opened the back door and Coco jumped out. He tipped a bellman to take care of her luggage and with an arm around her waist, walked Adeline through the large doors to the grand entrance-way.

Adeline kept quiet as he led her to a couch covered in red velvet and sat her down. "I'll check in for you," Chief said sternly. "Sit here. Relax. I'll be back."

"Thanks, Chief. I appreciate it."

The man nodded, looked at her for a long moment, as if contemplating whether or not he should leave her, then turned on his heel and headed for the thankfully short line at the front counter.

He hadn't been gone more than two minutes when someone sat on the couch next to her.

"I see you made it," Douglas practically sneered. "I just got here myself. It was stupid for us not to come together. A waste of company money."

Adeline huffed out a frustrated breath. Dealing with her boss was the last thing she needed or wanted to do at the moment, especially when she wasn't feeling one hundred percent.

"Hey, Douglas. We talked about this. I'm not going to claim the mileage, so it's not a waste."

He waved her words away with his hand. "Fine. You want to go to dinner tonight?"

Adeline was shaking her head before he'd finished getting the words out. God, didn't the man *ever* give up? "I don't think so. I don't feel that great. I'm just going to go up to my room and probably order room service."

"You're going to the opening speeches, right? That *is* why you're here. If you're too sick to go then maybe you should've stayed home."

Adeline could feel her blood pressure rising. This was the last thing she needed. She tried to stay calm. "Of course I am. Listening to Bob Iger talk about how

Disney has upped their game in the marketing department is a speech that I wouldn't miss."

"Good. Because afterwards I'm taking James Wolfe to dinner, and he's asked that you accompany us as well. He was impressed with your ideas for the new ads for his car dealerships and wants to meet you, discuss the results, and talk about where he should go from here to capitalize on the success of the current campaign."

Well, fuck. So much for her quiet night. "Fine. Where should I meet you two?"

Adeline didn't like the smug look in her boss's eye, but was too tired and out of sorts to think about it at the moment.

"Opening speech is at six. So how about seven-thirty right here in the lobby?"

"That sounds good."

"Who are you?"

The extremely irritated voice came from above them. Adeline looked up to see Chief standing next to the couch with his arms crossed over his chest. He was *pissed*, and it was easy to see.

"Chief, this is my boss, Douglas Hill. Douglas, this is my friend, Chief."

"You're dating him?"

It was an odd response, but Adeline hurried to say, "No, he's not my boyfriend. He's just a friend."

Chief hadn't moved a muscle.

"Is he the one who brought you up here?" Douglas asked, sitting up straighter.

"Yes."

Douglas held out his hand. "Good to meet you…er…Chief. Thanks for bringing one of my best employees to the hotel safe and sound. Guess you'll be headed back now, huh?"

Chief didn't reach for Douglas's hand. Simply stood there stoically and stared at him as if he was beneath him.

Adeline said quickly, trying to brush over the awkwardness, "Everything all set, Chief?"

He looked at her then and held out a hand. "Yeah, you're all checked in."

Adeline placed her hand in Chief's and let him pull her to her feet. She stumbled but caught herself. Even so, Chief put his arm around her waist to steady her.

Douglas's eyes narrowed at them as he stood, as if he was trying to figure out the exact nature of their relationship. "I guess I'll see you later then. I'll text if plans change."

"Thanks," Adeline told him absently, reaching down for Coco's leash.

Chief turned her and walked away from Douglas without another word, leading her toward the elevator. When they were well away from her boss, Adeline said softly, putting her free hand over Chief's at her waist,

"Thanks for checking me in. I appreciate it."

"He doesn't know about Crash?"

Figured Chief would pick up on that. She sighed, then said, "If he does, I didn't tell him. I like to keep my work life completely separate from my personal life. I haven't told Douglas, or just about any of my coworkers, about Dean. There's no reason for them to know anyway. It's not a big deal."

"You have plans with that asshole later?"

Adeline huffed out an exasperated breath. It looked like Dean hung out with men who were a lot like him. "Yes. But not like you're thinking. We're having dinner with a client. An important one, otherwise I'd blow it off."

"You tell Crash?"

Adeline shook her head as the bell over the elevator rang, indicating the car was there. Chief led her in and she said, "When have I had the time? Besides, he's at work. I'm gonna see him tomorrow. I'll tell Dean all about how I impressed the socks off the client at dinner when he gets here."

Chief's eyes narrowed as the elevator doors closed. "Think you better call him now."

"Look, Chief, Dean's not the boss of me. I am fully aware that he doesn't like Douglas. That doesn't negate the fact that I'm still his employee. I've got clients I need to assist and one of those is James Wolfe. Just because

I'm not thrilled that I have to have dinner with my boss doesn't mean I can skirt my duties. I'm here for my job. That means I need to actually *do* my job. No matter how much my boyfriend might not like it. Or his high-handed, closed-mouthed friend."

Chief chuckled low in his throat, and Adeline stared up at him in surprise. It wasn't exactly the response she thought she'd get. The smile and laugh looked good on him. Made him seem much more approachable and soft. He obviously didn't do it often, and Adeline couldn't help but hope some lucky woman would be able to make him laugh on a more regular basis.

"Right. But if I was your man, I wouldn't be happy to learn a day after the fact that my woman was breaking bread with a man who she disliked, didn't trust, and was even a bit scared of."

"What? I'm not scared of Douglas," Adeline protested. "Why would you say that?"

"When he sat next to you, you flinched and leaned away from him, pretending to pet Coco. You never looked into his eyes once, showing you don't trust him, and your body language screamed discomfort. It doesn't take a genius to see he's the last person you want to go to dinner with, sister."

The sister thing threw her, but Adeline ignored it for the moment as she had more important things to say. "You're right..." The elevator bell dinged to indicate they'd reached their floor, and Chief pressed against her back lightly to encourage her to exit.

As they walked down the hall to her room, Adeline continued, "I don't particularly like Douglas, but I'm not scared of him. We're in a public place. He's my boss. I've seen him every week at work since he was hired. It's not that I don't trust him, but it's not that I *do* trust him either. And it doesn't matter, it's just dinner."

"How many times has he asked you out before now?" Chief asked knowingly.

Damn. He'd obviously talked to Dean about this. "Only once, the first time. All the other times he asked because of work stuff."

"And how many times did you go?" Chief pressed.

"Well, none. We could get what we needed to get done at work."

"Right, so now you're away from home base. On your own, after hours. And he uses a client as an excuse to get you to go to dinner with him."

Adeline sighed and shut her eyes momentarily as they stood in front of her hotel room. She turned to Chief. "Look. I don't want to go out with him, but I kinda feel like I have to. I don't want to tell Dean now because he'll react the same way you are and I don't really have a choice. So in order to cause me less stress, I'll tell him tomorrow when he gets here and deal with his pissed-off reaction then. Okay?"

"Okay," Chief agreed, surprising the hell out of Adeline.

"Okay?"

"Yes."

Chief pushed the electronic key card into the slot in the door and opened it. Adeline stepped inside and Chief put his hand on her back and encouraged her to walk through the little sitting room to the bedroom in the back of the suite.

"Sleep," he ordered.

"I need to be up in an hour and a half to get ready for the opening speech," Adeline halfheartedly protested. She could totally use a nap. She was wiped.

"I'll make sure you're up," Chief told her calmly.

That made Adeline's head whip up. "What? You're driving back now."

"Nope. Plans changed. I'm going to dinner with you and your boss tonight." He said it with a completely straight face. No emotion, but in a flat way that encouraged no discussion.

Adeline eyed Chief for a moment. She wanted to protest, but tamped down the words. She licked her lips, then nodded. "All right. I probably should protest some more, but honestly, it actually makes me feel better. Although I feel like I'm taking advantage of you. Maybe it's because I'm still off from the seizure. Maybe it's because I feel like if I protested it wouldn't do any good anyway. But regardless, thank you, Chief. It would make me feel more comfortable if you were there tonight."

The relief in his eyes was easy to read. He was glad she hadn't balked. "Sleep," Chief repeated.

"An hour and a half," Adeline warned. "No longer. I mean it."

Chief's lips quirked once more, but never fully formed a smile. "Hour and a half. Got it."

Adeline shook her head and rolled her eyes, but wandered into the bedroom. She patted the bed, not caring if Coco left dog hairs on it for once, then curled onto her side and sighed. It felt good to lie down.

"Chief?" she called out, not moving.

"Yes, sister?"

There was that sister thing again. "Can you please crank down the air? Around sixty-six, sixty-seven if it'll go."

Not even a second passed before he called back, "Already done. Crash told me you preferred the cold."

"Thank you."

Chief didn't respond. Adeline smiled again. The man might not say much, but he sure was aware of everything around him.

She closed her eyes. All she needed was a nap and she'd be rarin' to go.

THREE AND A half hours later, Adeline was back in her hotel room, watching a pissed-off Chief pace back and forth in the small sitting room.

He'd woken her up after exactly an hour and a half of sleep. He'd gone downstairs with her and Coco and had stood with her while she registered for the conference. After learning he wouldn't be allowed into the opening speech without a registration badge, he'd bought a one-day pass for the conference without blinking.

He'd accompanied her to the speech by the CEO of Disney, then walked with her to meet Douglas and James Wolfe in the lobby.

But James hadn't been there. It was only Douglas.

Her boss claimed that the man couldn't make dinner after all, but since they had reservations, they could still go and discuss his account.

Chief hadn't said a word, but had taken her elbow and led her straight back to the elevators, with Douglas walking alongside.

"Come on, Adeline," her boss cajoled in an annoying, high-pitched tone. "We need to talk about Wolfe's campaign. You're starting to piss me off. This is very unprofessional behavior. You need to go to dinner with me now."

Chief had turned then, making sure he was between

Adeline and her boss, and taken a step toward Douglas. He'd stepped back. Chief took another step toward him and Douglas once again took a step back. They continued like this until Douglas's back was against the wall.

Chief leaned into him and, with his fists clenched at his side and words coming out clipped and flat, said, "She doesn't have to do anything with you and *she* isn't the one acting unprofessionally. She doesn't want to go to dinner with you. She doesn't want anything to do with you. You might be her boss, but you can't force her to do one damn thing she doesn't want to do. I suggest you back off, figure out where the fuck you left your professionalism, and pick it back up. Now."

It was the most Adeline had ever heard Chief say at one time. And. It. Was. Awesome. She wished she'd gotten it on video. Beth would've loved to have seen it.

They left Douglas standing against the wall, glaring at them, as they entered an elevator.

Now Chief was pacing her room, pissed.

Deciding to leave him alone and not try to make him talk, Adeline went into the bedroom and closed the door. She put on a pair of sweats and a sweatshirt—it was chilly in the room, after all—and then went back out into the sitting room to deal with Chief.

He was on the phone. Shit.

"I'm staying the night, brother," Chief was saying. Adeline knew who he was talking to. Double shit.

"Asshole tried to trick her into going to dinner. Said a client would be there when it was more than obvious he'd lied. When she tried to leave, he said some shit."

Adeline didn't like the way the conversation was going. "Let me talk to him, Chief," she ordered, holding out her hand for the phone.

Chief ignored her. "Yeah. I shut it down. But I don't want to leave her. Not after today."

Dammit. He wouldn't…

"Yeah, she seized. Bad. Grand mal."

Fuck. Fuck. Fuck.

"Yeah. Twenty minutes or so. She's still not herself. Groggy, not quite steady on her feet, and she's pale."

"Chief, give me the phone," Adeline demanded again, taking a step closer to him.

He looked her in the eyes, but continued talking to Dean. "Of course. I'll stick with her until you get here."

Adeline rolled her eyes and shook her head. She stepped right up to Chief and grabbed the phone. She knew the only reason he let her pull it away from him was because he was done talking to Dean, but she didn't care. She was pissed.

Turning her back on Chief and putting the phone to her ear, she didn't wait for Dean to say anything, but spat, "I'm fine. I'm a fucking adult and can take care of myself. I don't need you or your *brother* to babysit me."

"That asshole doesn't get to fuck with you when

you're five hours away from me and don't have me at your back." Dean sounded just as pissed off as she was.

"No, he doesn't get to fuck with me any time. Not just when I'm here and you're there. You don't have anything to do with this, Dean. This is my work. My job. You can't be all protectorly and shit when it comes to what I do for a living. Do you see me storming into the fire station and the fire chief's office demanding that you work less hours because I'm worried you'll get hurt? No. I trust you to do your thing and you need to trust me to do mine."

"It's not the same, beautiful," he bit out.

"The hell it's not," Adeline retorted. "It's exactly the same."

"You had a grand mal, Adeline," Dean said, his tone slightly less acidic.

"Yeah, I did. And you know what? I've had them long before you were in my life, and I'm still here walking and talking. I admit, I feel like shit. But I'm so used to it, it doesn't even make a blip anymore. I do what I have to do because it's *what I have to do*. People are out there living and working with more pain and feeling worse than I do."

"You don't need to deal with his shit on top of that," Dean tried again, his voice less pissed off and more tender, but Adeline didn't even notice.

She was on a roll. She was pissed. At the situation.

At her continued seizures. Upset that she was in Dallas instead of at home. Angry at Douglas. Pissed at Chief for calling Dean and blabbing about all the shit she was angry at.

"I do need to deal with this shit because it's my *life*," she screeched. "If *you* can't deal with it, fine. But do *not* decide what I can and can't do."

"Chief is staying."

"*God*," Adeline huffed angrily. "You know what? I don't care. He can make a pallet and sleep on the floor and feel like he's protecting me. But don't bother coming up here to Dallas, Dean. I'll deal with this like I have every other time in my life—by myself. I don't need you fighting my battles for me and I don't need you getting me fired." Her voice lowered and she said, "I *need* this job, at least until I officially get another. I like what I do. Don't fuck this up for me."

"Go to bed, beautiful. We'll talk later," Dean said, his voice flat and emotionless now.

"Whatever. I mean it, Dean. Don't come up here tomorrow. I'll be furious if you do. We can talk when I get home. I'll be less upset then."

He didn't respond and Adeline shook her head in defeat. She didn't even bother saying goodbye, merely took the phone away from her ear and clicked it off. She threw the phone on the nearby table and looked at Chief.

"Thank you for driving me up here but you'd better be gone when I get up in the morning. I mean it. You were out of line for calling Dean when you knew full well I didn't want him knowing anything about this shit."

Without waiting for him to respond, Adeline stomped to the bedroom and slammed the door. Putting her back against it, she slid down until her butt hit the floor. She curled her arms around her legs, put her head on her knees and cried.

Damn!

You were so close!

If that asshole wasn't here, she would've been yours.

His fists clenched and he paced the small sitting area in his hotel room. Back and forth he went. Five steps in one direction, then a quick turn and five steps back the way he came. Over and over he paced, thinking through what he knew about her and how he could get to her.

She didn't want to eat with you, so she'll pay for that.

She won't smile at you anymore? She'll pay for that.

She thinks her boyfriends are better than you? She'll pay for that.

Fucking cunt will pay.

But not before you get what you wanted all along.

You deserve it. You were so nice to her.

You would've worshiped her.

But now she'll deal with the consequences for not seeing how perfect you were for her.

An evil smile spread over his face as he imagined her look of terror when she realized her fate. Nothing would stop him now. Nothing.

Chapter Eighteen

———————— ◆ ————————

THE NEXT MORNING when Adeline's alarm went off, she lay in bed for a long moment. Her face felt swollen and puffy from all the crying she'd done and she knew her eyes would be red as well. She listened, but didn't hear any movement from the other room.

The conference sessions started at eight-thirty and she needed to get up and start getting ready, but took another moment to think about the night before. She'd said some mean things to Chief, and was ashamed of herself. Even though she was upset, her words weren't cool. At all. She'd apologize to him straight off.

Thinking about it, she was very grateful Chief been there last night when she'd met Douglas for dinner. If he hadn't been, she most likely would've gone ahead and dined with him even though she didn't want to. Confrontation wasn't really her thing, last night with Dean notwithstanding, and in order to make her life easier, she would've just agreed and had dinner with Douglas. He'd been asking her out for ages and she probably should've seen through his ploy. She probably needed to thank Chief for that too.

But she also needed him to know how fucked up it was for him to go behind her back and call Dean and blab about it. Even though she would've told Dean what happened, she'd felt like crap last night and the stress of dealing with her boss and that uncomfortable situation, paired with the fact she was starving because she never did get to eat dinner, and the fact she'd had a grand mal seizure for the first time in a long while, made her want to just take a few hours and process everything…and relax.

So much for that.

Being treated like she was eight-years-old had brought back too many memories of the way her family had treated her when she'd been growing up. Fragile. Like she was a ticking time bomb that could go off any second.

Chief had taken the independence she'd clawed and fought for out of her hands, and it had hurt. She didn't need her hand held or to be tattled on to her boyfriend. No matter how helpless Dean or Chief thought she was.

But when she thought of how she'd spoken to Dean, she knew she probably needed to apologize to him too. She knew he was protective. It wasn't a surprise. In fact, it was just one of the things she loved about him. She also knew how much he really didn't like her boss. So hearing from Chief that the man had tried to trick her into going on a date with him definitely hadn't sat well with Dean.

If the shoe had been on the other foot, and Dean had a chick constantly asking him out and then trying to trick him into going to dinner with her, Adeline knew she'd be just as upset.

She sighed. She'd screwed up and would definitely be apologizing to Dean. She wasn't sorry for telling him how she felt, she was sorry for *how* she'd done it. As much as she liked his protective and bossy side, he needed to know that he'd made her feel stupid and helpless last night. He needed to check that in the future.

Petting Coco's head once, Adeline threw her legs over the side of the bed and sat up. She swayed dizzily for a moment before getting her bearings. She really needed to eat something. She stood up and made her way to the door of the bedroom and opened it.

Peering into the sitting room, Adeline looked around, surprised Chief had actually listened to her. He wasn't there. In fact, there was no sign he'd *ever* been there. No sheets or blankets folded up after being used, no trash lying on the tables, no used cups…nothing.

There *was,* however, a note propped up next to the little sink.

I put a water in the fridge last night, so it would be

cold by morning. I also ordered room service for you, figuring you'd be hungry since you skipped dinner. It'll be here around seven-thirty.

And that was it. Well, shit. Chief had apparently stayed the night, and it was extremely thoughtful of him to get a water chilled for her *and* to order breakfast. Of course, he'd probably done it so she wouldn't have to go downstairs and talk to Douglas, but at the moment it didn't matter. She was starving and the mere thought of food made her stomach growl. Adeline didn't know where Chief was or if he'd be back to eat with her, but figured either way, he'd do what he wanted to do regardless of her feelings about it.

Unfortunately, as much as she might want to hide out in her room until she absolutely had to go to the first meeting of the conference and possibly run into Douglas, she needed to go downstairs anyway. Coco had to do his business. Adeline was already wearing sweat-pants and a T-shirt, so she threw a sweatshirt over her shirt, slipped her feet into flip flops, and picked up Coco's leash.

She didn't bother with his harness, but did strap on his vest. The last thing she wanted was someone questioning why she had a dog in the hotel when the property didn't allow pets. She definitely didn't need that hassle this morning on top of everything else she knew she had to deal with.

The hallway was deserted and the elevator was empty when it finally arrived on her floor. Grateful for not having to be courteous to anyone this early in the morning, and knowing she probably should've at least run a brush through her hair so she didn't look like a crazy escaped mental patient, Adeline walked swiftly away from the lobby and the front doors to a side door.

The service dog relief area was located away from the high traffic area of the front of the hotel. There was a small but functional grassy area especially for animals to use. The hotel had supplied a small trash can with a stand that held plastic baggies. As a responsible pet owner, she had some bags in Coco's vest already, but it was nice to have a hotel smart enough to provide some for those people who might not be as prepared as she was.

Thankfully, Coco did his thing relatively quickly, as usual, and they were on their way back upstairs within minutes. Adeline kept her head down and didn't look around as she made her way back to the elevator bank.

Glancing at her watch, she saw she had just enough time to get back up to her room and take a shower before the room service should arrive. Perfect. She had no idea what Chief had ordered for her, but at this point it didn't matter. She was so hungry; she'd eat whatever was delivered.

The arrow above one of the elevators lit up as a bell

rang, and Adeline stepped inside and pushed the button for her floor. Just as the doors were shutting, a hand reached between the doors, stopping them from closing, and they reopened.

Douglas.

The absolute last person she wanted to see this morning.

Especially when she wasn't wearing her work clothes or any makeup.

He stepped inside the small space, crossed his arms over his chest, and glared at Adeline. His back was to the doors and he stood with his feet shoulder width apart. He looked rough. He hadn't shaved and the stubble on his face, along with the frown and the ice shooting from his eyes, made him actually look a bit scary.

She'd been nervous around her boss in the past, and had thought he was acting extremely weird, but she honestly hadn't ever been frightened of him...until right that moment.

Adeline backed up until she hit the wall of the elevator and stared at her boss. Coco growled low in his throat and she risked a glance down at her dog. The hair on his back was standing straight up, and she'd never once seen him act as aggressively as he was right then. Coco wasn't a guard dog; he was a floppy, happy-go-lucky Lab. The most he'd do to someone was lick them to death. But Coco was definitely not happy with Douglas. Not that she could blame her dog; she wasn't either.

"Good morning, Douglas," Adeline said nervously, trying to break the tension.

"Is it, Adeline? Is it really?"

She swallowed hard and tried again. "I'm sorry about last night. I wasn't feeling well and my friend can get too protective."

He brought his hands up and put air quotes around his words. "Your 'friend,'"—he dropped his hands—"is a prick. This isn't a vacation, Adeline. Bringing him up here and trying to pass him off as merely a friend isn't professional. You're here to work, not fuck on the company's dime."

Adeline's eyes widened in shock. "Douglas, Chief is *not* my boyfriend. Honestly, he's just a friend."

A bell rang, announcing that they'd reached her floor. Douglas took a step out and put his back to the elevator doors and held out his arm, inviting her to precede him out of the small space.

Swallowing hard, Adeline shuffled forward, keeping Coco on her left side, away from Douglas. He followed her out of the small space and the elevator doors closed behind them. Walking swiftly, wanting nothing more than to get to her room and away from Douglas, Adeline headed down the hall. She had her key in her hand, ready to put it into the slot as soon as she arrived at her door.

"Seriously, Douglas. Chief is just a friend. Yes, I do have a boyfriend, but he's not here. I admit that he was going to come up and spend a few nights here with me, but something came up last night and he's not anymore. I didn't realize it was frowned upon, but I would never take advantage of company funds that way. So you don't have anything to worry about." She wanted to tell Douglas how offended she was that he assumed she would shirk her work duties and eschew the conference to spend time with Dean, but she decided he was way too angry to listen to her at the moment.

She stopped in front of her door and nervously turned to face her boss. The man hadn't said anything as they'd made their way down the hall. "I need to get ready for the first sessions of the day. I'll talk to you later…okay?"

"No, not okay. We're going to talk now," Douglas stated in a flat, even voice. He grabbed the key from Adeline's hand and pushed it into the lock.

"What are you—"

He didn't let her finish her thought. He put his hand on her throat and manhandled her through the now open door into the small sitting area of her hotel suite.

The door slammed behind them, but Adeline barely

heard it. Both hands came up to Douglas's hand at her throat and tried unsuccessfully to pry it off.

She heard her breaths wheezing as Douglas continued to back her into the room. Looking up at the twisted scowl on his face, Adeline realized for the first time that she was in big trouble.

She should've paid more attention to all those times when she'd felt uneasy around her boss. Should've taken Dean's advice and reported him. Should never have gotten into the elevator with him.

She hadn't thought for one second that Douglas would force his way into her room. She thought he'd bluster and bitch at her, then leave her to get ready.

Coco, sensing the danger his mistress was in, began to bark. Deep, menacing barks.

"Shut him up—or I'll do it," Douglas bit out, a knife appearing in his free hand as if by magic. He eased the pressure off her throat, but didn't let go.

Adeline's head spun, both with lack of oxygen and the realization that she'd ignored the warning signs of Douglas being unstable all along. He probably *had* followed her home. He had been lying in wait for her when she left her office. She'd been an idiot, and was paying the price for not wanting to rock the boat before she quit.

"Coco. Quiet," Adeline ordered immediately in a raspy voice, not wanting anything to happen to her dog.

He wasn't just her service animal; he was her best friend.

Luckily the well-trained dog stopped barking, but he growled low in his throat, following along behind Adeline and Douglas.

"Put him in the bathroom and tell him he better stay quiet. I'm not kidding. I'll gut him if he barks."

Adeline believed him. The man standing in front of her squeezing her throat, was nothing like the man she'd gotten to know over the last few months. She'd never really liked Douglas, but truly hadn't believed he'd ever lose it like he had.

She nodded slightly, her movement restricted by his grip, and pointed into the small bathroom. "Coco, enter. Stay. Quiet."

The dog wasn't happy, but did as Adeline ordered, still growling.

Douglas shut the bathroom door with a click and pushed Adeline into the bedroom, closing that door behind him as well.

Adeline's eyes were wide with fright and she held onto Douglas's arm to help keep her balance as he continued to shove her backward. This wasn't good. This so wasn't good. She tried to think fast. What could she say to defuse this situation before it got worse?

"D-Douglas," Adeline stammered, not sure what was about to come out of her mouth, but she didn't have to worry. Her boss didn't give her a chance to say anything more.

The back of her knees hit the bed and she sat down hard, Douglas following her, pushing her until she lay on her back on the mussed bedding, her boss hovering over her, his fingers still wrapped around her throat.

"You *knew* I had my eye on you, Adeline. For months I courted you. I went slow because you seemed to be shy. I didn't want to push too hard. You're so beautiful, with your jet-black hair and big innocent eyes. Knowing you had some sort of mysterious handicap made you all the more fragile. I wanted to protect you. To wrap you up in my arms and keep you safe. When you gave me those wonderful ideas to share with James Wolfe, I thought you were giving me a sign. That you wanted me too.

"I thought you were just being coy. That you wanted me to chase you. So I did. Time after time I asked you out, and thought it cute when you kept refusing. I was enjoying the chase. But then you changed. You started to get a mean look in your eye. I knew something had happened. Something awful. I was worried about you, but you weren't talking to me."

Adeline looked up at her boss in horror. He thought she was being coy? The hand at her throat tightened and she dug her fingernails into his fingers, trying to pry them loose. She wheezed in a breath, then another. She started seeing spots in front of her eyes as he continued to squeeze off her air supply.

"I followed you home one night," Douglas continued, his eyes boring into hers, hate flashing in the brown depths. "I watched you through your window as you talked to someone on the phone for over an hour. I saw how you laughed, smiled, and flirted with whoever was on the other end of the line. I knew it was another man. You hurt me, Adeline. You cheated on me!"

Just when Adeline knew she was going to pass out, Douglas loosened his grip, allowing beautiful air to get into her lungs.

She gasped for air and kicked weakly with her legs, trying to dislodge the large man on top of her.

He laughed, a maniacal sound that was the most frightening thing Adeline had ever heard. He lifted her as if she was a rag doll until her entire body was lying crosswise on the large mattress. He removed his grip from her throat for a moment, and swiftly sliced through the entire front of her sweatshirt, from the neckline all the way down to the hem. It fell open easily, leaving her in the Station 7 T-shirt she'd filched from Dean's drawer one morning.

Douglas's hand came back to her throat and he sneered down at her. "I could've overlooked you dating that fireman. I've been watching you ever since that first night, waiting. I assumed you'd get sick of him soon enough and you'd then turn to me." He ran the flat side of the knife up from her belly, over the tip of one breast to her cheek, the cold metal sliding up and down her face as he caressed her with it. The murderous look in his eye said he was contemplating what it might look like if he used the sharp blade instead.

His voice was almost calm as he continued his delusional speech. "I was ready to give you everything, Adeline. We were going to have beautiful babies. We'd run the company together. We had the world at our feet. Then yesterday I find out that not only are you dating someone else, who you should've kicked to the curb for me, you've been fucking an Indian too." He laughed then, another one of the kind that scared the shit out of her.

"A fucking *Indian*. I might've been able to handle it better if you'd chosen someone who looked like me to get off with, but no, you had to go and screw around with men so inappropriate and beneath you, it isn't even funny. To lower yourself enough to allow their filthy bodies inside your own. You defiled what was mine! You have to pay for that. If I can't have you, no one can."

If he'd been yelling, or otherwise showing anything other than the cold, remote calmness, Adeline thought she might have been able to do something to get through to him. But he knew exactly what he was doing. The fact that he'd been following her, had known all along she was dating Dean, but continued to ask her out anyway, was horrifying. How had she not known she was being followed?

She vaguely heard Coco scratching frantically at the bathroom door, but soon even that faded away as Douglas flipped the knife over and held it at her throat, the sharp tip pricking the sensitive skin there. Adeline raised her chin, trying to get away from the blade, but he tightened the pressure on her windpipe. Once more cutting off her air supply.

Adeline fought for her life now, no longer willing to lie passively underneath Douglas as he killed her. And she had no doubt that he was going to kill her.

She kicked her legs, her head tilted back, trying to keep the knife from sinking into her flesh, but couldn't get his weight off her. But as soon as she made the attempt, she stilled. Thrashing under him wasn't going to do anything but make the knife cut her.

Fighting the urge to try to peel his hand away from her throat, knowing it wouldn't work, she tried to thrust her fingers into his eyes, but he merely laughed as he moved his head up and away from her, and squeezed harder.

Gasping for air, feeling the nicks from the blade he was holding, Adeline looked up into Douglas's cold, dead eyes in despair.

"When you pass out from lack of air, I'm gonna cut off the rest of your clothes to see what should've been mine. To see the tits you've let *them* suck on. I'll open the legs you so easily spread for them when it should've been *me* you welcomed between them. I'm gonna wait until you regain consciousness, then I'll show you the pain you've dealt me. I'm gonna fuck you, Adeline. I would've made it so good for you, but I realize now you're nothing but a whore." His lip curled as he continued.

"You're a slut who spreads her legs for a fucking fireman and his filthy friends. Once I'm done with you, I'm gonna stick my knife so far up inside you, you'll feel it in your throat. No one will ever fuck you again, Adeline. You should've been mine, and I'll make sure I'm the last man you'll ever feel between your legs. And after I'm done, I'm gonna kill your dog, then I'm going to find those boyfriends of yours and cut them up too."

Adeline's eyes bulged out as she stared at Douglas in horror.

This was it. Maybe he'd stop before she actually died, maybe he wouldn't. But weirdly, the only thing she could think about was Dean. How she'd stupidly yelled at him the night before merely for being concerned about her. She'd lamented not having someone around who cared about her, and when she did have that person in her life, she'd treated him like crap. She regretted everything she'd said to him last night, even more so now. Every word.

She loved Dean. Loved him—and she'd never get a chance to tell him again.

Black began to creep around the edges of her vision again as Douglas continued to squeeze her throat.

"Please," she whispered. The word barely a breath of sound. "Don't."

Douglas brought his face close to hers, even as he continued cutting off her air. "I like hearing you beg, Adeline. I can't wait to hear you plead for your life. You'll beg me to fuck you before I'm done. Just like you should've been doing for the last few months."

The last thing Adeline remembered was the evil look in Douglas's eyes as she lost consciousness.

CRASH MET WITH Chief outside the front doors of the hotel and shook his hand.

"Thanks for staying, man, I appreciate it."

"There's no way I was gonna leave her alone after that shit went down last night, brother," Chief told his friend.

"She still sleeping?" Crash asked.

Chief nodded. "Was when I left, but I saw her out with Coco a few minutes ago."

"She didn't have a seizure last night?"

Chief shook his head. "No, I checked on her a few times and she was sleeping soundly. Didn't even stir when I opened the door."

"Good. She hasn't had a grand mal in months. I'm worried about the escalation of frequency of her seizures and the fact that she had a big one yesterday."

"Don't take what she said to heart, Crash. She wasn't herself. Not even close," Chief warned.

"I know. I should've taken more care when I spoke to her last night but I was pissed at her asshole of a boss. Not her. There was no way I was going to leave things the way they were, and no way I wasn't getting my ass up here to take care of her."

"The fire chief didn't have a problem in letting you bug out early?" Chief asked.

"Nope. It was a slow night, and one of the other guys agreed to come in early for his shift. I got a few hours of shut-eye then headed out."

Chief handed over a key card. "She's in seven-nineteen. I ordered room service. Should be delivered in half an hour or so."

Crash took the plastic card from his friend. "Thanks. I owe you one. Any time, any place. Name it and I'm there."

Chief shook his head. "You'd do the same for me. I didn't do this for a marker."

"I know. But you got one anyway."

Chief stared hard at Crash, but didn't say anything else about it. "Go on. I'll see you guys when you get home."

Crash shook the other man's hand. "Thanks again. I'll let you know when we're on the way home."

Chief nodded, then turned and headed for the valet stand.

Without wasting another moment, wanting to see Adeline, clear the air, and make sure she was all right after the day before, Crash strode toward the bank of elevators with his duffle bag thrown over his shoulder.

Within moments, he was on the seventh floor—and seconds after that he was running down the hall as fast as he could.

He could hear Coco growling from all the way down by the elevator. Something was terribly wrong.

It took Crash two tries to get the key to work but the lock mechanism finally clicked and he shoved the door open. His blood chilled at the desperate sounds coming out of the dog locked in the bathroom.

Crash dropped his bag and raced to the door of the bedroom, wrenched it open, and saw red.

A man was on the bed, hovering over Adeline, who wasn't moving under him. Her shirt had been cut open and she was bare from the waist up. The man had a knife and was in the middle of slicing her sweatpants open from her foot to her waist.

They both paused for a fraction of a second.

Crash growled, "You son of a bitch!" and stepped

toward the bed.

Moving quickly, the man slid the knife from Adeline's knee to her throat in the blink of an eye. "Take one more step and I'll slit her throat."

Crash stopped immediately, putting his hands up in the air in capitulation. This was a man on the edge, the stubble, wrinkled clothes, and crazed look in his eyes making it obvious he'd do just as he threatened. Crash couldn't do anything that would make the situation worse. Not when it came to Adeline's life.

He had a pretty good idea who the man was. There really was only one person it *could* be. All the things Adeline had told him about her boss over the last couple of months took on a whole new meaning now.

"Douglas Hill, I presume," Crash said in a low, controlled voice, trying not to escalate the situation.

"Oh no, you had your chance with her. It's *my* turn now!" the crazed man spat.

"Did something happen this morning?" Crash asked.

"Yeah. Something happened this morning. This bitch has been leading me on for months. Teasing me. Getting me all worked up, then playing coy and backing off. She's been playing hard to get, and this morning she decided she wanted me after all."

It was ridiculous, because there was no way the unconscious woman lying on the bed, with blood dripping from nicks on her throat and her clothes cut from her body, was there willingly.

"Okay, I didn't realize that's what this was," Crash commented, his mind racing as to what his next move should be. He should've sent Chief a message before entering the room, but there was no way he would've stopped for the several seconds it would've taken, not when Adeline needed him.

The choice of what his next step should be was taken from him when Coco finally clawed his way out of the bathroom and sprang out of the small room, barking frantically.

"Dammit!" Douglas spat, flinching at the loud sounds coming from the dog, his movement cutting another small line in Adeline's vulnerable throat.

Crash thought the dog would come barreling into the bedroom where he and Adeline were, but instead, Coco made a beeline for the door to the suite, held open by Crash's dropped duffle bag, and out into the hall.

Crash realized Coco had done the one thing that would help end this standoff sooner rather than later—making enough noise to wake the dead as he ran up and down the hallway. Someone would call the front desk and complain, sending security up to investigate.

"It looks like you're going to have to wait," Crash noted dryly. "Put down the knife and we'll figure this out."

The second Douglas turned his attention back down to Adeline, and away from him, Crash moved.

He threw himself forward, aiming his hands for the wrist holding the knife to Adeline's throat first. He hit Douglas and both men rolled, the knife lost somewhere in the sheets on the bed. Crash had thirty or so pounds on the other man, but Douglas had rage and insanity on his side.

The two men rolled over a few times and Douglas locked his hands around Crash's throat, but by doing so, left his own body vulnerable.

Choking might have worked on the smaller and weaker Adeline, leaving her unable to defend herself, but it had little to no effect on Crash, except to give him the opportunity to defeat Douglas once and for all.

Crash jabbed his fingers into Douglas's eyes, and when the man roared in pain and sat up, Crash punched him as hard as he could between the legs. It might've been a low blow, literally, but Crash didn't give a shit.

After the punch, Douglas rolled off Crash, clutching his balls in his hand, and it was only a matter of a few more well-placed hits to make the other man fall unconscious on the floor, with blood pouring out of his broken nose and cracked lips.

Crash scrambled off the floor and onto the bed next to Adeline. Ignoring the fact that she was bare from the waist up, he put his fingers on her throat, feeling for a pulse. It was there, and fairly strong. He breathed out a relieved sigh then continued his assessment of her body.

There were clear red marks in the shape of Douglas's fingers on her throat, which made Crash want to beat the man lying on the floor all over again. He brushed a lock of her jet-black hair away from her face, bent down and kissed the tip of her nose. "Come on, beautiful. Open your eyes for me. You're safe. He won't hurt you again."

He pulled back and brought the edges of her shirt over her chest, covering her.

"What in the hell is going on in here?" a hard voice said from the doorway.

Crash had been so focused on Adeline, he hadn't realized security had finally shown up. Coco had done exactly what he'd set out to do: get help for his mistress.

Crash turned slowly, making sure his hands were visible at all times, and spoke to the two men standing in the doorway, their hands on the Tasers attached to their belts. "My name is Dean Christopherson. This is my girlfriend, Adeline Reynolds. This is our room; you'll find both our names on the registration." Thank God she'd insisted on adding his name. "I entered our room this morning to find this man,"—he used his head to indicate the unconscious Douglas—"on top of her with a knife to her throat. It looks like he choked her, and was in the process of cutting off her clothes. We fought, I disabled him."

"Holy fuck," the second man stated unprofessionally, reaching for his walkie-talkie to call for backup.

"She needs to go to the hospital," Crash stated unnecessarily.

"That her dog raising bloody hell out in the hallway?" the first security guard asked.

"Yes. His name is Coco. He's her service dog. He was locked in the bathroom and when he got out, he ran out of the room to raise the alarm."

"He did a good job," the man answered dryly. "Will he respond to you? We couldn't get near him. Now that we've got the situation under control, maybe you'll see if you can't get him to calm down."

"I'm not leaving her," Crash stated adamantly.

Just then, Coco stopped barking. The cessation of sound was almost alarming.

Torn between wanting to make sure the dog was all right and not leaving Adeline, Crash looked apprehensively at the door.

After a few tense moments, Chief appeared, holding Coco's leash. Crash let out a sigh of relief. "Thank God," he stated.

"What the fuck?" Chief barked, not intimidated in the least by the two hotel security officers. "I had a bad feeling and thought I'd come up to make sure you both were all right before I headed back to San Antonio."

Taking another step into the room, and finally seeing Douglas's bleeding body, Chief's face turned to stone and he took a few steps inside the room, his eyes not leaving the unconscious man on the floor.

"Sir?" one of the security officers said hesitantly. "If you would please stay back until the situation is under control."

Chief's gaze went from Douglas to Adeline, and his face hardened further. "Motherfucker. I'm an idiot. He was watching her. It's no coincidence that he got to her in the twenty minutes I left her side."

Crash agreed, but didn't comment. He slowly lowered his hands.

"Sir?" the officer said again. "You need to step back and wait in the hall."

Then, if possible, the situation got worse.

Coco sat at Chief's feet and started pawing his leg—alerting him to the fact that Adeline was going to have a seizure.

Chapter Nineteen

ADELINE WOKE UP slowly. She hurt. Her neck. Her arms. Her shoulders. And she had no idea where she was or what had happened. She smelled antiseptic and there was an incessant beeping that was annoying because it wasn't stopping.

Feeling as tired as if she'd stayed up all night, Adeline kept her eyes shut, trying to work through where she was and why she felt so off. After only a moment, she remembered.

The conference.

Douglas.

Not being able to breathe.

And his threats on what he'd do to her when she woke up.

Her eyes popped open and she flinched at the bright light. Without thinking about anything other than getting away, Adeline rolled as hard as she could to her left—and ran into some sort of metal bars.

"No!" she croaked, not recognizing her own voice.

Sitting up, she scrambled to get her legs free from the confining blanket covering them and tried to scoot downward to exit the bed that way.

"Jesus, Adeline! Stop! You're safe! I'm here."

She paused and whipped her head to the right. Dean.

"Dean?"

"Yeah, beautiful. It's me. I'm here, you're okay. You're in the hospital."

"D-Douglas…" Her voice trailed off. She was so confused, and had no idea how Dean was there, or even where "there" was.

"He's been arrested." He took her head in his hands and forced her to look at him. "You're safe. Hear me?"

Adeline nodded, not taking her eyes from his. "He-he…forced me into the room. He was insane. Saying that I led him on, that he wanted to date me, that he'd been courting me." She paused, trying to remember what else he'd said.

"Go on, get it all out."

"He thought I was having sex with both you and Chief. He had his hand on my throat and I couldn't get him to let go. He was going to hurt me with his knife."

At that, Dean enfolded her awkwardly into his arms. He lowered the safety rail on his side of the bed and sat down, bringing her into his embrace fully.

"D-D-Did he hurt me?" Adeline choked out.

Knowing what she meant, Dean hurried to reassure her. "No, beautiful. I got there in time. Then Coco broke out of the bathroom and barked his head off, running up and down the halls until more help came. He didn't get that far. I swear. You're okay."

Adeline pulled back and whispered, "Why were you there? I told you not to come."

He smiled at her tenderly. "I know you did. But I never was a very good listener. I left work around one-thirty in the morning. I decided that we'd argue in person. There's no way, knowing you'd had a crap day and night, I was *not* going to come up to be with you. Adeline, I love you. There's no doubt in my mind that you're the woman I want to spend the rest of my life with. Things won't always be smooth between us, we're both too passionate and hardheaded for that, but I'll do whatever I can to make sure too much time doesn't pass before we talk it out and make up. That's what I was doing."

"Thank God," Adeline breathed. "I was so scared."

"I'm sorry I didn't get there sooner."

Adeline laid her head on Dean's chest and snuggled into him as best she could. "You got there. That's what counts."

After a moment, she lifted her head again. "Where's Douglas?"

"Jail," Dean told her without pause. "Things got a

little crazy at the hotel, but with your condition and Chief's account of what happened the night before, he was taken in. Unfortunately, you'll need to talk to the detective sooner rather than later, to give *your* account of what happened, to make sure he stays behind bars. But for now, all you need to know is that you're safe."

"Things got a little crazy?" Adeline asked nervously.

Dean sighed and brought a hand up to smooth her hair back from her face. "Yeah. Coco alerted and you had a seizure."

"Oh shit."

"Yeah."

"It was bad, wasn't it?" Adeline asked.

He nodded. "Grand mal. Lasted quite a while. If I'm being honest…you scared me to death, beautiful."

"I knew I felt weird," Adeline commented. "But I'm okay?"

"For now."

She knew what that meant. "I'll make an appointment when we get home to talk to my doctor about scheduling the surgery as soon as possible," she whispered.

Dean kissed the side of her head. "Will you marry me?"

Adeline's head whipped up at his words. She stared at him with wide eyes. "What?"

"Will you marry me?" Dean repeated calmly.

She continued to stare at him in disbelief.

He chuckled. "Marriage, beautiful. Man and wife. Rings, you in a white dress, me in a tux, all our friends there." He got serious and kissed her gently on the lips before continuing, "I love you, Adeline Reynolds. I want to marry you. Spend the rest of my life with you. Make babies with you. I would do it tomorrow if we could. But the bottom line is that I want you to understand, from the tips of your beautiful toes to the top of your head, that I love you no matter what. In sickness and in health, Adeline. I don't care about the outcome of your surgery except for the fact that it'll reduce your seizures."

"And if I don't know who you are afterward?" Adeline asked in a whisper.

"I'll still love you."

"I can't do that to you," she protested. "It's not fair."

"You're not listening to me, Adeline. I'm never going to love another woman the way I love you. Never. Whether I marry you or not. Whether you remember me after the surgery or not. It's not going to change the way I feel. If it happens, I'll simply have to work hard to make you love me all over again. If I could do it once, I'm confident I can do it a second time." His cocky smile warmed her. "If the shoe was on the other foot, if I got hurt on the job, knocked in the head and didn't remember you…would you walk away?"

"No," Adeline gasped, horrified. "Never."

Dean didn't say anything, simply stared at her, his point made.

A tear escaped, and Adeline didn't even try to stop the ones that followed. "Yes, I'll marry you. I love you, Dean. So much that I'm scared something's going to go wrong. I don't want to lose what we have."

"We won't. I swear it." He brushed away the wetness on her face with first one thumb, then the other.

He tipped her head up and kissed her gently and sweetly. "As soon as the docs give the okay, I'll get you home and we can make plans for both our wedding and the surgery. That sound all right?"

Adeline sucked in her lips then reluctantly nodded.

"What?" Dean asked.

"It's just that…the conference. There were a lot of really interesting sessions I wanted to go to."

Dean chuckled and looked around surreptitiously, as if making sure they were alone, then whispered, "Chief is still there. He took your place and is taking notes for you."

"What?" Adeline asked in shock. "He is?"

"Yup."

"Why?"

"Because he knows how important it is to you."

Tears filled her eyes again. "But…I don't really even

know him. I was so mean to him last night and I haven't even gotten to apologize yet. I don't get it."

"Adeline. You're my girlfriend. He knows that I love you. That means *you're* as important to him as I am. Which means he'll bend over backwards making sure you get what you need…just like driving you up to Dallas and making up an excuse to do it, and sleeping on that miserable excuse for a couch all night to make sure you were safe. Just like I'd do for Sledge and Beth, if it was her. It's what true friends do."

"Oh shit, now I'm crying again," Adeline moaned. "It's just so sweet…I didn't expect it."

"You should also know…"

Dean paused dramatically and Adeline couldn't help but chuckle. "Lord, what?"

"He's handing out your business cards to as many people as he can and letting everyone know you had to leave the conference early, without saying why, and that you're looking for a new position."

Adeline put her hand up to her forehead and rubbed.

"If that place that interviewed you last week really wants you, they'd better step up their game. I got a text from Chief this morning and he said there were at least four people who really seemed interested. They'd seen the James Wolfe campaign, and after he told them you, not Douglas, were the brains behind it, they couldn't take your card fast enough."

"He's gonna make some woman a wonderful husband," Adeline noted. "If he's this nice to me, a chick who's just his friend, I can't imagine what he'd do for someone he loved."

"I'm not sure he'd realize a woman was interested in him that way if she hit him over the head," Crash said dryly. "He's kind of oblivious."

"Really? That surprises me. He doesn't seem to miss much," Adeline noted, wiping the rest of the tears out of her eyes.

"I haven't talked to him about this, mind you, but I think he's simply used to being looked down upon because of his heritage, so he assumes anyone who wants to sleep with him would only do so either because he's a firefighter or because of his looks."

"That's ridiculous," Adeline spat, more like her old self. "I can't believe women would do that . . . well, I get the one-night-stand thing, but to be that shallow is screwed up. Seriously, I'll have a talk with him."

Dean laughed out loud. "Yeah, let me know how that goes."

"Okay, maybe a talk isn't the best idea, but still. That's crazy, Dean!"

"It is what it is. I'm hoping that he'll meet a woman out of the blue, kinda like I met you, who will knock him off his feet and make him see what he's been missing before he can think too much about it. He's a lot like me, protective and bossy, so whoever he finds is gonna have to be able to overlook his flaws . . . just like you've done with me. Now, let me go find a nurse. I was supposed to notify them the second you woke up. The doctors wanted to keep you here until you woke so they could make sure you were okay. They might do a few tests and they'll send the results back home to your doctor. We'll get out of here as soon as we can though."

"I'd appreciate that. Thanks for being here."

"You don't have to thank me, beautiful. There's no place I'd rather be. Oh, and Coco is currently being spoiled rotten by the nurses. They've kept him at the desk, keeping him entertained."

"Awesome," Adeline said tiredly.

Dean leaned down, kissed her one more time, ran his fingers lightly over the bruises on her neck, and said, "Lay back down and relax. I'll go find a nurse."

"I love you, Dean."

"And I love you, beautiful. Rest. We'll be on our way home shortly."

Adeline lay back and closed her eyes. Her neck still hurt, as did her arms. She still felt off, but somehow her spirit felt lighter than ever.

Dean asking her to marry him before her surgery told her everything she needed to know. He would be there for her . . . no matter what. Through sickness and health.

Chapter Twenty

---◆---

TWO MONTHS LATER, Adeline sat in bed, her sister sitting cross-legged at her feet, Coco snoring lazily next to her. It had been both a deliriously happy and tough couple months for her.

On the happy side, she'd been offered the job by the company she'd interviewed with before the fateful conference and confrontation with Douglas, and they'd been more than willing to wait until after her surgery for her to start.

Because of everything that happened with Douglas, and a conversation with the lawyer Dean had procured to represent her, her current company had agreed to maintain her on their payroll as she recuperated, thus keeping her insurance active. Adeline didn't ask how the lawyer had helped them come to that decision, but she wasn't going to protest. Having the money situation taken off her plate was a relief.

Dealing with her medical issues wasn't as fun, however. She'd been through video EEG monitoring, MRI scans, as well as neuropsychology testing. The doctor had even had a brain mapping done to try to evaluate the surrounding areas of her brain to determine what kinds of issues she might experience after the surgery.

Her procedure was a resection surgery. The surgeon removed the part of the brain that was causing her seizures, in her case part of the temporal lobe. Luckily, this was not only the most common type of surgery for epileptics, but also the most successful, with sixty to seventy percent of patients being free of seizures that caused unconsciousness as a result.

She had to continue taking medicine, but over time her doctor hoped she'd need less and less. There had still been risks, of course. She could have lost her memory, lost either her vision or speech, and even suffered from paralysis.

But Dean hadn't let her dwell on the negatives. He'd kept her focused on the positives, taking each one of her seizures in stride, and not seeming to let it bother him that they'd increased to around two a day before her surgery.

When he was working, her sister or Beth kept her company, Beth having no problem being at Dean's condo instead of her own house...especially with Coco there. Spending time around her dog had cemented Beth's decision to adopt Second, and training him so he could be her assistance dog. She'd found that there was something calming about being around a dog, and when Coco jumped into her lap and licked her face after she'd had a panic attack, Beth told Adeline that she was able to pull herself together much faster than if she'd been by herself.

Alicia, Beth, and Dean had pitched in, along with the rest of the guys at the station and her family, to help plan the wedding. It hadn't been fancy, but it'd been as beautiful as Adeline could ever have imagined. They'd decided to have it in the early afternoon, when she'd be least likely to have a seizure.

The lawn behind the fire station was set up with tents and tables, and they'd used the ladders of the firetrucks to make a sort of arch. Dean knew a retired county court judge who'd agreed to officiate. Adeline's parents and sister were there, as were all of Dean's law enforcement friends, their girlfriends, and of course, every firefighter who wasn't away on a call.

Not only that, but Dean's parents showed up with his little sister in tow. Dean had wanted her there, but wasn't sure they'd be able to make it work, since she couldn't travel by herself. Laura had screamed when she'd seen her big brother and had run toward him with a smile on her face a mile wide. It was one of the most touching things Adeline had ever seen in her life.

When Dean introduced Adeline to his sister, it took a while for Laura to warm up to her, but by the end of the day, she'd freely hugged and kissed Adeline as if she'd known her all her life.

The wedding itself was both beautiful and hilarious at the same time. Laura kept getting up off her seat and coming up to the altar and hugging her brother in the middle of the ceremony. His firefighter and cop buddies weren't afraid to give Crash wedding advice…also in the middle of the ceremony, and Adeline hadn't been able to stop smiling.

She had held it together until Dean had recited the words "in sickness and in health" during his vows to her. He'd paused right before that line, leaned forward, and taken her chin in his hand. He tilted her head up and kissed her, saying the words against her lips. It was beautiful, and such a Dean thing to do.

They'd spent the rest of the night partying and enjoying the time spent with their friends and families, only disappearing once when Coco alerted, going back into the same small room they'd been in when she'd had that first seizure all those months ago. Somehow it seemed appropriate.

Dean was given a week off after their wedding and they'd spent it holed up in his condo instead of traveling somewhere for a honeymoon. They'd made love on every surface and piece of furniture, and had poured over online websites looking for a house that appealed to them both.

Even with all the good stuff in her life, Adeline was very ready when it finally came time to have the surgery. She'd been worrying and stressing over it and was relieved when it came time to head to the hospital early one morning.

The surgeons had clipped her hair short over the section of her skull that would be removed during the operation. She'd cried a little, but Dean had simply kissed the side of her head where the surgeon would cut into her brain and reminded her that it would grow back.

The last thing Dean said to her before she was wheeled out of her room was, "Love you, beautiful. In sickness and in health. I'll see you when you're out."

Crying right before undergoing brain surgery wasn't exactly what she'd expected to be doing, but cry she did.

She didn't remember going under the anesthesia, but vaguely recalled the surgeon talking to her and asking her to do things like lift a finger, or move a foot, in the middle of the operation. It took about four hours, and she'd spent one night in the intensive care unit, and another four days in a regular room. The first couple of days had been extremely painful, and she'd spent a lot of time sleeping through the pain, thanks to the heavy doses of narcotics she'd been given.

The first time she was truly aware of the world around her, she opened her eyes to see Dean asleep in the recliner next to her, Alicia reading a magazine in another chair at the foot of her bed, her mom sitting next to her sister watching television and, surprisingly, Chief leaning against one of the walls of her room.

Her first thought was relief that she'd immediately recognized each of them, and the next was how much her head hurt.

"Dean?"

His eyes popped open as if she'd yelled his name and he immediately stood up and hovered over her.

"Hey, beautiful."

"I remember you." It wasn't exactly what she wanted to say, but her eyes were heavy and moving was painful.

"I'm hard to forget."

Her lips quirked upward and she blinked—a long, slow closing of her eyelids, then raising them slowly as if they weighed a hundred pounds. "Love you," she slurred.

"I love you too, Adeline. The surgery went great. You haven't had a seizure since. The doctor is optimistic," Dean told her softly.

Adeline closed her eyes and said simply, "Okay."

She felt the pressure of his lips on her forehead, then his whispered, "Sleep, beautiful. I'll be right here."

As if his words were the permission she'd been waiting for, she drifted off again.

As THE DAYS went by, the pain slowly ebbed to manageable levels and she'd been allowed to go home. She didn't have the energy to do much more than shuffle to the bathroom and back to bed, but the doctor had said that was normal and not to push it.

She'd only had one small seizure, and it had been over almost before it started. Adeline had called it a miracle, but Dean had only smiled and kissed her gently.

After two weeks, Adeline made Dean go back to work. He was driving her crazy, hovering and being paranoid about every little ache and pain she had. He'd only agreed to go if someone stayed with her.

So Alicia was now sitting on the end of her bed, tasked with being with her for the day, and her parents were coming over that evening to spend the night. Beth and Penelope would be visiting tomorrow, and her parents were coming back over to spend the next night as well. Then Dean would be back on the third day.

It wasn't exactly ideal. "I feel like I'm a pain in the butt and hate that everyone has to babysit me," Adeline complained to her sister.

"We're not babysitting you, sis," Alicia said with a laugh. "If anything, it's really nice to be able to spend time with you. You've been working really hard and I've missed hanging out."

"Yeah, okay. Good point," Adeline conceded.

"Any word on Douglas?"

"He's currently in a mental health facility. The prosecuting attorney told us that it was likely the case would never go to trial because Douglas was diagnosed with dissociative identity disorder. He'd been taking medicine to control it since his teens, but had recently stopped taking it when he joined the company for whatever reason. One of his alters apparently got obsessed with me, to the point where he was following me around and taking pictures of me without my knowledge. When I didn't fall into his plan to date him, he got pissed."

"Jesus. I hadn't realized," Alicia said, eyes wide.

"I know, neither did I. In Douglas's apartment, the police found a compartment in his floor where he'd hidden pictures, papers from the job, and even a paper cup I'd probably used. There were also handcuffs and rope that they think he was going to use to tie me to the bed or something. He's said some stuff to his doctor to the effect that he wanted to keep me and never let me go." Adeline shivered at the thought, but continued, "He, and his lawyer, are denying culpability in the kidnapping and assault charge due to the crime being committed by a different identity state. It's all kinda confusing and scary, but the prosecuting attorney told me and Dean that if it did go to trial, and they tried to claim not guilty by reason of insanity, it most likely wouldn't fly and he'd be found guilty."

"And how are you with all that?" Alicia asked.

"Honestly? I don't care what happens to the man, as long as he stays away from me and Dean. The detective said he'd keep us informed on what happens with him, and the attorney said the same thing. For the moment I'm safe, and I refuse to waste any more time thinking about him."

"I'm not sure you're dealing with what happened to you," Alicia said in concern, putting a hand on her sister's leg. "You didn't talk to a psychiatrist about it."

"I don't need to," Adeline said, then shook her head and held up a hand when her sister opened her mouth to protest. "I *don't*. Look, I know I almost died. If Dean hadn't decided to ignore my hissy fit the night before, I *would* be dead. I get that. But I'm *not* dead. And Dean came up to Dallas to talk to me, to make things right between us. He ignored the mean things I said to him on the phone. I'm okay with what happened because I realized that no matter how independent I am, no matter that I'm a thirty-four-year-old woman with a disability I've lived with my entire life, it's okay to lean on others to help me out.

"Yeah, it sucks that it took a psycho to make me see it, but Chief stayed the night with me to make sure I was okay, even after I was a bitch to him and told him to leave. He stayed because he cares about me and Dean. Then Dean did the same thing, driving up in the middle of the night, after working all day. I couldn't get away from Douglas by myself. But that's okay because Dean and his friend had my back."

"I don't get what that has to do with seeing a psychiatrist," Alicia said honestly.

"All my life, I've felt like a burden. To you, to mom and dad, to the people around me, and it's all because I always tried to be so independent. But Dean made me see that independence doesn't mean I can't lean on someone else. When I have a nightmare, Dean holds me and lets me talk about it. When my head hurts, he gets me drugs. He lets me be me, and I know down to the marrow of my bones that when I need him, he'll be there. That's why I don't care one thing about Douglas. If he gets out of prison, Dean and his friends will be there to protect me…and I'll let them. I'm not afraid of him."

Alicia's lips curled into a huge smile. "You really are okay about it, aren't you?"

"I am."

"You know that Matt and I will also be there if you need us, right?"

Adeline nodded. "Yeah. I do. Thank you."

"You're welcome. Tired?"

"A little."

Alicia swung her legs off the bed and stood. "I'm gonna make peanut butter cookies while you nap."

"My favorite," Adeline said, informing her sister of something she already knew.

"Yup."

"Love you, sis."

"I love you too. I'll pop back in later to check on you." Alicia squeezed Adeline's leg and slipped out of the room.

For the thousandth time since she'd woken up in the hospital to see Dean hovering over her, and realizing she remembered him and everyone around her, Adeline felt like the luckiest woman in the world.

THAT NIGHT, ADELINE woke up when Dean sat on the bed next to her. The light in the bathroom was on, softly illuminating the room. She opened her eyes and furrowed her brow in confusion. "What are you doing here? Shouldn't you be at the station?"

"Yeah," he whispered, keeping his voice down so he wouldn't wake up her parents who were sleeping in the guest room across the hall, "but I wanted to see how you were doing."

"You couldn't have sent a text or called?" Adeline asked, still half asleep.

"Not the same as seeing my wife in person. You feeling okay?"

"I'm fine, Dean. Promise."

"Good." He tenderly brushed a lock of hair from the unshaved side of her head out of her face and behind her ear.

Adeline felt her heart melt. God, she had the best husband. She pulled her arm out from under the covers and put it on his knee. Feeling mischievous, she inched her hand upward until it rested on his cock. She felt him twitch under her fingers.

"What are you doing?" he asked with one brow cocked, but she noticed he didn't protest or otherwise move her hand.

He'd been right by her side, from the moment she went in for the final tests before her surgery until she'd kicked him out of the house and made him go back to work the day before. Everything he'd done had been for her, now she wanted to do something for him.

Adeline moved her hand until she was cupping him through his pants. She squeezed lightly, then ran her palm up and down his hardening length.

"Fuck, that feels good," Dean said huskily.

Feeling bold, Adeline brought her other hand out of the covers and undid the button to his cargo pants and slid down his zipper. She scooted over on the mattress, giving her husband room next to her.

"Lay down, Dean," she ordered softly.

SUSAN STOKER

He went to turn to lie next to her and Adeline shook her head. "No, just like that. Your head down there and your feet up here."

"Are you sure?" he asked, not moving.

"I'm very sure. You've done nothing but give to me since my surgery. Let me do this for you."

Dean slowly moved his legs up to the bed, shifting only enough to push his pants and boxers down over his crotch, then he lay back, propping himself up on his elbows. His erection rested on his belly and he had a goofy grin on his face.

He was in the perfect positon for Adeline to reach him with her hand without straining. She propped her pillows up so she could rest back on them and still be able to see what she was doing. Then with her right hand, she grasped his hard cock and stroked.

Immediately, a soft groan left his mouth and his eyelids dropped to half-mast.

"Shhhh. Don't wake my parents up," Adeline cautioned with a saucy grin. "The last thing I want is for them to come rushing in here thinking I need them, only to find my hand around my husband's cock."

She stroked him faster, using the pre-come that was already leaking from the tip to lubricate his length, allowing her to pump faster.

A few minutes later, Dean dropped his elbows, falling to his back as he groaned under his breath. "God, beautiful. Your hands feel so good. Fuck."

"You got hard really fast, Dean. Haven't you been taking care of yourself?" Adeline asked, genuinely curious. She figured he'd been masturbating in the shower each morning. She certainly hadn't felt close to wanting to fool around, but thought he'd for sure be getting himself off.

"No. I didn't want to come without you."

His answer sent a warm and fuzzy feeling shooting through her and she felt the first twinges of arousal since the surgery. She wasn't up to making love yet, but was relieved she was finally feeling back to normal.

She tightened her hand, slowing her strokes again so they were unhurried and methodical. "That's crazy, Dean. I don't think it's healthy for you to hold it in."

He chuckled. "In a minute or two there won't be any more holding it in. Faster, beautiful. Please."

Complying immediately, Adeline moved her fist faster up and down his length. One of Dean's hands came up to fondle his balls as she continued to stroke him.

"Concentrate on the tip...fuck that feels good," Dean crooned as she did as ordered. His other hand got into the action as well, slowly stroking the base of his dick as her palm rapidly moved up and down over the tip of his cock. The pre-come that was now constantly leaking out of the mushroom head more than lubricated her palm and the sounds of her caresses seemed loud in the quiet room.

Adeline felt his orgasm move through his cock even before he groaned low and long in his throat. He half sat up and his buttocks tensed as his dick throbbed under her hand. Keeping it over the head so he wouldn't make a bigger mess than he was already about to make, Adeline watched as Dean released into her palm. She gently held him as he twitched and pulsed under her hand.

Finally, he let go of himself and fell backward in a heap. Adeline caressed his softening length and kept her hand around him as they lay there silent for a long moment. Eventually, Dean sat up and grabbed a couple of tissues from the nightstand. He cleaned her hand first, then wiped himself down, pulled his underwear and pants back up and fastened them. Then he turned and put his hands on either side of Adeline's waist and leaned down, nuzzling her neck and the skin behind her ear.

The smell of sex was heavy in the air and Adeline felt almost as relaxed as Dean obviously did. She put her hands on his chest and caressed him as he whispered in her ear.

"Thank you, beautiful."

"You're welcome." Adeline beamed up at her husband.

"You know, that wasn't why I came home."

She kept smiling. "I know. And I hadn't planned on that, but you've done nothing but care and do things for me. I wanted to do something for *you* for once."

"For the record, you can give me a hand job anytime you want. I'll never complain. But you don't owe me anything. Never. It's been my pleasure and privilege to watch over you and help you get better. And it's been a miracle to witness exactly how successful your surgery was. You've had only that one small seizure since the operation and it makes me thankful each and every day for modern medicine."

"Me too."

"As much as I'd love to return the favor, you're squinting and I know that means you're in pain. When was the last time you took a pill?"

"Lunch, I think."

Dean leaned down and kissed her lips, lingering just a moment to brush his tongue over her bottom lip, then pulled back and kissed her forehead. "I'll be right back."

In a couple moments, he was back with a pill and a glass of water. He helped her sit up and she swallowed it down. Dean got her situated back on the pillows then leaned over her again. "Beth and Penelope will be here in the morning?"

Adeline nodded. "I think around nine."

"Good. I'll call around lunch and check in."

"You don't have to."

"I know, but I want to."

"In that case, I'll look forward to hearing from you," Adeline said with a smile.

"Go to sleep, beautiful."

"Love you, Dean."

"And I love you too, Adeline Christopherson."

"I CAUGHT CRASH sneaking into the fire station last night," Penelope told Adeline with a smirk. "Any idea where he'd been?"

Adeline smiled, but didn't say anything.

They'd eaten lunch and Penelope, Beth, and Adeline were sitting in the living room. The TV was on low in the background, but they weren't watching it. Coco was sitting between Adeline and Beth, his head resting in Beth's lap while she absently petted him. Penelope was sitting nearby in an oversized leather chair.

"He came to see you last night? But your parents were here, right?" Beth asked, confused.

"Yes and yes. He said he just wanted to check on me. It was the first night we'd spent apart since my surgery."

"Oh my God, that's so sweet!" Beth exclaimed.

"He had a mighty big grin on his face," Penelope remarked.

Adeline threw one of the pillows she'd been holding at the other woman and everyone laughed.

"All kidding aside, I think it's great," Penelope told Adeline. "Not the sneaking home to get some, but the fact that he's so in love with you he doesn't want to spend even one night away from you."

"For the record? We didn't make love. My head still hurts too much for that. But he might've still gotten some satisfaction while he was here." Adeline blushed when the other two women whooped and cheered. "But yeah, even though it's not feasible for us to spend every night together, especially not with his work schedule, I had no idea how hard that first night would be. It took forever for me to get to sleep, and it was such a nice surprise to wake up to him sitting next to me."

"I'm so happy for you two," Penelope said with a hint of sadness in her voice. "You're both so amazingly strong and you couldn't have found better men...and I'm not just saying that because you're with my brother, Beth."

"You'll find your guy," Beth told her best friend. "I know it."

Penelope shrugged. "Maybe, maybe not. I'm so not ready to be in a relationship. There's too much shit going on in my head to ever think I'd make a good girlfriend."

"You're still attending the group sessions, aren't

you?" Beth asked, referring to the group therapy sessions for victims of kidnapping. It was where they'd met when Beth first came to town.

"Now and then. I think I've gotten all I'm gonna get out of them," Penelope said, then waved her hand, dismissing the topic. "But enough about me. Let's talk about houses! Have you guys found something you both like yet, Adeline?"

Adeline didn't really want to let the topic of Penelope's mental state drop. There was something behind her eyes that wasn't good. An emptiness that was disconcerting. It was as if she was there laughing and talking with them, but her soul was crying.

Not knowing the other woman well enough to push, but promising herself she'd talk to Beth about it later, Adeline began to talk about the different houses she and Dean had been considering.

They spent the rest of the afternoon talking about topics ranging from houses, to sex, to assistance dogs, to the best thing to eat when you'd drunk too much. Around dinnertime, Adeline's parents arrived and the women said their goodbyes, promising to come over again soon and chill. They also made vague plans for a night out when Adeline was feeling more up to it.

Around eleven that evening, an hour or so after Adeline had gone to bed, there was a knock on her bedroom door.

Her mom stuck her head into the room and asked, "You awake, baby?"

"Yeah, Mom. What's up?"

"Your dad and I were watching the news and there's a huge warehouse on fire. It's bad, and there are tons of firefighters downtown fighting it. I thought you should know."

Adeline gasped. She'd been so concerned about her own surgery and what was going on in her life, she hadn't once stopped to think about the realities of what it was Dean did for a living.

Taking a deep breath, she forced herself not to panic. "I'll get dressed and come out and watch with you…if that's okay."

"Of course. Let me know if you need anything." Her mom shut the door behind her.

Adeline snatched her cell phone off the bedside table. No missed calls and no texts. But if Dean was fighting the fire, he wouldn't be able to stop and call her.

He was fine. She believed that to the marrow of her bones. Dean and all his friends were good at what they did. Really good.

She climbed out of bed and threw on a pair of sweats, then shuffled into the living room, still holding her cell phone.

Two hours later, her parents said good night and

headed off to the guest room. There hadn't been any more updates on the television, and she hadn't heard anything from Dean. She *had* heard from Beth, who texted to say she'd hacked into the fire band channel where the incident commander was giving instructions and information to the firefighters and police officers on site. She'd been sending updates about the fire, how it'd been only five percent contained, then ten, then twenty. At one point she messaged to say there were two firefighters down, but she didn't know who they were.

Adeline didn't take her eyes off the small phone screen, torn between terror that Dean was lying trapped in a burning building and the conviction that he and his friends were just fine. She finally fell asleep around two in the morning on the couch, Coco sleeping on his side on the floor near her.

Once more she was awakened by the feel of Dean sitting next to her. But this time she was immediately awake and alert. "Are you all right?"

He smiled gently at her. "I'm fine."

"Everyone else?"

"All fine too."

Adeline breathed out a sigh of relief. "Good."

"How long have you been out here?" Dean asked, leaning down and kissing her forehead.

She smelled the faint scent of smoke, but since his hair was damp, it was obvious he'd showered before coming home. "What time is it?"

"Six."

Adeline shrugged. "My parents went to bed around one."

"You up for breakfast?"

"With you? Always."

He helped her up and they went into the kitchen. For the first time since her surgery, she felt almost no pain. When the bacon was frying, Dean went and got her medicine, and she took the pills with a big glass of orange juice.

When the eggs and bacon were done, they settled into chairs at the dining room table. Dean took her hand in his. "You okay?"

Adeline nodded. "I was scared, I won't lie. But I know you and the others are good at what you do. Beth was listening to the commander in charge of the scene and I got a little worried when I heard about the trapped firefighters, but then I decided that if, God forbid, it was *you* who was trapped, I would've heard about it from someone. Your boss, one of your friends, Beth, *someone*. Then I remembered our vows. In sickness and health. It truly hit home that my fears before my surgery, about you leaving me, were ridiculous. You would've no more left if something went wrong than I would if you were hurt on the job. I love you, Dean. I'm proud of what you do and even though I don't particularly enjoy seeing the fires and stuff on the news, I know you're doing what you love, and if there's any chance, I mean *any* chance, you'll come home to me. So yeah, I'm okay."

"God, I love you," Dean said reverently, gently pulling her to him with a hand on the back of her neck. He kissed her, then pulled back just enough to rest his forehead on hers. Whispering, he asked, "When are your parents leaving?"

Adeline giggled and whispered back, "Not soon enough."

Still keeping his voice down, Dean said, "I can't wait to taste you again. To watch as you come hard for me as I'm sucking on your clit. If you think you're up to it, we can start slow and easy."

"I'm not sure I'm up for multiple orgasms, but maybe a little fooling around. I've missed your touch." Adeline confirmed immediately with a smile.

"I love you."

"And I love you."

Dean pulled back and kissed the side of her head right above the still healing wound. "I'll be careful, beautiful. If you feel even one twinge of pain, let me know and I'll stop."

"I will."

"Good. Now eat. You need to keep your strength up."

Adeline smiled at her husband as Dean sat back. Living with a firefighter wasn't easy, but then again, neither was living with someone with epilepsy. It was a matter of give and take, and she was content to do both.

Happily forking some eggs into her mouth, Adeline couldn't help but think about Dean's single friends. After a hellacious, dangerous night, they were going home to empty houses and apartments. It seemed heartbreaking that they didn't have the love that she and Dean did.

AROUND ONE IN the afternoon, Chief pulled his SUV into his driveway and saw that his lawn had been freshly mowed. He was surprised, but grateful as well. He was exhausted after having stayed until any chance of the large warehouse rekindling had been suppressed. His shoulder hurt from where a section of a wall he'd been standing near had collapsed. He'd moved fast enough so he wasn't trapped beneath it, but it'd glanced off his shoulder when he'd turned away from the falling wall.

Chief knew he hadn't hired anyone to cut the grass for him, even though it was about a week and a half longer than it should've been since it was last mowed. Once again, he thought about selling the house and buying a condo or townhouse...someplace that had monthly dues so he didn't have to worry about maintaining the lawn. Crash had the right idea there for sure. He was crazy for thinking about buying a house. Maybe they should just switch residences.

He smiled at the thought, then noticed there was a beaten-up-looking mower sitting in the driveway of the house next to him. After parking, Chief headed that way. He'd been meaning to cut his grass, but between his long shifts, Adeline's surgery, and just plain being exhausted, he'd let it go too long.

"Hello?" he called out.

A woman walked out of the open door of the garage at the sound of his voice. Chief had seen her in passing before. He hadn't ever talked to her, and didn't know her name or who else might be living with her. He didn't have a lot of time to make nice with his neighbors, choosing instead to keep his distance.

Chief had learned his lesson when he was young and new to San Antonio. Using the casino proceeds he'd received from the council back home, he'd bought a small house in an upscale neighborhood. But instead of being welcomed with open arms, he'd been shunned and harassed until, disgusted, he'd sold the house and moved. It was hard to believe racism toward Native Americans still existed today, but he'd seen it up close and personal.

So instead of trying to get to know anyone, as he'd done before only to have it blow up in his face, Chief worked longer hours and didn't bother making any attempts to be friendly. But now that someone had gone out of their way to mow his lawn, he felt as though he needed to at least say thank you.

He noted that his neighbor was pretty, even though she was blonde. Chief had never been attracted to women with blonde hair; they seemed too…Anglo for him. He'd always chosen to go out with women who had features similar to his own, to the people he'd grown up with, darker skin and brown or black hair. He'd learned early in his life that it was easier to blend in if he stuck to people who looked like him.

One glance at his neighbor and it was obvious she wouldn't blend in no matter where she went. Her hair was so blonde, it was almost white. At the moment it was pulled back into a messy knot at the back of her head. Her eyes were a bright blue, almost as though she was wearing colored contacts. She was tall, nearly as tall as his six feet. She was wearing sneakers, which most likely put her around five eight or nine. And she was muscular. The yellow tank top and jean shorts she was wearing did nothing to hide the strength in her arms and legs. She looked to be in her mid to late twenties, maybe a bit older, it was hard to tell and he'd never been a good judge of age.

Recognizing the stirring of desire in his body, Chief bit out, probably harsher than he would've if she'd been shorter, darker, weaker, and less appealing, "Your man around?"

She didn't say a word, but her lips parted twice as if she was trying to decide what she wanted to say.

"Your husband? Boyfriend?"

When she continued to stand there, mute, Chief muttered, "Fuck it," and reached around to his back pocket for his wallet. He winced when the action pulled the already sore muscles of his shoulder. He pulled out a twenty-dollar bill and held it out to the silent woman. "Here."

He could see the word "what" form on her lips, but she still stubbornly kept quiet.

"Give that to your boyfriend for mowing my lawn. I appreciate it. I've been busy. I'll do my best to keep it cut from here on out, but if he wants to keep it up, I won't complain. Twenty bucks for each time he cuts it. That work?"

This time she bit her lip, looked back into the garage, then faced him again and nodded slowly.

Done with the awkward conversation—if it could be called that; the woman talked less than he did, and that was saying something—Chief gave her a chin lift and headed back across her lawn, through his own freshly mowed grass to his garage.

Without giving his odd neighbor another thought, Chief lowered his garage door and headed inside. A long, hot shower, a big glass of iced tea, and his mattress were calling his name. Thank God he had the next two days off. He needed every minute to recover from the clusterfuck that had been the warehouse fire.

The bitch of it was, they'd learned this afternoon that it had been the work of an arsonist. Millions of dollars' worth of merchandise had gone up in flames, not to mention the property damage of the nearby buildings and the safety of each and every firefighter who had spent hours trying to put out the fire.

He never heard the woman he'd left standing in the driveway next door whisper to his back as he stalked away, "My name is S-S-Sophie. It's good to m-mcct you. I'm not m-married and I was happy to cut your grass to thank you for your s-service to our city."

He never saw her look down at the twenty dollar bill in her hand and say sadly, "I didn't want your m-money. I just wanted to introduce m-myself."

And he didn't hear her mumble to herself as she pushed the mower back into her garage and shut the door behind her, "S-so much for m-making a good first impression."

Look for the next book in the Badge of Honor: Texas Heroes Series, *Shelter for Sophie* in August 2017.

Discover other titles by Susan Stoker

Badge of Honor: Texas Heroes Series

Justice for Mackenzie

Justice for Mickie

Justice for Corrie

Justice for Laine (novella)

Shelter for Elizabeth

Justice for Boone

Shelter for Adeline

Shelter for Sophie (Aug 2017)

Justice for Erin (Nov 2017)

Justice for Milena (TBA)

Shelter for Blythe (TBA)

Justice for Hope (TBA)

Shelter for Quinn (TBA)

Shelter for Koren (TBA)

Shelter for Penelope (TBA)

Delta Force Heroes Series

Rescuing Rayne

Assisting Aimee – Loosely related to DF

Rescuing Emily

Rescuing Harley

Marrying Emily (Feb 2017)

Rescuing Kassie (May 2017)

Rescuing Bryn (Oct 2017)

Rescuing Casey (TBA)

Rescuing Wendy (TBA)

Rescuing Mary (TBA)

Ace Security Series
Claiming Grace (Mar 2017)
Claiming Alexis (July 2017)
Claiming Bailey (TBA)

SEAL of Protection Series
Protecting Caroline
Protecting Alabama
Protecting Fiona
Marrying Caroline (novella)
Protecting Summer
Protecting Cheyenne
Protecting Jessyka
Protecting Julie (novella)
Protecting Melody
Protecting the Future
Protecting Alabama's Kids (novella)
Protecting Kiera (novella) (June 2017)
Protecting Dakota (Sept 2017)

Stand Alone
The Guardian Mist

Special Operations Fan Fiction
www.stokeraces.com/kindle-worlds.html

Beyond Reality Series
Outback Hearts
Flaming Hearts
Frozen Hearts

Writing as Annie George:
Stepbrother Virgin (erotic novella)

Connect with Susan Online

__Susan's Facebook Profile and Page:__
www.facebook.com/authorsstoker
www.facebook.com/authorsusanstoker

__Follow Susan on Twitter:__
www.twitter.com/Susan_Stoker

__Find Susan's Books on Goodreads:__
www.goodreads.com/SusanStoker

__Email:__ Susan@StokerAces.com

__Website:__ www.StokerAces.com

__To sign up for Susan's Newsletter go to:__
http://bit.ly/SusanStokerNewsletter

__Or text:__ STOKER to 24587 for text alerts on your
mobile device

About the Author

New York Times, USA Today, and *Wall Street Journal* Bestselling Author Susan Stoker has a heart as big as the state of Texas, where she lives, but this all-American girl has also spent the last fourteen years living in Missouri, California, Colorado, and Indiana. She's married to a retired Army man who now gets to follow *her* around the country.

She debuted her first series in 2014 and quickly followed that up with the SEAL of Protection Series, which solidified her love of writing and creating stories readers can get lost in.

If you enjoyed this book, or any book, please consider leaving a review. It's appreciated by authors more than you'll know.

CPSIA information can be obtained
at www.ICGtesting.com
Printed in the USA
LVOW11s1609010317
525810LV00001B/19/P